PRAISE FOR SHIRLEY JUMP AND THE HARBOR COVE SERIES

"It's her relationship with her family that puts the heart in this adorable friends-to-lovers romance from bestseller Jump...The Monroe sisters' dynamic gives the story its Hallmark feel...This is sure to please."

—*Publishers Weekly*

"Perfect for readers looking for stories that feature both familial and romantic love in a small town."

—*Library Journal*

"I highly recommend *The Marvelous Monroe Girls* to anyone who loves a book about complex sisterly relationships."

—TheBashfulBookworm.com

"A great opener to this new series with a sweet romance at [its] core."

—CarriesBookReviews.com

"A beautiful small-town vibe that makes you feel like an invited guest."

—WhatIsThatBookAbout.com

THE MARVELOUS MONROE GIRLS

SHIRLEY JUMP

FOREVER

New York Boston

Forever
Hachette Book Group
1290 Avenue of the Americas, New York, NY 10104
read-forever.com
twitter.com/readforeverpub

Originally published in trade paperback and ebook by Hachette Book Group in January 2022.
First mass market edition: December 2022

Forever is an imprint of Grand Central Publishing. The Forever name and logo are trademarks of Hachette Book Group, Inc.

The publisher is not responsible for websites (or their content) that are not owned by the publisher.

The Hachette Speakers Bureau provides a wide range of authors for speaking events. To find out more, go to www.hachettespeakersbureau.com or call (866) 376-6591.

Library of Congress Cataloging-in-Publication Data

Names: Jump, Shirley, 1968- author.
Title: The marvelous Monroe girls / Shirley Jump.
Description: First edition. | New York, NY : Forever, 2022. | Series: Harbor Cove |
  Identifiers: LCCN 2021032995 | ISBN 9781538720288 (trade paperback) |
  ISBN 9781538720660 (ebook)
Subjects: LCGFT: Romance fiction. | Novels.
Classification: LCC PS3611.A87 M39 2022 | DDC 813/.6--dc23
LC record available at https://lccn.loc.gov/2021032995

ISBNs: 978-1-5387-2028-8 (trade paperback); 978-1-5387-2650-1 (mass market);
978-1-5387-2066-0 (ebook)

Printed in the United States of America

OPM

10 9 8 7 6 5 4 3 2 1

To Momma.
What I wouldn't give for one more late-night
conversation, one more laugh,
and one more hug.
I miss you every single day.

THE
MARVELOUS
MONROE
GIRLS

ONE

The best memories from Gabby Monroe's childhood were sprinkled with chocolate chip cookie crumbs. On too many nights to count, a trail of sugary crumbs marched across her pink-and-white comforter and then tumbled down to the white Berber carpet, like an inviting road for a mouse. Whenever Gabby woke up with crumbs on her bed, it meant the three Monroe sisters had stayed up way too late, giggling and whispering and growing as close as peas in a pod.

Grandma dubbed them the Monroe Musketeers, because where one went, the other two often went, too, whether that was on an adventure along the creek that ran behind Grandma's house or under Gabby's blankets after lights-out to read a book by flashlight.

Eventually, all three girls had grown up, and their paths diverged, and Gabby's bed became a neatly made queen in her own little house. There were no whispers at night. No giggles. And most of all, no cookie crumbs.

As each of them graduated high school and moved

on and out, a sharp distance began to build between them. Over the last year or so, Gabby could feel Meggy and Emma slipping away even more, like they were a trio of boats adrift in the ocean.

Maybe it was the cost of burying the truth over the years, or maybe the fissure had begun the day Momma died, but whatever had happened between her and her sisters, Gabby knew it was time they came back together. For Grandma's sake, if nothing else. So she'd done what she always did—concocted a plan that would put the three of them in the same room for a few hours, before Emma took off on another adventure and Meggy got buried in her business, and the ocean between them widened a little more.

Which was why, on a too-warm day in early spring, the three of them were standing in Grandma's dusty, dim, hot attic, looking for anything historically related to Harbor Cove, as well as for Momma's wedding dress, in the myriad of boxes stacked along the pitched walls. In the past half hour, they had opened one box and had two arguments.

The happy family reunion she'd planned was already swerving into tense territory, and the promise Gabby had made that day in the cemetery, when she'd stayed behind to whisper a solemn vow over a freshly dug grave, echoed inside her.

I'll keep us together, Momma. I promise. I'm never going to let you down again.

Once upon a time, the Monroe Musketeers had been a team. Now they were…distant friends.

"I remember Momma giving me this tea set for my birthday," Emma said as she opened a box and pulled out a tiny white saucer. Her French braid cascaded over one shoulder, so long it brushed against her wrist. Emma was the wild one, a mustang that didn't want to be contained, ready to flit away on impromptu weekend hiking trips or weeklong yoga retreats at any second. In between, she worked at a boutique hotel as an assistant wedding planner. The fact that she'd had the job at the Harbor Cove Hotel for more than a year now was a miracle in and of itself. "Remember us having tea parties with our stuffed animals, Meggy? And Momma would sew little place mats and napkins for us to use?"

"No, I really don't. In fact, I remember Momma giving this to me, not you. I swear, the two of you have a totally different family history written in your heads than I do." Margaret had a smudge of dust on her cheek, and her normally sleek dark hair had become a frizzy mess making a desperate—and futile—attempt to escape her severe ponytail. Anyone who knew Margaret knew that nothing around her was ever out of control. She owned the jewelry store in downtown Harbor Cove, a custom-design shop catering to persnickety customers much like Margaret herself.

Today was the first time all three of them had been in the same place for longer than a few seconds in weeks. Gabby was not going to let Margaret screw this up.

"Can we please not argue about a toy?" Gabby said. "Momma wouldn't want us to—"

"Momma isn't here, in case you've forgotten." Her sister's sharp tone spoke of annoyance and impatience.

"I've *never* forgotten that, Margaret. I just…" She sighed and ran a hand through her hair. She didn't want to alarm them about Grandma, because it wasn't like Eleanor Whitmore was sick, exactly. Just…not herself. An argument during their visit would simply make things worse. "I need you guys to work with me, okay?"

"What do you think I'm doing up in this attic? God, I swear it's a thousand degrees in here." Margaret fanned herself and made a face. She'd worn what Gabby liked to call her "work armor"—a wrinkle-free navy pantsuit and a pair of sensible tan heels, both of which sent the message that Margaret was undoubtedly heading to work. On a Sunday morning. Again. "What's so important about finding all this junk anyway?"

"Do you have a single sentimental bone in your body?" Emma asked. "Come on, this is history we're looking at. Our history."

"I don't have *time* to be sentimental." Margaret scowled. "Or to rummage through a bunch of stupid boxes just because Gab got on some tear about a trip down memory lane."

"That's not it at all, and you know it," Gabby said as she took the box with the tea set from Emma. "Business has been down all over Harbor Cove for the better part of a year. The business committee thought this tricentennial celebration might be just the thing to ignite a little interest and revenue. I would think you'd want the boost for your own store, Margaret."

It sure mattered to Gabby's struggling vintage dress shop. She'd opened it a year ago, proudly naming the shop Ella Penny Boutique, an homage to her name, Gabriella, and her mother's name, Penny, hoping that would also bring her fledgling foray some good luck. She had thought business would come easily. After all, Harbor Cove was a tourist town, and anything unique or fun seemed to sell insanely well during the warmer months. But as the year wore on, business slowly dropped to a trickle, and

Gabby realized she needed to do something to get back on track—or close her doors and figure out what else she could do with her life.

A couple months ago, she'd gone to several other small business owners in town to brainstorm something that could boost everyone's sales. On a cold January afternoon, they'd come up with the idea of Celebrate History in the Harbor as a way of using the upcoming tricentennial to showcase the vintage clothing, antiques, and jewelry that historic Harbor Cove was known for. Now all Gabby needed was one retro wedding dress—a dress with a story and emotional ties—to bring attention to Ella Penny Boutique.

It wasn't just her mother's name on the sign that drove Gabby's need to make the shop a success. It was more—maybe a need to prove she wasn't an aimless thirty-year-old who couldn't figure out what she wanted to be when she grew up. Gabby had done everything in the years since she'd graduated from UMass—waitress, transcriptionist, clerk, administrative assistant. Not a one of those jobs had felt quite right, as if she'd been wearing shoes a tad too big or too small. Then she'd seen an empty storefront downtown and cobbled together enough money to rent the shop and slowly fill it with inventory. Now that idea, too, was falling flat. Gabby couldn't afford yet another failure. This business boost had to work.

It absolutely had to.

"Yeah, Margaret, quit being a Grinch and just get on board." Emma looked cool and calm with her light cotton maxi skirt and the clunky silver-and-turquoise bracelet that echoed her blue eyes. Emma's facial features were the most like their mother's, all delicate and porcelain and beautiful.

"Fine. But I want that tea set." Margaret reached for the box in Gabby's hands, but Gabby was faster and swept it behind her back. Margaret scowled. Then she paused and peeked past Gabby's shoulder. "Hey, isn't that Jake outside?"

"You will not distract me with the mention of someone I have known since I was six," Gabby said. Of course she knew Jake was here. Maybe it was because they'd been friends for as long as she could remember, but every time the boy next door—now a tall and often annoying man—was near, Gabby was aware of him, maybe too aware. It wasn't that Jake wasn't handsome or that he didn't have a nice smile. He was just…Jake. "Besides, you both know as well as I do that nine days out of ten, Jake is over here and not at his own house. So that's not exactly a news flash."

"Because he has a crush on you," Emma said, her voice singsong and teasing.

"Oh. My. God. We are not in middle school, and no, he does not. Besides, it was his cousin who asked me out, not Jake." After the disastrous end to her short-lived, fiery relationship with Jake's cousin Brad, Gabby had vowed to swear off any man with the last name Maddox. Just because Jake had always hovered on the edge of Gabby's life, was a handsomer version of Brad, and had a pulse did not make them a potential couple. "Anyway, back to the—"

"He has grown up quite nicely, don't you think, Emma? If you ask me, a lot nicer than that cousin of his," Margaret said. She tried to sidestep Gabby, but once again, Gabby was faster. That's what Margaret got for skipping pretty much every single one of the weekly yoga classes the girls took at the Harbor Cove gym.

"All boys grow taller, but not all boys grow up, as Grandma says. And Jake is in the latter group. Both the Maddox boys are." Gabby held the box to her chest. "Now let's settle this silly argument so we can get back to why we're up here in the first place. Celebrate History in the Harbor is only three weeks away, and Momma's dress is perfect because it's an original Betsy Josephs. They're doing a whole retrospective on Betsy at the town museum—"

"Which is just a glorified room in the back of the community center," Margaret cut in. "And Betsy wasn't exactly Michelangelo. She was a tailor."

"Who made a dress for a Kennedy."

Margaret rolled her eyes. "The second cousin of a Kennedy. Not the same thing. Honest to God, that's a tangential connection at best."

"Well, it's a tourist draw, and with the peak season just around the corner, Harbor Cove needs all the tourists we can get." *And so do I.* But Gabby didn't say that because it would worry her sisters and Grandma. The shop would be just fine. Just. Fine.

Gabby opened another box and found a bunch of dusty Halloween decorations. Damn it. "Where is that trunk? Grandma has so many boxes up here."

"Either way," Margaret said, taking advantage of Gabby's distraction to snatch the tea set box away, "this is mine, and I'm taking it home."

"Have the two of you ever considered that maybe, just maybe, Momma rewrapped it and gave it to Emma?" Gabby said. "As in... regifted it?"

"She would never have done that." Margaret, the authority on everything, of course.

"Remember when Momma regifted the punch bowl

that Mrs. Hartman gave her?" Honestly, how did no
one in this family remember a single thing from their
childhood? If anything, Gabby remembered too much,
and sometimes...well, sometimes that made life a little
harder. Hence today's plan, which, so far, was going sideways at a fast clip. "And she turned that crystal bowl into
a planter for Cousin Charlie?"

"Oh yeah." Emma dropped onto a dusty wooden
chair and reached into the box at her feet, one filled with
newspaper cutouts and memorabilia from over the years,
sifting through it without really looking at anything.
"Momma was pretty practical that way."

Their mother had been more than practical. She'd
been...magic. Beautiful and warm, and always taking
the girls on adventures or coming up with little games to
play on rainy days. Gabby missed her every single day,
sometimes as deeply as she had the day Momma died. It
hadn't been easy for any of the girls, especially Margaret,
who, as far as Gabby knew, had never had a moment that
wasn't stoic. Emma had only been five, Gabby just eight,
but Margaret had been nine, and in a flash, the oldest
Monroe girl had become an adult.

If only Gabby had been more responsible that day,
taken her promise to Momma more seriously, then their
mother never would have been on that dark road at night
and never would have ended up—

No. She couldn't think about that now. If she did,
she'd fill up with regrets and start to cry. It would become
a whole thing, and she couldn't afford the time to pause
for a breakdown or an explanation.

Gabby loved being in this dusty old attic, full of
moments frozen in time. All her best memories, as well
as some of her worst ones, were in this Bayberry Lane

house. From the long, stormy afternoon of the funeral reception, when Gabby had tried to make herself scarce in the crowded yet empty rooms of Grandma's house while sad-eyed mourners drifted in and out, giving the girls pitying looks and distant hugs, to the hazy afternoons when their father made a harried visit, his mind somewhere else, his heart permanently shattered. When things were bad, Gabby would sneak away to the attic and burrow beneath a knitted afghan on the faded armchair in the corner while dust motes floated in the air and the soft murmur of voices echoed in the stairwell. She'd read books or play dolls, or later, write in a journal about acne and boys and disappointment.

Grandma was always the one to find Gabby. Never Dad. No, he'd checked out the day his wife had died and never quite checked back in, at least not with his own family. There were things that Gabby knew, things she'd never told a soul, because they would tarnish the memories everyone had and hurt her sisters.

Over the years, the Daddy she had known as a kid became Dad, a less warm, less connected name. He'd left the girls in the wake of his grief, maybe on purpose, maybe not, but still, he'd left and moved on to another family, another life. A life he may have had waiting in the wings all along, a secret that Gabby had told no one, not even Jake. If it hadn't been for Grandma…

Gabby pushed those thoughts firmly out of her mind. It was far better to focus on the tea sets and rummy games and cookie crumbs. That world was the one she liked, the one that was like sinking into a familiar movie, where she knew the ending and could be guaranteed a happy catharsis.

"Let's get back to work," Gabby said, returning to

the pile of boxes she'd been moving a moment earlier, and in the process disrupting a cloud of dust. "This attic is so cool, isn't it? It's like visiting old friends every time we find something."

Margaret scoffed. "Did we have the same crappy childhood? Because it wasn't as romantic as you seem to think, Gab." Margaret took one of the plastic teacups out of the box and held it up to the light. A pattern of faded pink roses marched around the edge. "Sometimes I wish..." She shook her head, tucked the cup back into the box and, along with it, the fraction of vulnerability that had flickered on her face. "Anyway, let's get this finished. I need to get to work."

"You do know it's Sunday, right?" Gabby said.

"And you do know I don't need a reminder?" Margaret shot back. "What does Grandma always say? Eyes on your own book, Gabby."

"Fine. I'm just pointing it out. I thought it would be nice for all of us to—"

"Will you quit living in the past, Pollyanna?" Margaret interrupted.

"I'm not doing that. I'm...trying to help everyone out." Didn't her sisters understand that there were days when Gabby couldn't do enough to make up for that day? For one tiny mistake that had had enormous repercussions?

Stop it. She wasn't here to think about things she couldn't change, choices she couldn't undo. Secrets she couldn't share. Gabby shoved the biggest box along the back wall to the right, sending a fresh cloud of dust into the air. She coughed, waving it away, and then saw a glimmer of wood and brass.

Finally. "Hey, guys, look! I found the dress!"

"About damned time." Margaret sighed. "Now can I leave?"

If Margaret left, the entire happy moment that Gabby had pictured in her head wouldn't happen. When she'd come up with the idea of participating in the fair with Momma's dress, she'd pictured the three girls laughing and crying and sharing memories of their mother and their childhoods. "Help me pull this out, Margaret."

"Fine. But I better not get dirty. I have to—"

"Go to work. I know. Can you please, for five minutes, be present with the rest of us?" Gabby gestured toward the other end of the trunk and grasped the brass handle on her end. "This was supposed to be a chance for us to be together and honor Momma and—"

"Oh my God, Gabby. You talk so much, we're going to be here all day. Come on, let's just get it over with." Margaret yanked up her side—surprisingly strong for a woman who worked behind a desk most days—and the two of them lugged the steamer trunk out of the shadows and into the light.

Gabby lifted the brass latch, exposing the inside of the trunk to the dim light in the attic, and gasped. Ten years since she'd looked inside this cedar box, and she'd been expecting the worst. "Oh my...it's still perfect. I was so worried." She reached inside and then peeled open a cardboard box with a cellophane window, revealing a frothy creation of organza and satin. As Gabby gently lifted it out, the fabric rustled in the quiet of the attic, a whisper of memories from before the girls were even born. "It's prettier than I remember."

When she'd lived at Grandma Eleanor's, Gabby had snuck up to the attic at least a dozen times to visit Momma's wedding dress. She'd draw the soft fabric to

her face and inhale, swearing she could still catch the
scent of Momma's perfume in the folds. As Gabby got
older and taller, she'd slip the dress on over her shorts
and T-shirt and then stand in front of the full-length
oval mirror and imagine Momma on her wedding day,
beautiful and beaming and perfect.

Then Gabby had moved into a little house of her own,
and her life got rushed, and the dress sat in the steamer
trunk, forgotten and, she'd feared, moth-eaten. But no,
the dress had been spared, and although it had yellowed
some over the years, it was nearly as perfect as the day
Momma had worn it to walk down the aisle of the Harbor
Cove Methodist Church. Gabby could just imagine Dad's
eyes, the smile on his face that he seemed to have lost a
long time ago, and the way he must have taken his bride
into his arms and pledged forever. Whether he meant it or
not she had no idea, but Gabby's version of that day was
a fairy tale.

In the distance of her memories, she could remember her father, the way he'd say "I'm so glad to see
all my favorite girls" every night when he got home
from work. Momma would kiss him and giggle, and the
girls would hang on Daddy's arms as he duck-walked
over to the dining room table. Some nights, their father
would drape the tablecloth over the edges of the table,
making it into a tent, and then read books to them by
flashlight. Momma would make shadow animals with her
hands before crowding under there with them until the
clock ticked past bedtime. In those days, life had been
perfect.

"I know that look, Gabby. Don't go getting all
daydreamy and mopey. You have that love-story-fantasy
face, and real life isn't anything like that." Margaret's

sharp tone interrupted Gabby's memories. "We found what we came for, and now I can go."

"For Pete's sake, Meggy. You haven't seen Momma's wedding dress in forever." She thrust the full-length gown in her sister's direction. "Here. I swear, you can see her in it when you touch it."

Just remember her like I do, Gabby thought. *And maybe you'll stop being so distant and we can all go back to being the family we once were.*

Margaret didn't say anything. She fingered the edge of a cap sleeve just long enough for Gabby to hope for a moment of sisterly reminiscing. But instead Margaret stepped back. "What was Momma thinking?"

Gabby pivoted toward the mirror and held the dress up to her chest. Now that she was an adult, the dress was almost a perfect match for Gabby's frame and height. The only thing Gabby didn't have—or want—was a groom. Brad still lingered at the edges of her thoughts, more of a needle reminding her of their painful and abrupt breakup. There was no way Gabby wanted to fall in love with any-one and end up brokenhearted or, worse, betrayed. "What are you talking about? Her dress is beautiful. She was stunning on her wedding day."

Margaret seemed to come out of whatever daze she'd been in. "Of course she was. Sorry. I was just…thinking about something else."

Where the girls once had exchanged daily phone calls and texts, recently there'd been mostly radio silence on Margaret's end. For months, her eldest sister had claimed it was work keeping her tied up, but as time wore on, Gabby began to wonder if maybe there was something more going on, especially given that odd, distant look in Margaret's eyes, and the fact that she and her husband,

Mike, had missed more family dinners than they'd attended. "Is everything okay with you, Meggy?"

"Will you quit calling me that?" Margaret scowled. "I'm not five, and I don't need a nickname. I wish you both would just leave me alone."

Everything about Margaret's body language said *Don't ask*, so Gabby let it go—again—and went back to digging through the trunk. She swore she saw Margaret exhale a sigh of relief when the subject got dropped. "I wonder if Momma's veil is still in here, too," Gabby said. "Last time I was up here, I think I put it back in—"

"You guys..." Emma's voice trailed off. "Um, there's something here you should see."

"Did you find the wedding announcement?" Gabby moved a quilt to the other side of the trunk and tugged out the box with her mother's glittery white shoes. Kitten heels with rhinestones marching along the edges and toes. Beside the box was a smaller one marked *Veil*. Awesome. "I thought it might be nice to frame the announcement and hang it in the shop beside the dress."

"No. I found something...else." Emma got to her feet. She held out a stack of newspaper clippings. "You all need to see this."

Gabby set the shoes back in the trunk and then turned to look over Emma's shoulder, giving the pages a cursory glance. "It's a bunch of Dear Amelia columns. I know about those. Grandma collects them."

Emma nodded. "I know that. But if all she collects is the past columns...why does she have the letters, too?"

"What do you mean?"

"See?" Emma flipped past the first pages of newsprint until she came across a stack of letters, some handwritten, some typed, some on white paper and some on blue, some with monogrammed stationery and some just plain copier pages. "Why would Grandma have these?"

"Let me see." Margaret took a few pages from her sister and began to read. "Maybe she just thought they were good advice or something."

"But why would she have the *original* letters?" Emma asked. "The only one who would need—or have—those would be Dear Amelia herself."

Gabby shrugged. Their grandmother had worked as a typesetter at the local paper for at least three decades. Maybe she'd brought home the wrong folder one day or something. "Do you think Grandma knew the real Dear Amelia?"

"If she did, she totally would have told us." Emma gave Gabby a clipping. "Wouldn't she? I think the truth is something else. Read this one and tell me who it reminds you of."

Gabby's gaze skipped over the lines on the faded newspaper. She read the town paper most days but usually just focused on the pages for neighborhood news and the occasional garage sale or estate sale where she could pick up some vintage dresses to carry in the shop. She always checked out the creative ads Jake designed, only to get great ideas for her own ads. But she couldn't remember the last time she'd read the *Harbor Cove Gazette* from cover to cover, much less the entertainment pages that were scattered with comic strip panels, a daily word jumble, and the Dear Amelia column.

The corners of the decades-old page in her hand were so fragile that they threatened to crumble, but the picture of a generic kindly woman and the familiar script for the Dear Amelia column looked as they always had. " "The road of life is paved with squirrels who couldn't make a decision,'" she read, and then skipped down to the next paragraph, "'That really frosts my socks,'" and the next, "'That's the kind of guy who would make a girl cash bad checks.'" She glanced up as the words tumbled in her mind and gears clicked into place like a clock suddenly springing to life. Her heart hammered in her chest. This was impossible. "That sounds exactly like..."

"Grandma." Margaret took the sheet from Gabby's hand and read the same words Gabby had just spoken aloud. "Grandma says these exact phrases all the time."

"Maybe they just stuck in her head after reading the columns at work? I mean, she did typeset them, so she had to be staring at them a lot, right?" Emma said.

"Or maybe they're in the column because..." Gabby took a deep breath and looked at her sisters, all of it making sense in some weird, couldn't-possibly-be-true way. "Grandma wrote them."

"As in wrote the Dear Amelia column?" Emma shook her head. "No way. We'd know if Grandma was Dear Amelia."

"Would we? It's supposed to be a secret, and if people in Harbor Cove found out, they'd be on Grandma's doorstep—"

"Like pigeons at a picnic." Margaret pointed to a line of type in another column. "These are totally Grandma's words. Remember her hundred-dollar lectures?"

"The ones where she kept us up super late and talked our ears off about the dangers of dating and doing drugs?" Gabby laughed. "I think I got the two-hundred-dollar lectures. I always seemed to be in trouble for one thing or another."

"'You should sit your daughter down,'" Margaret began to read over Emma's shoulder, "'and remind her that nothing but trouble happens after midnight. Boys who are interested in her for more than just a quick moment in the sun will show up on time, with their tie knotted and their best smile, and they'll stay until you kick them off the porch like a dog who has overstayed his welcome. Those are the kind of boys who grow up to be husbands who—'"

"Take care of their wives and watch out for their little girls," Gabby and Emma finished, not from the pages but from memory because they had heard those words dozens of times before. Not to mention how often Gabby had recited them to herself after Brad broke her heart. Turned out that Maddox men weren't the kind who stuck around.

"Oh my God. It *is* Grandma." Gabby dropped into the faded armchair, and a puff of dust erupted around her. Their dear, loving grandmother, who had been there for all three girls anytime they needed her. Recently, Grandma had mentioned something about feeling unneeded. Gabby had attributed it to the three girls growing up and living their own lives, but maybe there was more to Grandma's mood. "How long has she been Dear Amelia?"

Emma dug in the box before her and flipped through a folder. "The letters date back almost twenty-five years."

"That's crazy but also kinda cool." Margaret dusted off her dress pants and smiled, and for a moment, it was those thundering nights with the cookie crumbs all over again. Then the expression melted and Gabby could practically see her older sister pull away. "Well, I'll leave the two of you to it. I need to get to work."

"Don't you want to know more about this? It's as if we're uncovering a mystery in our very own house. We're like a team, like when we were kids. I've missed that.

Haven't you?" Gabby asked, desperate to have Margaret come back from wherever she'd gone.

Gabby needed her sisters. Needed her family. She'd been treading water for so long all alone, carrying a burden on her own shoulders, protecting Meggy and Emma, just as she'd always done. If they could just talk, hang out, maybe she wouldn't feel so lost anymore.

"Sounds like you both have solved the big mystery," Margaret said. "So now we can all get back to our regularly scheduled lives. Life is not a novel, and we are not here to do some remake of *Little Women*, Gabby. I tell you that all the time, but you don't listen." She checked her phone, distracted, halfway gone in her head. "I gotta go."

Margaret started making her way down the stairs that led to the second floor of the house.

"Meggy? You okay? You didn't answer me."

"Yes, of course." But Margaret kept going as she said it, avoiding Gabby's gaze and disappearing a second later.

"Did you think she was acting weird?" Gabby asked Emma. "Like, distant or something?"

Emma shrugged. "Margaret is usually distant or something. She's not exactly the warm and fuzzy one."

Gabby laughed. "True." Whatever was bugging her sister, Margaret would undoubtedly keep it to herself.

"And..." Emma paused.

"What?" She saw the hesitation in Emma's face, the words on the tip of her tongue. "Go ahead and say it."

"You worry too much, Gabby. We're all functioning adults, more or less. You've been trying to make up for Momma being gone all your life, and that's a hole you can't fill." Emma took her sister's hand. "Just worry about you. It'll all be fine."

It was far from fine, but Gabby simply nodded and blinked back her tears. "Yeah, I guess you're right, Em."

"Girls?" Grandma's voice carried up the staircases, echoing in the nooks and crannies of the roomy Victorian. "Are you almost done? I put on a pot of coffee, and I have a batch of cookies getting ready to come out of the oven."

"So I say we go ask Grandma about this column thing," Emma said, lowering her voice even though their grandmother was two floors below them and the sounds of the old house carried better up than down. "Right now."

"Maybe…" Gabby flipped through the papers and saw an opportunity in this mystery. "We could do a little research first. Sort of poke around and see if we're right. The Sunday paper came out today, right? That means this week's column is in there. Maybe we should take a sneak peek at the letter and see if it still sounds like Grandma. I mean, maybe she doesn't write it anymore, or maybe she does. Either way, I'm pretty sure if she hasn't told us yet, she won't tell us now."

"Like ask without asking? We can ask questions, but not in a super-obvious way?" Emma laughed. "I like the idea of a little subtle sleuthing."

Gabby gathered up the wedding dress and the veil, draping them carefully over her arm. She'd come back later for the shoes, and if she could talk her sisters into another hunt, maybe find that wedding announcement, too. Emma grabbed a photo album and a stack of newspapers with headlines about Sputnik and President Kennedy, as well as a box of pictures. She'd told Gabby earlier she had a project in mind for those, but Gabby hadn't had a chance to ask what it was.

Right now, all Gabby wanted to know was whether Emma was right. For a second there—a blip, really—the girls had been excited about something together. Maybe this was the key Gabby had been looking for to rebuild those bonds that had been fraying for far too long.

Every day, Gabby felt like she was trying to grasp strings that were just out of reach. The business, the debts, the late notices, and now her sisters. If she could get one thing back on track, maybe the rest would fall into place, and they'd all truly be okay. "Let me take that folder, and we can analyze these later. Over wine."

Emma shot her a grin. "Sounds like my kind of plan. Although we'll have to do it pretty quickly. I've got a week of vacation burning a hole in my pocket. I'm dying to go to Morocco. Maybe Paris. Someplace...different. Exciting."

"You're going away again?"

"You bet your butt I am." Emma smiled. "I want a job that takes me somewhere exciting, and I can't find that stuck here. Somewhere far, far away from this tiny little nowhere town. I want to wake up in a place where I don't speak the language or know what anything on the menu is."

"But then you'll be far away from us."

"That's why God invented air miles, Gabs. Just come visit me."

"Or maybe you can find excitement right here. Like in this little mystery." Before her sister could disagree, Gabby tucked the dress back into its box, along with the veil. She slid the folder between the panels of the skirt before the two of them went downstairs. Gabby stowed the box by the front door, then she joined Emma and her grandmother in the kitchen. A pile of mail sat on the counter, with the latest edition of the newspaper on the countertop, still rolled and secured with an elastic band.

Their grandmother stood beside the stove, lifting warm cookies with a spatula to check their golden-brown bottoms, while the coffeepot finished brewing and another batch of cookies baked in the oven. She was a slight woman with a fondness for pink who kept her long silver hair in a perpetual bun. Today, she had on a floral short-sleeved blouse with a pair of well-worn jeans that had a dusting of flour across one hip.

Gabby loved her grandmother fiercely, this woman who had stepped in and become mother and father and everything in between to three lost little girls even while she deeply grieved the loss of her only child. Grandma had stayed strong, becoming the one who packed the lunches and checked the homework and kissed the skinned knees of Meggy, Gabby, and Emma.

The familiar radio that sat on top of the breadbox blared a tinny Van Morrison singing about a brown-eyed girl. Grandma's hips swayed in time with the music. "Where's Margaret?" she asked.

"She left." Gabby put her back to the kitchen counter and sidestepped a few feet, as casually as she could, until her hand landed on that day's paper. Emma slipped into place beside her, and as Gabby spoke, louder than normal, she scooted the rolled newsprint into Emma's hand. "Said she had to go to work. You know Margaret, the biggest overachiever in this town."

Grandma sighed. "That girl is always working."

"Busy is Margaret's middle name," Gabby said. "You know that."

"True. She always was the one who couldn't sit still for too long." Grandma pulled the carafe out of the coffeemaker and poured the rich, dark brew into two mugs while Emma slipped out of the kitchen undetected. "There's creamer in the fridge, Gabriella. And iced tea for Emma."

"You know us well, Grandma." She crossed the room and pressed a kiss to her grandmother's cheek. The soft scent of Estée Lauder wafted between them, a scent of childhood and warmth and love. Gabby wrapped an arm around Grandma and worried that her grandmother felt thinner than last time she'd embraced her. In the last few weeks, Gabby swore she'd heard a note of melancholy in Grandma's voice, but whenever Gabby asked if anything was troubling her, Grandma had insisted she was fine. "Are you taking your heart medication?"

Grandma turned and faced her granddaughter. A stern smile curved across her face. "You girls worry too much about me. I'm seventy-five, not a hundred. And just because I've been a little down doesn't mean I won't pop back into my cheery self. It's just tough getting old and not being as...current as I once was."

"Current? You're the coolest grandmother we know." There was a soft ding of an incoming text message on Gabby's phone.

"Either way, it doesn't matter. Although I do miss the days when you girls needed my hugs and advice." Grandma turned and cupped Gabby's face in her soft, weathered palms. "You three had been through so much. Such little girls with such big weights on your shoulders."

"Made easier by a really strong grandma." The familiar words, exchanged dozens of times over the years, brought a smile to Gabby's face and a shimmer of tears to

Grandma's eyes. Grandma had no idea how much Gabby had leaned on her strength, or how grateful she was for a parental role model who showed the girls a world of grace and compassion. "Enough of that. Didn't you mention cookies?"

Gabby tugged open the fridge, taking a peek at her phone and the image Emma had sent while she feigned spending extra time searching for the creamer. Emma slipped back into the kitchen with a flashed thumbs-up and a sleight of hand that set the newspaper back in place.

When she closed the fridge, Gabby caught a glimpse of Jake out of the corner of her eye. He was climbing a ladder with a can of paint in one hand, his broad profile made into a dark shadow by the bright sun behind him. Margaret was right—Jake had grown up to become rather handsome, if a girl liked a man with a rangy build and dark brown hair that was just a tad too long, not to mention a permanent smile on his face like he was some kind of loon.

He caught her staring and flashed her one of his trademark goofy grins. Then he gestured for her to come outside. *Want to help?* he mouthed, hoisting the paintbrush.

She pointed to her ear and shook her head, as if she hadn't just read that man's overpronounced words on his lips. Okay, yeah, maybe he did look kind of hot with a white T-shirt that rippled across his chest and flecks of pale gray paint on the muscles of his arms. Didn't mean she was going to do anything other than tease him the same as she always had.

Plus, every time she looked at him, she was reminded of his cousin, and the way Brad had treated her heart like it was a scrap of trash. Brad was taller, not as lean, and didn't have the dimple that Jake had, but in every other way, the two of them seemed to be carbon copies. The same affable grin and easygoing manner, but in Brad, that masked a driven, competitive man who had been successful at everything he tried. Even making Gabby fall in love.

She didn't want to repeat that mistake with another Maddox man. *None of us are any good at commitment*, Brad had said just before he got on a plane. *Don't be as foolish as my mother was and think we can be anything else.*

Besides, Gabby and Jake had always been friends and decided years ago that they wouldn't do anything silly like muddy those waters with a relationship. Except for that one time on the dance floor at the senior banquet, Gabby had never even thought about kissing Jake. No, Brad had been the one she had a raging crush on most of her life. And the one who had broken her heart as easily as snapping a twig.

She had bigger things to worry about, she thought. Like a sad grandmother, a business that was on the brink of collapse, and a town that was looking to her to come up with an event big enough to save them all.

TWO

Jake Maddox knew he was being an idiot.

Hanging off the side of Eleanor Whitmore's home on a warm spring afternoon, with a bucket of paint in one hand and a brush in the other, just to get a glimpse of the girl he'd been in love with since the first grade—it was dangerous in a hundred different ways.

Not that he minded helping Eleanor with little projects around her house. Gabby's grandmother had been like his own for most of Jake's life. He'd spent more time at Grandma El's than in his own chaotic, tense, unpredictable home. A father who was gone more often than he was at the dinner table and a mother who was rarely out of bed before noon and then back on the couch with a scotch in her hand by three o'clock meant Jake had done a lot of raising himself. On the rare evenings his workaholic father was around, he spent most of the hours between dinner and bed reminding Jake that he wasn't living up to some impossible Maddox standard.

Jake had met Gabby in first grade but had barely

exchanged a handful of words with the exuberant girl who sat two rows behind him. That was, until one spring afternoon when she'd changed his life, a moment that meant more than he could ever tell her.

His mother had moved out the night before, heading to Scottsdale to live with her brother while she "figured things out." Jake woke up to a banana and a note on the counter, and a father who was running late for work while shooing his son out the door with only a handful of answers. Jake walked to school by himself, dazed and confused, wondering how his mother could leave behind her only child so easily.

His teacher assigned a family tree as homework. Jake stood outside the doors of Harbor Cove Elementary as dozens of happy-to-go-home students parted around him like a wave. He stared at the long sheet of paper with its little circles for pictures and lines for memories. Then he crumpled it into a ball and tossed it into the trash, just as Gabby came around the corner.

"What'dja do that for?" she asked. Her green eyes were wide and curious.

For a second, he thought she was talking to someone else. Most of the kids in school either teased or ignored Jake. They didn't see past the cast on his leg or the way his body leaned a tad too far to the right. He was different, and he'd learned to keep his head down and not draw attention. But this girl, this emerald-eyed friendly girl with a riot of rich brown curls, was staring directly at him, not his leg, not his brace, not all the corrective surgery scars, but him. "I...I...don't know what to put on the paper."

She shrugged. "Just make it up. I'm gonna put a dog on mine. We don't have one, 'cause my momma is allergic. But I really want a dog in my family. A big dog, with lots of fur and floppy ears."

"I don't have a mom right now." He hadn't told anyone that, hadn't even admitted the truth to himself because maybe, if he pretended it hadn't happened, she'd be there when he got home from school. "My dad says she ran away."

Gabby bent over, fished the paper out of the trash, and smoothed it against a concrete pillar before handing it back to Jake. "I think you should draw your mom anyway."

"Why?"

"Because your mom could come back. My momma says you always gotta have hope, or you don't have anything at all." She'd given him that wide smile of hers, missing one tooth, leaving a little gap that only made her seem cuter somehow. "Wanna come to my grandma's with me? We can have cookies, and I can help you draw a dog on yours, too."

Somehow, that invitation to conquer a homework assignment that had seemed impossible ten minutes ago lightened everything. She'd given him a ray of hope— a hope that in a way did come true—and a reason to smile. He'd gone with Gabby and been welcomed into her warm and boisterous family as if he'd always been a part of it.

After that, they drifted into a routine, walking home from school together and stopping at her grandmother's for snacks before hurrying down the sidewalk to their own houses for supper. Even on the weekends, Jake had tagged along with Gabby more often than not, captivated by the warm family and the dinners around the table and the hugs that seemed to happen every minute of the day.

Then Gabby's life had been upended, and on that day, Jake had been there, too. Only this time, he was the one giving the hugs and mourning the loss of Gabby's mother in a way he'd never mourned anything before or since.

Over the years he'd become protective of them, this family he had grown to love, and when his cousin broke Gabby's heart last year, it had taken everything inside of Jake not to break Brad's jaw in response. His cavalier, smart, charming golden-child older cousin had gotten the one thing Jake had always wanted—Gabby's love—and then thrown it away like a toy that had outlived its use.

The tears in her eyes and the slump in her shoulders told him how badly she'd been hurt. It had taken a solid six months for the Gabby he knew to begin to return, and for their friendship to get back on an even keel.

That, Jake told himself a thousand times, was enough. Gabby had always been the only person who saw him as himself, who never made him feel awkward or out of place. When the first of the casts he'd endured over the years was removed at the end of first grade and Jake had to spend his summer undergoing painful physical therapy, Gabby had sat beside him and made him laugh or just chattered about a blue jay she'd seen that day or the way the moon looked the night before. She'd been the bright spot in those tough years while his mother was away. Hell, she'd always been a bright spot, and although he'd accepted—more or less—that her heart belonged to another Maddox man, he'd never been able to shake that tiny whisper that someday she'd see how very much he cared about her.

Today, Gabby and her sisters had shown up at Eleanor's house a little after ten in the morning. He'd been here since eight, touching up the trim on the northern side of the house. New England nor'easters had a way of peeling the paint right off the shingles, as Eleanor liked to say, so Jake gave the shake-style siding a little buff and shine every spring when the weather turned warm again.

"You going to stay up there all day, Jake Maddox, or come inside and have some iced tea and cookies?" Gabby shielded her eyes with her palm and propped the other fist on her hip.

Damn. Every time he looked at her, his heart did a little jump. She had grown into a beautiful woman with high cheekbones, a wide smile, and long brunette curls that the summer sun always tipped with copper. Today, she was wearing jeans and a snug black T-shirt that showed off her curves.

And he was just as smitten as he had been in high school, when he'd followed her around like a lovelorn puppy.

She's not even interested in you.

"What kind of cookies?" he shouted back.

"What do you mean, what kind of cookies? You eat every kind of cookie known to man, last I heard. Don't you be getting picky on me, or I'll eat your share."

He climbed down the ladder and set the can and paintbrush on a makeshift bench he'd set up on a couple of sawhorses. "You eat my share of cookies, and I will throw you in the bay. Again."

She laughed. "The last time you did that, I was eleven. I can outrun you now."

"Oh yeah?" He hopped off the last step. "Prove it."

Gabby spun on her heel and darted across the lawn. Jake scrambled after her, outpacing her in a matter of seconds with his longer legs. She dashed behind an oak tree, laughing and winded. "No fair," she gasped. Anyone watching them would think they were both thirteen, not thirty. "You didn't give me a heads-up."

He grabbed the trunk of the tree and swung around it to face her. Her cheeks were flushed, her chest heaving, and a few flyaway curls had escaped her ponytail. He had the strongest urge to kiss her. All it would take was a little lean in her direction and—

Instead, he reached out and tapped her head. "You're it."

She rolled her eyes and then burst out of her not-so-secret hiding place just as Jake pivoted and sprinted across the lawn. He could hear her laughter behind him as he skidded to a stop at the back door of the two-story Victorian-style home. Gabby bent over, heaving in deep breaths. "Since...when...did you...start running so fast?"

"Since I started running." He grinned, oddly proud that he'd beaten her. There'd been years when no one thought Jake would walk, much less run, and except for a slight hitch in his gait when he was tired, most people didn't realize what he'd endured as a child. "I had to do something to keep up with you."

"Well, I am younger than you."

"By two months."

"Oh my goodness, you two sound like you're still in grade school, the way you tease each other," Eleanor said as she came out to the porch. She shook her head, but a smile played on her lips. "Now, quit all that nonsense and come inside. I made peanut butter chocolate chip cookies."

"Aww, my favorite, Grandma El." Jake grinned at Gabby. "Because she likes me best."

"That's just because you have her fooled into thinking you're a nice guy." Gabby tapped him on the nose as she brushed past him and into the house. "But I know better."

You think you do. He watched her saucy sashay over to the table and wondered if she'd ever stop seeing him as anything other than the annoying boy next door and the cousin of the man who had stomped all over her heart. He could hear the implied *you're just like every other Maddox man* in the joke about him not being nice, lumping him right in there with Brad.

He had no doubt she believed that, too. For a solid month after their breakup, Gabby hadn't spoken to Jake, maybe because he was guilty by association and DNA. The painful thirty days of silence was a reminder that he would be stupid to mess with a good thing. If Jake was forced to choose between Gabby being his ex-girlfriend or Gabby being his friend, he'd take the heartache and longing over losing her again any day.

He poured himself a glass of iced tea and took a seat at the table with Gabby on one side, Emma on the other, and Grandma El at the end. He couldn't count how many times he had sat in this very spot with the Monroe girls and their maternal grandmother surrounding him as if they were all part of the same family. He'd been here more than he'd been with his bitter, driven, critical father, even spending so many Christmas days in this house that Grandma El had started hanging a stocking over the fireplace with his name on it.

"The paint job is shaping up nicely," Grandma El said to Jake. "I love seeing all those ducks just hop into rows."

He chuckled. Gabby's grandmother was known for her interesting phrases and small-town wisdom. She'd grown up somewhere in the South and then moved to Massachusetts when she got married, which had left her with a mashup of Southern charm and Bostonian manners. "With any luck, the last of the ducks will be up there next Saturday. I only have the peak over the attic to do."

"Oh, you shouldn't do that yourself." Grandma El put a hand on Gabby's. "Gabby, why don't you come over next weekend and help Jake? He really shouldn't go up that high by himself."

"I'm pretty sure there's only room for one person on the ladder, Grandma." She took a bite of cookie, and a dusting of crumbs brushed her chin. Jake resisted the urge to reach out and swipe them away with the back of his thumb, or worse, kiss away the sweetness.

Grandma waved off Gabby's words. "You're not going to be *on* the ladder. You can be in the attic, holding on to it for him and passing him iced teas or lemonades."

"As his personal waitress?" Gabby laughed. "As much as I'm sure Jake is a perfectly capable adult male—"

"Only on Tuesdays and Thursdays," he quipped.

Gabby grinned, and his heart did that little flip thing again. "—I can help him if it will ease your mind, Grandma."

"Thank you. It will. A mind at ease is easy to please." She reached for the pitcher and topped off her iced tea.

"Besides, no one wants Jake to end up splattered across the lawn. I just weeded the flowerbeds last week." Gabby grinned again, her grandmother admonished her, and Emma laughed.

"Something like that would end up in the *Harbor Cove Gazette* for sure," Emma said. "Might even make front-page news."

On either side of Jake, Gabby and Emma exchanged

a conspiratorial glance. Gabby gave Emma a little nod and then sat back in her chair, feigning innocence and nonchalance. Anytime Gabby did that, there was trouble brewing.

"Grandma," Gabby said, her voice soft and sweet and innocent, "I was wondering if you had seen the Dear Amelia column this week. It was quite the quandary."

Since when did Gabby use words like *quandary*? The little lilt in her voice and the devilish gleam in her eyes told Jake that something was definitely going on. And the Dear Amelia column? Jake had worked at the *Gazette* for more than two years now and heard the newsroom's Monday morning quarterback discussions about whatever wisdom Amelia had doled out that week. And now Gabby was fascinated by the same section she usually made fun of? Since when?

"Oh really? I hadn't noticed." Grandma El said. "I've just been so busy."

"Some husband wrote in and said he was all worried because he and his wife had drifted apart after their baby was born. You—" Emma cleared her throat. "Amelia told the husband to get creative on date night and find what bonded them before the baby."

"Like going back to the coffee shop where they met or something," Gabby added.

"I thought that was a great idea." Emma added a nod for emphasis. "Didn't you, Gabs?"

"Oh yeah. Low pressure on the romance, and with caffeine. Good combo." Gabby fiddled with her mug. "Although…it seemed like Dear Amelia was kind of frustrated in her reply. She said something about people making the same mistakes over and over again instead of listening to wisdom from others."

"Well, when someone gives perfectly good advice that's ignored, it could frustrate a patron saint. Too many young people these days don't see the value in the wisdom of those older than them, which can leave one feeling as irrelevant as yesterday's newspaper. Anyway..." Grandma El sighed. She shook her head as she broke off a chunk of cookie and set it on her plate. "Either way, let's hope that young man fixes what's wrong in his house, because family is important. I think this whole world would be better off if good advice were heeded and if men paid less attention to their lawns and jobs and more to the women they have been blessed with. Speaking of family, Gabriella and Emma, have you two talked to your father lately?"

Jake could feel the tension in the room shift. The girls' relationship with their father had been rocky for many years and was the one subject Jake never dared to broach with Gabby. She didn't talk much about her father. They'd had some kind of fight years ago, and now they were barely on speaking terms. If there was one person who understood avoiding family drama, it was Jake.

Gabby cupped her mug with both hands and took a sip of coffee, avoiding Grandma El's inquisitive gaze. "He's been busy."

"He's never too busy for his daughters."

Gabby scoffed. "Tell that to Dad. Anyway, Grandma, I should probably get going. I need to work on that display and...some other things." She grabbed a cookie and then pushed away from the table. She dropped a kiss on her grandmother's cheek. "I'll see you tomorrow."

"I, uh, should get to painting the trim. Thanks for the snack, Grandma El." Jake wrapped a handful of cookies in a napkin.

"I saw that." Grandma El grinned. "Which is why I made extra cookies and also fixed you an iced tea to go." She nodded toward the countertop.

"And that is why you are my favorite grandmother." He gave her a one-armed hug, snatched the cookies and tumbler from the counter, and hurried after Gabby. He really needed to fall for a different girl, or maybe just move to another planet. Because everyone he dated, everyone he talked to, all ended up compared to Gabby at some point. While the one man she had loved had no idea what he had lost. "Hey, Gabs."

She was already halfway out the door, the sun streaming behind her, making her hair sparkle. She'd always been beautiful, but in the last year, as she built her own business and, with it, her confidence and strength, she'd become even more so. Beautiful and smart as hell, in an understated, *I can beat you at chess* way. Why the hell had Brad been so stupid as to let her get away?

"What's up?" she asked.

"What was all that back there? You and Emma looked like you were plotting a coup."

She gestured for him to follow her. He stepped onto the porch and pulled the front door closed. The tang of fresh paint hung in the air, mingling with the scent of the beginnings of spring. New grass, budding trees, hopeful flowers. "Have you noticed my grandmother seems a little... down lately?" she said, her voice low.

Now that she mentioned it, he realized Grandma El's sunny personality had been dim for a few weeks. "Yeah, it's been weird."

"I think there's a good reason why." Gabby cupped a hand around her mouth and whispered, even though they were alone outside. "My sisters and I have been doing a little...sleuthing."

"Sleuthing? You sound like Nancy Drew." He laughed. "Were you searching for clues behind the old clock tower or under the hidden staircase?"

She rolled her eyes. "No. We're not trying to figure out a crime. More like...a possible family secret."

"Well, I'm practically a relative, so you should tell me."

She propped a fist on her hips and gave him a scowl. "Jake Maddox, just because you hang around eighty-five percent of the time does not make you a relative."

"Eighty-five percent? Hmm. That seems like a pretty exact percentage. Are you keeping track of how often you see me?" And why did he hope like hell she was?

Give it up, man. Give. It. Up.

She brushed past him, and he caught the bright strawberry-lemon scent of her shampoo. "I have things to do that do not revolve around you."

He trotted alongside her. "Things like what?"

"Don't you have a house to paint?"

"It can wait. It's waited all winter for me to get up on that ladder. What's another five minutes?"

"I have to get over to the shop soon and place some orders. See? Stuff." She paused as she toed at a leaf on the driveway. "Anyway...uh, have you heard from your cousin? I was just wondering if his trip was over or...well, it doesn't matter. I shouldn't have asked."

There was his own clue—as big as a billboard. She was still hung up on another Maddox man. "I don't talk to him much." He didn't add, *Because I want to strangle my blood relative for hurting you.*

"Forget I said anything. Besides, he's the moron who broke up with me, right?"

"And lost a wonderful thing," Jake said.

Gabby laughed and gave his arm a soft punch. "Don't you 'wonderful thing' me, Jake Maddox. I know you, and I'm not going to fall for your corny pickup lines. Try them out on someone else."

"Who says I'm trying to pick you up?" He arched a brow in her direction.

She just rolled her eyes. Across the street, Antonia Lopez emerged from her house with a baby on one hip and a grumpy look on her face. Her dark brown hair was wrapped in a bun secured by an elastic band and a wish, given how many tendrils were escaping and how the baby kept grabbing and pulling the runaway curls. She gave Jake and Gabby a quick and exhausted half wave and then peeked inside her mailbox. In the background, Luis, her husband, was walking the perimeter of the lawn, weed-whacking along the outside of the fence.

"I need to go talk to Antonia," Gabby said, and dashed off before Jake could ask why. He was half tempted to follow her. Instead, he took his time heading back to the ladder and paint can, glancing over his shoulder at the one woman he needed to quit looking at.

"Hey there, Antonia! So nice to see you on this bright and beautiful day," Gabby called out as she crossed the street. "How are you today?"

"Just fine." She sighed. "Alex is teething again…"

The rest of the conversation was caught in the breeze. Jake retrieved the paint can before he headed for the western corner of the house, where he'd noticed a few places he needed to touch up. As he did, he saw Gabby out of the corner of his eye, catching up with the neighbor and making funny faces at Alex, who reached out and tugged a lock of Gabby's hair.

Gabby laughed, her entire face lighting up like a sunrise, and Jake wondered for a half second what it would be like if she looked at him like that. The way she'd once looked at Brad, who'd been too stupid to hold on to the one prize any smart man would give his right arm to have.

THREE

Perfect.

Momma's wedding dress fit the mannequin in the bay window at the front of Gabby's shop as if it had been custom designed. She'd put it up there first thing Monday morning and was so glad she spent all that time in the attic searching for the dress. The sweetheart neckline, cap sleeves, tucked waist, and flared satin skirt with an organza overlay were simple, elegant, and stunning. The sheer rhinestone-edged veil cascaded down the mannequin's back like a wave of sea foam, frothy and light.

Gabby had flanked it with a pair of dresses made by a local girl who'd just graduated from Parsons School of Design. Serena tended to design dresses with a retro flair, with scalloped necklines and tea-length skirts that belled, the exact kind of design that Gabby loved and wore herself. Serena's designs perfectly offset the white with pastel spring colors. They were close to what Gabby had envisioned, although she would have gone with three-quarter sleeves, and maybe a hem detail.

"Aww. That mannequin looks just like her," Emma whispered with a catch in her voice and a shimmer in her eyes. "It makes me miss her so much."

Gabby clasped her youngest sister's hand, just as she had the day Dad sat the three girls on the love seat in Grandma's front room and broken their world. Emma had been just five years old, so little, so scared, so confused, and all Gabby could do was hold her hand and keep whispering, *It'll be okay*, although it never really was and never really would be. "Me too, Ems. Me too."

Then and now, Gabby had made promises she couldn't keep, told lies she could hardly bear, all to protect her sisters. There were things that Em and Meggy didn't need to know, wounds they didn't need to open.

A heartbeat of silence passed between Gabby and Emma. Then the two of them went inside the shop and her little sister made a beeline for her oversize leather tote. She rustled in there for a moment, clearly gathering her emotions. "I, uh, think this idea of yours to combine historical moments and mementos with the town anniversary is brilliant," Emma said. "Especially this early in the spring. People are looking for a reason to get out of their houses now that winter is over, and I think it'll be a good kickoff to the season, and a nice early event for the tricentennial this year."

Gabby wanted it to be more than that. No one in her family knew how much her shop had struggled, especially as the world moved away from in-person buying and more toward online shopping. She desperately needed a website with an easy shopping cart feature, along with a whole lot of marketing to get the word out, but neither had been possible while she was drowning under a pile of bills and a constant worry about making rent.

When she'd opened Ella Penny, she'd thought it would finally be the thing that gave her direction and motivation. The thing that Gabby had been meant to do because it combined her love of fashion with her love of history and family. But as the months wore on and the store's profit margin barely stayed out of the red, her enthusiasm waned, and she had to fight the urge to throw in the towel.

If she could just get the ball rolling with this Celebrate History in the Harbor event, then maybe everything would turn around and she'd find that spark she'd been searching for.

Gabby shrugged off the dark thoughts and forced a smile to her face. "Thanks. There are just so many great artisans in Harbor Cove. I think Margaret is carrying handmade jewelry just for the event, and you've got that mini art gallery off the lobby of the hotel."

"We already sold two pieces, and it hasn't even kicked off yet," Emma said. "I also found this great photographer who specializes in antiquing photos. He took a couple of the ones from Momma's wedding, blew them up, and added a touch of sepia to them. They look like they're retro. It's so cool. I thought we could hang some here, some at the hotel in the bride's room, and some at Margaret's store."

"And mess with Margaret's décor?" Gabby grinned at the idea of upsetting Margaret's organizational-freak apple cart, far more fun than thinking about the fact that her store's rent was due in six days. "You know how she feels about anything that spoils the 'clean lines and sophisticated hues' of the jewelry shop."

"Which is exactly why I picked this one..." Emma turned and pulled a frame out of the pile she'd brought with her and held it up. "Specifically for Margaret's shop."

The playful image of Momma and Dad standing beside a three-tier wedding cake and smearing white frosting and vanilla sponge onto each other's faces filled the sixteen-by-twenty-inch frame. It was bright and happy, with the smiles on their faces echoing the deep love they had for each other and the aching hole that Momma's death had left.

In all of their lives. Momma had been the light of their world, the sun everyone else orbited around, and losing her had caused the entire Monroe galaxy to spin on a wobbly axis. At least for the girls. As for Dad...he hadn't waited more than a heartbeat before moving on, if that long.

Momma had been the one who made Gabby believe in true love, until Dad had burst that romance-novel bubble with a sharp dose of reality. Neither of her sisters knew about what she'd seen that day in the kitchen right after Momma died, and if Gabby had any say in the situation, they never would.

"What do you think she would be like if she were still alive?" Gabby asked. "What do you think our lives would be like?"

"You know her. She'd be dashing in and out of our businesses, checking on us, helping to stock shelves or book guests, then telling the entire world that her girls had the best companies and jobs in all of the continental United States. Even though I was so little when she died, all I remember is how proud she was of us."

"Always busting her buttons, as Grandma would say."

Emma's features softened, and she danced a fingertip across the image of their mother. "I bet she'd also be talking up every single man in a fifty-mile radius, trying to matchmake you and me with someone who would love us as much as Dad loved her."

Gabby scoffed. Dad hadn't loved Momma—if he had, there would have been no way he would have even looked at a woman like Joanna so soon after losing the love of his life. "I've dated every man in a fifty-mile radius, and all I can say is that single looks better every day," Gabby said. She'd tried dating apps, speed dating, and even the singles mixer that Harbor Cove held just before Christmas. Lots of one-off dates, but no one who gave her that goose-bumps feeling. Maybe it didn't exist in the real world, or maybe she was simply overthinking it all.

Well, there had been one person she'd thought was different from all the rest. Brad Maddox had been charming and handsome, smart and accomplished. He'd pursued her like she was the last Christmas tree on the lot and made her feel special and wanted.

Until he sent a text just before he hopped on a plane: *This isn't working for me. Best of luck.* Then nothing. The abruptness, the silence afterward, and the callous way he'd treated their relationship made her want to swear off dating entirely. That look in Momma's eyes was a fiction that didn't last.

"Do you miss him?" Emma asked, as if she'd read Gabby's mind.

Gabby could have played dumb, but pretending to smile would have taken a lot more emotional strength than she had right now, especially after the day with her sisters and the worry about Grandma. And staring at Momma's portrait, so in love and so happy, made Gabby long for a dream she knew rarely came true. "Sometimes I think I do. But maybe I'm just rewriting the history in my head and making the relationship with Brad better than it actually was."

When Brad had been around, he'd been charming, whisking her off to romantic dinners in fancy Boston restaurants or having dozens of flowers delivered to her house. Every one of those, she realized later, had been an apology of some kind because Brad was rarely available and barely a part of her life. He worked long hours at Maddox & Maddox, expanding the personal injury law firm into multiple locations over the five years he'd been there. A month or so after they'd started dating, it was as if he'd stopped working on wooing her. He hardly ever texted or called, and if she saw him more than once in a week, it was a miracle. Gabby had read somewhere that a relationship like that, with sporadic meetings, stayed in a constant honeymoon phase, and they had, for about a year. Most of the time, she'd vacillated between annoyance at his unavailability and excitement when he returned. It had been an exhausting roller coaster that had consumed her. It wasn't until after it ended that she realized how insane he had made her feel.

"I always thought you deserved better," Emma said.

Gabby shrugged. "I just don't think I'm going to find that happily-ever-after. I'll be that spinster fitting dresses until my arthritic hands can't hold the pins anymore."

Emma rolled her eyes as she tucked the photo back into her tote bag. "Now, that is a depressing view of your future. If it wasn't eleven o'clock in the morning, I'd go out and buy us a bottle of wine to drown our dating sorrows with."

"Don't tempt me, because it's definitely five o'clock somewhere." Gabby laughed. "Speaking of matchmaking, I talked to Antonia yesterday."

Emma's eyes widened, and even though the sisters were alone in the shop, her voice dropped to a conspiratorial whisper. "Do you think her husband is the one that Grandma was answering in the paper?"

"Her husband fits all the details. Married for three years, a two-year-old, and a busy wife who seems to think her husband has been too busy mowing the lawn to pay attention to her. I'm just saying, I think it's her." Gabby picked up one of the portraits and hung it on the wall. "I invited her into the store today to do a little shopping. I'm going to try to get the behind-the-scenes scoop and maybe see if I can nudge her in the right direction."

"You are sneaky. I love that about you." Emma laughed. "Oh! I almost forgot about my little project I told you about. I wanted to give you these." She rummaged in her bag and pulled out an envelope. "In the attic, I found a whole stack of pictures of Momma, and made some copies for you and Margaret."

"Thank you." Gabby took the envelope, but before she could open the flap, Emma tapped her on the shoulder.

"Speak of the devil. Here comes Antonia."

Grandma's neighbor was coming down the sidewalk, wrestling her stroller toward the shop. Every few feet, Alex threw his stuffed giraffe on the ground, and Antonia stopped to pick it up. She sighed and then pushed on before repeating the whole process a few seconds later. She fit every definition of an overwhelmed young mother.

Before Antonia could reach the door, Gabby had it open and ready, a friendly smile on her face. "Hi, Antonia! I'm so glad you came by."

"Honestly"—Antonia sighed and tucked a lock of dark hair behind her ear—"I'm just glad to get out of the house. Alex is adorable, but oh my, is he driving me crazy. I barely have time to breathe."

"I bet that's tough. Like when you want to go on date nights and stuff." Okay, that might have been way too obvious. Gabby vowed to dial it back a notch or two.

Antonia waved a hand. "I don't remember what dating is like, it's been so long. I know Luis is trying, God bless him. He said something crazy this morning about going out for coffee—and Luis doesn't even drink coffee. When I said no, he said it seems like I've abandoned him for the baby or something crazy like that." She brushed her hair off her forehead and sighed again. "Doesn't he understand I'm an exhausted mommy who feels more like a pooper scooper than a sexy wife? Once upon a time, I had a figure that"—a grin flashed across her face— "va-va-voomed, if you know what I mean."

"You still do. And I think you should get something pretty that wows Luis and makes you feel as gorgeous as you are." Gabby quickly pulled several hangers off the rack, a selection of fit-and-flare styles, which would accentuate Antonia's curves. "We have these great dresses that are marked down and—"

"I can't." Antonia shook her head. Her chocolate eyes filled with regret. "I mean, going out is a whole thing. I need a babysitter and—"

"I'll babysit!" Emma popped into the conversation, overeager and a little too quick. She gave Antonia a sheepish grin. "Sorry, I get excited about babysitting. I just love kids."

Gabby bit back a laugh. Of the three Monroe sisters, Emma was definitely the least likely to have children. Emma had vowed long ago to never get married and never settle down, so the idea of her watching over a busy toddler would be completely impossible, if they weren't doing this all for Grandma.

Antonia's gaze darted between Gabby and Emma and a squirming, unhappy Alex, who was clearly trying to make a prison break from the stroller. "Wait…you mean it? You would help me?"

"Sure. When I'm not assisting the wedding planner for the hotel, I help out with the kids' summer camp program. I know how to make one laugh." Emma bent down. "Hey, Alex! Look at this little guy! So cute, right?" She squeezed the giraffe sitting atop the stroller bar and made a funny face. The toddler giggled and watched Emma as she danced the stuffed toy back and forth. "See?"

A flicker of envy ran through Gabby. She was thirty, and sometimes she felt like she had missed the trail that led toward marriage and family. Except, who did she know who had that fairy tale? Pretty much no one. Sure, everyone had that starry-eyed moment, but it didn't seem to last. Far better to concentrate on making the store profitable, because in the end, being practical, not romantic, was the smartest option.

"Having a date and a babysitter would be so wonderful! You have no idea how much we need to get out and be alone." Antonia reached into her bag for her cell phone. "Maybe I should ask Luis what he wants to do."

"Or maybe just surprise him," Gabby said, gently pushing Antonia's hand down. For this to work, and for Luis—assuming he was the one had written wrote the letter—to think his plan was successful, Antonia couldn't tell him it had been the girls' idea because he might assume they'd read the column and put the pieces together. "You should get all pretty, leave Alex with Emma, and take *Luis* out for a change. He's obviously trying to bring the magic back, and maybe you can...nudge it along. Make him feel like his efforts haven't gone unnoticed." And maybe Luis would write in to Dear Amelia and tell her all about how well her advice had worked, giving Grandma a little optimistic boost.

Just as Antonia was about to answer, the bell over the door rang, and Jake strode into the shop. Damn it. That man had the worst timing of anyone she knew. She shot him a glare, which he ignored. "Hey, Jake, we're kinda in the middle of—"

"I'm here to ask you to go get coffee."

The sentence hung in the air of Gabby's shop for a long second. Emma shot Gabby a glance, but all Gabby could do was stare at this man who had just come into her store on a Monday morning and—

Asked her on a date? That was impossible. Jake wasn't interested in her. Sure, there'd always been a little flirtatiousness in their repartee, but that was more teasing than actual flirting. Besides, she was sure as hell not interested in him, at least not that way.

Gabby shook her head. "I'm a little busy, Jake, and—"

"And Lori comes in at eleven thirty, which means you'll have time to take a break," he said. "I know you drink coffee most of the day, and I'm offering to buy you one at the Lucky Bagel."

"Must be something in the air," Antonia said. "My husband just asked me to do the same thing yesterday. Even mentioned going back to the shop where we had our first date."

"Saw it in the Dear Amelia column," Jake said with a little knowing wink in Gabby's direction, "and it sounded like a good idea."

Gabby's throat tightened. Did he know that she and

Emma were conspiring to help Grandma feel needed again? Did he suspect anything about her offer to Antonia? And how the heck did Jake know so much about Gabby's schedule anyway? Maybe that 85 percent of the time was closer to 99.

"Uh, right, but why are you asking me? Don't you have some blonde tripping over herself to make you smile?"

He arched a brow. "Where did you hear that?"

"I heard someone mention it at the grocery store a while ago, but..." She shook her head and felt a weird little surge of jealousy in her chest. The last she'd heard, Jake was dating one of the preschool teachers in town. For some reason that had bothered her, yesterday and today, and she'd dropped two not-so-subtle digs about another woman in his life. What was wrong with her? "It was a long time ago. And I shouldn't pry."

"We're practically family, right? Prying comes with the territory." He leaned one elbow on the counter. "And for your information, there's no woman tripping over herself in my life right now."

"Well, that's good. Or not. Whatever makes you happy." Why was she so flustered? She didn't care if Jake dated anyone, or if that pretty, friendly teacher was out of his life. Not one bit. Gabby nodded toward Antonia. "I have a customer, Jake, so if you'll excuse me..."

"No problem. I'll wait." He crossed his arms over his chest and settled into the space by the register, a long, lanky man who made jeans look so good that the view should have been illegal.

He ignored her second glare, and every subsequent one she sent him as Emma played with Alex and Antonia tried on the dresses. After the third one, Antonia fell in love with a crimson square-neck one that nipped at her waist and had a thick black leather belt. It offset her dark curls and deep brown eyes, making every part of Antonia look more vivid and daring.

"Gabby, you are so good at choosing the perfect dress for my figure. And the color? It's to die for. I feel eighteen again in this." Antonia turned left and right, sending the skirt out like a spinning umbrella. Across the room, Alex was immersed in a tower of chunky blocks that Emma would build and he'd knock over. "I love it!"

"It's gorgeous, Antonia," Emma said. "You look like a movie star. Luis is going to be totally wowed."

"Thank you. I have the perfect pair of black heels to wear with it, too." Antonia paused to admire her reflection in the triple mirror. Even with no makeup and her hair in a messy ponytail, Antonia had been transformed by the happiness on her face. "It's so pretty, but…such a big expense for one night. I mean, where am I even going to wear this?"

"Well, the dress is half price, and I can slip in a neighbor-to-neighbor discount on top of that, making it practically free. Oh, and I almost forgot! Bella Vita restaurant is doing a co-promotion with my shop where they give away one gift card per week to a lucky couple." Gabby handed Antonia an envelope and hoped she didn't notice the freshly glued seal or the fact that there was no such advertisement in the shop. Gabby had bought the gift card this morning on her way to work, thinking she would find some way to give it to Antonia and Luis. It had been an expense she could ill afford, but if the whole thing ended with Grandma smiling, the cost was worth every dime. "I think you and Luis should be the lucky couple to win this week."

"Oh, I can't," Antonia said, but a look of longing lingered in her eyes and on her face. "I shouldn't."

"You can, and you should," Gabby said. "Now let me ring you up so you can get out of here and get ready for your date night."

Emma kept Alex occupied while Antonia changed and paid, and Gabby wrapped her purchase in bright pink tissue paper and then tucked it into a thick shopping bag with the shop's logo. A few minutes later, a much happier Antonia was on her way home with a tired toddler who was already starting to nap in his stroller.

"I have to go, too," Emma said as she grabbed her oversize leather bag and started rummaging through it for her car keys. She shook the bag, heard the jingle, rooted around again, and then repeated the process until she finally found her keys, an everyday occurrence with Emma, who was smart as a whip but had a tendency to forget where she'd put her keys or her phone. "I have a bride coming in at two for a tour, and another one who is picking out her linens at four. But I should still be out of work in plenty of time to go to Antonia's at five so she and Luis can go to dinner. Hopefully they have a lovely romantic evening that he just *has* to tell Dear Amelia about." She grinned and crossed her fingers. "See you later, Gabs. I'm so glad that the plan is working. Oh, and Jake, thanks for recommending the hotel to the Harper family. Diana told me you were the one who mentioned it to her. You are so good to our family."

He shrugged. "It was nothing. I was talking to one of the *Gazette*'s advertisers, and she asked me if I knew of a venue for her daughter's wedding. The hotel was the first thing that came to mind. Besides, your family is more my family than my own. And it's a small town. We should all help each other out, shouldn't we?"

"You are a good man," Emma said as she gave him a sideways hug. "Some smart woman should snatch you up."

"Why would I want any other woman when I'm surrounded by you two?" He grinned as he reached out to hold the door for Emma. She tossed him a "Thank you" and then headed for her car.

When the door shut again, leaving just Gabby and Jake in the store, the room seemed to become very quiet despite the Muzak on the sound system. Gabby fiddled with the racks, rearranging clothes that didn't need to be rearranged. "Uh, Jake, about the offer to get coffee—"

"I need your opinion, Gabby," he interrupted. "You're my best friend, and I trust your advice."

"Oh...my opinion. Sure, sure. No problem." Why did the word *friend* cause a little sinking feeling in her stomach? That was what she was to Jake, and what she would always be, and that was a good thing. She had no interest in dating anyone right now, and especially not in dating another Maddox. And she sure as hell didn't want to tie her future and her life to someone else. "Throwing in a coffee makes it all irresistible. I'm sure you know I'll give you about anything when you pay in coffee."

Oh my God, had she just said that out loud? She'd been trying to make a joke, not an innuendo. Crap. "I...I didn't mean anything. I just meant..."

"I know what you meant, Gabby." He nodded toward the street, where Gabby's part-time employee was just getting out of her car. "Look, Lori's on her way in, and I really need to make a decision, and you're the person who knows me best. So what do you say? Shall we?" He put out his arm in a mock chivalrous move.

Gabby was half tempted to take it, but with this funny feeling in her stomach, touching Jake would just complicate everything. Keeping it simple and light, as it had always been, was the best course of action. "I'll meet you over there in a couple minutes. I have to give Lori a rundown on the sale before I go."

"Sounds good." He opened the door, and Lori scooted in, thanking him as she did. "Mocha latte with skim milk, right?" he called back to Gabby.

He knew her favorite coffee? She couldn't remember a single time when she'd told him that, but Jake, in typical Jake fashion, had heard that detail and memorized it. Brad had never remembered so much as her birthday month, never mind the exact date or something as simple as how she took her coffee. The thought that Jake had paid attention softened her stance a bit. "Emma's right," Gabby said. "You do take good care of us Monroe girls."

"That's my job." He gave her a smile that only made that weird, off-kilter feeling in her gut multiply. "See you soon, Gabby."

"Is it just me or does that guy get hotter every time I see him?" Lori stowed her purse under the counter and pulled her hair back into a barrette. The twenty-three-year-old had graduated from college with a degree in fashion and taken the job at the shop over the summer, fallen in love with one of the frat boys from Emerson, and stayed here ever since. Gabby loved the way she could calm any nervous shopper and help her find the perfect dress.

"Jake? He's just a friend." But as Gabby went over the sale details with Lori and then headed down the block to the Lucky Bagel, the word *friend* felt odd on her tongue. It was just the coffee invite that had thrown her off. She'd misinterpreted it, clearly. She'd grab her mocha, give him some advice, and then go back to work. Just like normal. Which was exactly where Gabby wanted to be right now.

She found Jake inside, sitting in one of the booths with a mug of black coffee before him, alongside a mocha with a coaster on top to keep it warm. The two cups flanked a plate of brownies. Damn that man for knowing her so well. "Thanks for the mocha. And the sugar rush."

As she slid into her seat, she realized that he didn't look much like Brad at all. Where Brad was polished and meticulous, Jake was a little rougher around the edges and...

Comfortable.

It was an odd word to describe a man, but every time Gabby looked at Jake, she thought of words like *warm*, *cozy*, and *comforting*. She wanted to curl into his chest and take a nap or just listen to his heartbeat. Crazy thoughts. It had to be because she knew him so well. Nothing more.

"Least I can do." From inside his jacket, he pulled out a rolled-up oversize envelope she hadn't noticed before and set it on the table. "Now, before I show you this, you have to promise not to laugh."

"Are you suddenly developing a sensitive side, Jake Maddox?" The words were a gentle tease. She knew how he'd been bullied as a kid, made fun of constantly for the operations to repair a birth defect, followed by casts and braces, all the way through third grade. Jake had been the shyest kid in her class, and almost from the minute she saw him standing far apart from the other students, she'd felt like she should protect him.

He'd been there for Gabby when her mother died and when her father disappointed her over and over again. They'd developed a kinship over their similar family histories, and that made Gabby understand Jake in a way she was pretty sure very few people did.

He drew in a deep breath before he spoke. "So, there's this photography contest for *Vista* magazine. I've always wanted to enter, but I never thought anything I had was really good enough. But I have this picture—"

He opened the envelope, tugged out a sheet of paper and set it on the table. An image unfolded before her, spread across an eight-by-ten photo. A wood-and-metal school desk, the square surface covered in dust, with a plastic chair turned slightly to the right, as if the student who'd been there had just dashed out to recess. Papers were scattered across the floor, caught mid-ruffle in a breeze coming through the broken window. The sun was just starting to rise in the background, casting a muted haze through the foggy playground, making it seem ghostlike behind the empty classroom. "Is this our old elementary school?" she asked.

He nodded. "It's been empty for almost ten years, ever since the town closed it after all that storm damage it suffered."

"I remember." Hurricane Sandy had reached her destructive hand into Harbor Cove, demolishing most of the school with a wicked wind and pounding rain. The town had moved the elementary students into the middle school for the rest of the school year. Then they built a wing for the younger kids over the summer, combining all eight grades into one building far from the shore. "Jake, this is tragic and beautiful and just...it takes my breath away and makes me think at the same time. How did you capture this?"

"Woke up ridiculously early and trekked out there every morning for two weeks. There was a fog rolling in one morning, and it just gave the entire scene this haunted quality. Or maybe I'm seeing stuff that isn't there. This is probably too much, or too dark, or too whatever."

"It's too amazing, that's what it is." She glanced up at him. His hazel eyes were more green than brown today, and he had a day's worth of stubble on his chin, giving him a rugged, cavalier edge. "Are you going to enter it?"

He shrugged. "I don't know. I'm supposed to be a lawyer, making big bucks for my father's firm. Not 'pursuing some frivolous hobby that's never going to pay the bills.'"

"You hated being a lawyer. And that's your father's voice saying it's a silly hobby. You're great at your job and you're an amazing photographer. You're already starting to argue with me," she said as he opened his mouth, "and don't do it. I see what you post on Facebook, and even your casual shots with your phone are awesome. You should go after this. I mean, how are you ever going to fulfill your dreams if you don't take risks?"

"Have you met me, Gabby? I'm the most risk-averse person I know."

He was indeed. If there were an award for logical planning with no spontaneity, Jake would win. Before he quit the job at his father's law firm, he'd worked for six months at the paper in his spare time, making sure he could do the job. Jake never made a move that wasn't carefully pro-and-conned. "Which is exactly why you should do it." She covered his hand with her own and gave it a squeeze. "Get out of your comfort zone, Jake. You're wearing a hole in the sofa."

For a long second, Jake didn't reply. In that space, Gabby remembered the Jake from elementary school. Painfully quiet and painfully aware that he was different from the other kids. He'd always been on the periphery of their group of friends, until somewhere around middle school when he bought his first camera and found something he loved to do—something he loved so much, he walked away from his father's law firm to pursue it.

He was a brilliant photographer. She'd seen most of his work, and Jake had a keen eye for the story behind the picture and a way of bringing it to life with angles and lighting. Even the ads and layouts he designed for the *Gazette* had a modern, fresh take, something that had boosted the paper's sales even as others saw their subscription numbers dwindling; then as the paper began moving into the digital market, Jake had come up with the idea of exclusive photo content for web subscribers. People raved about his work because he was somehow able to capture the essence of the small towns that the *Gazette* chain served. Residents loved the behind-the-scenes look at their world, if the number of likes and comments was any indication.

"Take the chance, Jake. It could work out beautifully." Then she realized she was still holding his hand. She quickly released him and grabbed her mug, taking a long sip before setting it back on the table because, for some reason, her hand was shaking.

"Yeah, that's easier said than done." He gave her his suspicious eye, something she knew well from all the trouble she'd talked him into when they were younger. "Speaking of things outside our comfort zone . . . what was all that with Antonia Lopez today? And you suddenly having some gift certificate deal? And Emma saying something about the plan working? What are you guys, Charlie's Angels?"

She averted her gaze and reached for another bite of brownie. "Nothing. Just helping a neighbor."

"Nope, not buying it." He crossed his arms and leaned across the tabletop, winnowing the space between them to a few inches. "I read that Dear Amelia column that you and Emma suddenly seemed so interested in that you had to ask your grandmother about it. I thought that was an odd conversational topic, given the fact that you never read it before and the fact that you used the word *quandary* in a sentence."

"It was just interesting. That's all." She gave him a little glare. "And I'm smart, you know. I use big words."

"This little...whatever you have going on...it wouldn't be the source of this family mystery you mentioned, would it?" He arched a brow. "Like maybe you think Grandma El is Dear Amelia?"

Damn, the man was smart. Jake had always been able to spot a Monroe girl lie from thirty yards away. Gabby picked up her mug again and kept it in front of her face, hoping the heat in her cheeks wasn't a dead giveaway. "Of course not."

"Well, speaking hypothetically, if she was, and if you and Emma were trying to...let's say manipulate the outcomes of her advice, might it help to align with an ally who works full-time at the paper and can get a peek at the column before it goes to print?"

"Now who's using big words?" She cocked her head and studied him. "Did you start subscribing to that word-of-the-day app thing again?"

"Don't try to change the subject, Bella-Ella," he said, using the nickname he'd coined when she was six years old. He was the only one who called her that, an endearment she found both annoying and touching. "I know you noticed that Grandma El has been a bit down lately." He paused, giving Gabby enough time to nod in agreement, and the two of them shared a flicker of worry. "So if you and Emma are scheming to cheer her up by creating a few happy endings for the people who write to her...then I'm all in."

She sat back and studied him. "I thought you were risk-averse."

"When it comes to caring about the Monroe women," Jake said, plucking a bite of brownie from the plate and popping it into his mouth, "I already took that risk a long time ago."

FOUR

Eleanor had spent most of the last three decades worrying about her granddaughters. She'd always chosen to see that responsibility as a blessing, not a chore. From the day Margaret was born and Penny had brought over the squirming, grumpy, seven-pound-eight-ounce miracle of joy, Eleanor's world had shifted to revolve around first Margaret and then Gabriella and Emma, the three little girls she loved more than anything in the world.

If there was one thing Eleanor was good at, it was being needed. Her late husband, Russell, had been a good, strong man who rarely cried and struggled to express an emotion other than stoicism. He'd told her once that he'd needed her to soften him and ground him. So she'd been the anchor and he'd been the ship that brought them from Savannah to Boston, buying a house too big for a family of three and building a life in this little town.

Penny announced she was pregnant just two weeks after Russell had died, a little bit of joy in a house that was trapped beneath the shadows. When Penny had Margaret, Eleanor held that baby and realized she could be happy again. Not the way she'd been happy with Russell, but in a new way, with a new purpose. As each of the girls came along, Eleanor babysat and baked cookies and spoiled them as any grandmother would.

Life had been good. Bright. Sweet. Then a car accident stole the life out of all of them. Davis, Penny's husband, had been useless after his wife died, as lost as a dinghy in an ocean, and Eleanor had taken the girls in, putting her own grief to the side. She'd had purpose again, and a house full of giggles and running feet. The days flew by, and for a while, it was as if Eleanor was reliving Penny's best childhood moments, only in triplicate. She could see her daughter's grace and spunk in each of the girls, a little bittersweet gift from God.

Then the girls had gone and grown up and started their own lives, and the big house that had seemed so full just a few years ago felt emptier and sadder every year. Margaret, the most driven of the three, had poured herself into her jewelry business, quite probably at the expense of her marriage, given how little Eleanor saw the couple together nowadays. Emma, the headstrong wild child, was always one bad day away from running off to Guam or Russia or whatever place captured her fancy. And Gabriella…

Well, Gabriella had been struggling for a while, but she was doing a good job of pretending that whatever was bothering her didn't exist. Putting everyone else's happiness ahead of her own.

Something Eleanor knew a lot about. She sighed, and then she dumped out the tea that had gone cold while she sat at her kitchen table and missed people who were never coming back. She headed into her tidy little office and pulled out the folder of emails she'd printed yesterday afternoon. Once upon a time, she'd had to drive over to the *Harbor Cove Gazette* and retrieve the letters in person, but now they came into her inbox. She printed them out, just to have the feel of a real letter, a nod to the nostalgia of ebony ink and heavy stationery. In a world gone digital, sometimes it was nice to hold something tangible and real.

The only person who knew her secret, and who had vowed to never share it, was Leroy Walker, the editor for the *Gazette* chain. Many years ago, Leroy had hit a bad patch in his marriage, and Eleanor had been his sounding board. Next thing she knew, he was proposing that she write the advice column for the chain, and offered to pay her a nice chunk of change and for only a handful of hours of work that she could easily do after hours.

She'd agreed, as long as he kept her real identity anonymous. *People are more likely to tell their secrets to someone they don't know*, Eleanor had told him. *So I'll be able to be the kindly stranger who gives them wisdom, with a little bit of sass on top.*

That was exactly the persona she'd mastered in the Dear Amelia column for going on twenty-five years now. It had given her a purpose outside of raising a family, and a fun little peek into the inner lives of the people in Harbor Cove. Sometimes, those lives were full of tragedy and loss. Other times, their problems were as simple as asking a neighbor for a favor. She had seen the world shift over the years she'd written the column, but in the end, relationships were what set everything right again.

And yet, every week when she flipped open the folder and pulled out the letters that had come in, she thought

that it felt like people just didn't seem to care about advice
or common sense anymore. Or what a grandmother had
to offer. She sighed again and then set to work, drafting
her response to the lonely hearts letter before her. Dear
Amelia had plenty to say—

But Eleanor wondered more and more these days if
anyone was listening.

❧❧❧❧

Jacob Theodore Maddox. Jake typed his name into the
entry form, and this time managed to make it through his
address and phone number before he deleted the entry and
closed the page to the website. Again. The photo he had
shown Gabby sat beside him on his desk at the *Harbor
Cove Gazette*, almost accusatory in its glossy finish.

Coward. Just do it.

This was crazy. It was a contest, not a gladiator fight
to the death. A hundred dollars out of his pocket for the
entry fee. He should enter the damned thing and get it
over with.

The stack of ads for the week sat by his right
hand. Atop the pile was one for his father's law firm,
with a picture of Brad's successful, confident face in the
upper corner. *He should have been my son*, Jake's father
had yelled when Jake quit his job at the firm, *because
he doesn't waste time on silly hobbies and daydreams.
That's all those pictures you take are, Jacob. A daydream.
One of these days you're going to grow up and stop being
such a coward.*

Gabby was right. He had gotten too used to being
in his comfort zone, and for good reason. The last time
Jake had taken a risk, almost everything in his life had

imploded. His grandfather had once told him that a smart man stuck to the well-traveled road because then there weren't any surprises or land mines.

"Maddox, you have that ad copy for me yet?" The sharp bark of his boss, Leroy Walker, startled most of the new people at the paper, but Jake had known Leroy for ten years and knew full well the paper's editor was more bluster than bite.

"Just sent it over to typesetting," Jake said. The newspaper's offices filled the second story of a former accounting firm in downtown Harbor Cove. The wooden floors creaked when people walked across them, and the windows had a drafty chill in the winter, but the place was old and historic and the perfect setting for a newspaper. The heavy rumble of printing presses and typewriters had been replaced by the quiet hum of computers and servers, but at least the building had the charm of the past. "By the way, the owner of the Bella Vita had a lot of last-minute changes. He couldn't make up his mind on the typeface or the image."

Leroy sighed, and a frown crossed his dark face. "Again?"

Jake nodded. Every week, Francesco Rossi hemmed and hawed about his ad in the paper, and nine times out of ten, he ended up running the same one he'd run the week before, and the week before that. "He says his ex-wife was the one with all the advertising sense."

"Maybe so, but she also nearly bankrupted him before they got divorced."

"Frank is one of those guys who sees the best in everyone." Harbor Cove was a small town, with a small-town paper, which meant Jake knew pretty much every business owner in a ten-mile radius. Bella Vita had been a favorite of the locals for decades, but over the last two years, the restaurant's profits had begun to dip. Frank was a master chef who made the most brilliant Bolognese sauce Jake had ever tasted, but when it came to advertising, marketing, and increasing profits, Frank was at a loss.

"True." Leroy leaned against the wall of Jake's cubicle and crossed his arms over his broad chest. He had a penchant for loud Hawaiian shirts, and today's bright blue with yellow parrots was bold yet befitting a man who wasn't above the occasional practical joke. "Speaking of people without any sense..."

"Don't start, L," Jake muttered. "I used to like you, you know."

He chuckled. "I'm just trying to nudge you down a better path."

"I have a job right here. A job I happen to love."

"And you're great at it. I might end up like Frank if I keep saying this, but you're a hell of a photographer, Jake. You should be behind the lens instead of hunched over a Mac all damned day. This place wouldn't be the same without you, so I'm only half-serious about telling you to go find some greener, more lucrative pastures."

"You don't think designing a two-for-one special at Earl's Diner is using all my skills?" Jake grinned. "We have this same argument every week, and every week, I tell you the same thing."

"That you're happy where you are." Leroy arched a brow. "You sell that story so well. I think I've heard it about ten thousand times."

"Hence why I'm in advertising, because I can convince Santa he needs a convertible." Jake shut down his computer, leaned back in his chair, and stretched. "Want to grab a beer?"

"Only if I can talk you into leaving this two-pony town for bigger and brighter lights."

"You can try, but my answer will be the same." Brad was the one who chased bigger and brighter, shifting the firm away from the lesser-paying contract law and into the big-bucks world of personal injury law. Jake didn't need any of that. Yeah, maybe he didn't make the money Brad did or drive a fancy car, or live in a house big enough for a family of twenty, but he was content, and there was something to be said for that.

How are you ever going to fulfill your dreams if you don't take risks?

Gabby's words had haunted the edges of his thoughts ever since they'd had coffee. Quitting the law firm had been a risk, but one that he'd almost had to take, because working with his critical, hard-driving father had been miserable. Jake didn't have the love for the kill that his father and Brad had when they went into court. He'd been more open to settlements than lawsuits, mediations instead of judgments. He'd never be the kind of lawyer his father wanted him to be, and leaving had cost him what little of a relationship he'd had with Edward Maddox. Mom lived far from Harbor Cove in Scottsdale, and although he talked to her once a week, they'd never really rebuilt their bond after she'd left. Jake had found a home here, among the computers and the artwork and his camera, but it had, admittedly, become a comfortable, predictable home.

Maybe it was time to shake that up. Get off the comfort-zone sofa, as Gabby had said, and see where he ended up. Maybe. He'd decide that another day.

As Jake got to his feet, he noticed a pile of papers

in Leroy's hand. "Hey, is that the proof for Tuesday's edition?"

"Yep. Hot off the presses."

"Can I take a look?" Jake riffled through the pages and then stopped. "I'll be damned," he muttered as he scanned the page and caught snippets of the words in the entertainment section. "It worked." He glanced up. "Are you done with the proof? Can I take this one with me?"

"Are you that anxious to read all about Cassie Wallace opening a new dog grooming parlor and the rummage sale at the Methodist church?"

"Well, if it's between beers with you and the early edition of the *Gazette*…" Jake chuckled. "I'll meet you over there. I just have to make one stop first."

The dress shop, with its cheerful pink-and-yellow-sherbet awning and classic white paint, had been a match for Gabby's vivacious personality since the day she opened the doors. Jake had painted that awning himself and hung the sign over the door. A curlicue script of deep green letters read *Ella Penny*, bold against a white backdrop.

Inside, he could see Gabby handing a bag to a woman. Gabby's face was animated and happy, her smile wide, and for a second, he wished he were the one buying a gift and hearing Gabby's lighthearted banter.

When Gabby had first opened, Ella Penny had been bustling with customers nearly every day. She'd started her shop at the height of tourist season, and the crowded downtown foot traffic made for lots of potential sales. But the last few times Jake had come by here, the store had barely had more than one or two people shopping. It made him wonder if Gabby's business was struggling or if maybe the winter slowdown had been tougher than usual this year.

In the old days, Gabby would have talked to him about it. But ever since she'd dated his cousin, there'd been a coolness in their friendship, with Gabby keeping more and more things to herself lately. She'd withdrawn everywhere in her life, he'd noticed. She rarely posted on social media and didn't seem to go out with her friends as often as she used to. Maybe it was just a little winter doldrums getting to her.

The door chimed as he entered, and Gabby looked up. The smile lingered on her face for a beat before her gaze shifted back to the customer. "Have a nice day, Sandy. I'll give you a call when I get some more sweaters in stock."

"Thank you so much." Sandy Williams gave Gabby a wave and headed for the door. She was a gregarious woman in her early seventies who ran the garden club in town and had a booth selling succulents and annuals at the weekend farmers market in the summertime. "Good afternoon, Jake."

He nodded. "Ma'am."

She blushed. "If I were twenty years younger..."

"You'd still be too good for me." Jake grinned and held the door and then waited for Sandy to pass through. She gave him a smile before getting in her car.

"Flirting with my customers again?" Gabby asked.

"It's a tough job, but I'm happy to do it." It was so much easier to make a joke than to admit the truth—that the only woman he wanted to flirt with was Gabby, who clearly had no interest in flirting with him. "Business seems kind of slow lately. Everything okay?"

"Of course. All sunshine and roses." But her smile fell flat, and she averted her gaze.

"I could always run an extra couple of ads in the paper, Gabby. No charge. Or maybe some kind of coupon promo."

"It would be crazy to turn down free advertising, so I'll take you up on that offer." Her face brightened. "But really, I'm fine."

"And if you aren't, you know I'm here for you, right?"

"Of course. Because you're my *friend*."

The way she emphasized the last word made him feel like she was drawing a line in the sand and telling him to stay firmly on his side. A tingle of worry ran up his spine, but he brushed it off. If Gabby said she was fine, surely she was.

He reached in his back pocket and pulled out the stack of papers he'd taken from work. He spread them on the counter in front of Gabby. "By the way, it seems your little plan worked."

"It did?" She snatched up the pages and scanned the Dear Amelia column. "'Dear Amelia, thank you so much for your advice. My wife and I went to dinner last night, and it was wonderful. She got a babysitter and a new dress, and it was just like when we first got married. Thank you for helping me get back a little of that spark we both have been missing lately.'" Gabby shot him a smile, a wide, happy, contented gesture. "It really worked."

"Seems so. Or maybe you just got lucky."

"Well, if I got lucky once, I can get lucky again." Gabby ran her finger down the page, skipping to this week's request for help, muttering words under her breath. "Restaurant work, divorced, lonely." She jerked her attention back to Jake. "I think this is the guy at the Bella Vita. Didn't he get divorced a couple years ago?"

"His name is Frank Rossi, and yes, he and his wife split up, but that's not necessarily him."

"And what powers of deduction have you used to decide that, Sherlock?"

"The same poor ones you have used, Watson. There are a lot of restaurant owners who are divorced and lonely in this world." Actually, Jake couldn't think of another one, but that didn't mean that Frank had written in to the town paper in between his constant dithering about his weekly ad.

"Maybe…" Gabby tapped her bottom lip. "He saw how happy Luis and Antonia were on their little date, and it got him thinking that he might like to meet someone, and—"

"Gabs, this is not a romance novel." Because if it were, this conversation would be going in a different direction, one that ended with Gabby being his date at the bar instead of Leroy. "There are dozens of customers in Frank's restaurant every night. Doesn't mean he saw those two or that he's the one who wrote that letter."

"But what if he is?"

Jake rolled his eyes. "You know nothing good comes from scheming, right?"

"I bet something will." Her eyes shone. "In fact, I'll prove it to you. What are you doing right now?"

Staring at you. He cleared his throat. "I was going to go have a beer and—"

"You're coming with me." She reached out and grabbed his hand and the newspaper with her other hand. "And we're going to Grandma's for a visit."

FIVE

Gabby set the paper on the counter and stood to the side, trying to look nonchalant. If this was going to work, Grandma couldn't suspect a thing. And yeah, maybe being here meant Gabby was avoiding her store and the lack of customers, but she told herself she was doing something for her family, and that trumped work anytime. If there were a gold medal in Ignoring Things You Don't Want to Face, Gabby would win it for sure. Tomorrow, she vowed. Tomorrow she would pore over the books and google some articles on increasing retail store traffic.

"Grandma, isn't this cool?" Gabby said. "Jake brought by a sneak peek of this week's newspaper."

"Oh really?" Grandma bustled around the kitchen, opening the jar of tea bags, dropping one into a delicate china mug, and grabbing a cloth napkin. For as long as Gabby could remember, Grandma had opted to use cloth napkins, whether it was for a quick breakfast in the kitchen or a sit-down dinner with everyone. It was a quirk that Gabby loved, a little throwback to tradition that made her think of old sitcoms and the TV families sitting down for dinner.

"Yup. I know how much you love the op-ed section, so I thought you might like to see it earlier than the rest of Harbor Cove, like a real VIP," Gabby said as she nudged the page with the Dear Amelia column closer to Grandma.

"Oh, dear, I don't know. I'll wait for the paper to hit my doorstep. It's fine." Grandma dunked her tea bag before setting it on the small plate. The warm scents of lemon and honey filled the air. "I'm just going to take my tea and watch some television tonight."

Gabby glanced at Jake and caught a reflection of her own worry in his eyes. So odd for Grandma to sit at home on a nice night like tonight. Everything about Grandma had been out of character over the last few weeks. "You're not going to walk with the neighbors? Or knit? Or work on your scrapbooks?"

"No, dear. I'm just...tired." She sighed. "You two have a good evening. I'm not much for company. I'm sorry."

There was no mistaking the gloomy tone in Grandma's voice. It worried Gabby, worried her in a way that made her want to pace and plot. That was what she always tried to do—find a way to make things better, smooth out the rough edges, ensure everyone's happiness. The day Momma died, Gabby had vowed to be different. To be more responsible for her sisters, to worry more and forget less. Because she knew deep down inside that if she hadn't forgotten Emma's backpack—

Well, that was a path Gabby tried never to travel in her mind. All the what-ifs and if-onlys in the world wouldn't change the rain-slicked roads and the pickup going too fast, and Momma's sedan sliding through the intersection. Or the fact that Dad hadn't been there to pick up the pieces.

Gabby had felt responsible then, and she felt responsible now. So she put on a happy face, told everyone she was fine, and tried to fix whatever went wrong. But every time she turned around, it seemed as if the family that she had was slipping farther and farther out of her grasp. First her sisters, and now Grandma. What if Gabby took her eyes off the ball and caused another loss in her family? What if they all drifted apart? What if something happened to one of them? What if—

"Grandma, why don't you walk with me?" Gabby said, shaking off the dark train of thought. She couldn't change the past, but she could do her best to make the present better. Grandma needed her granddaughters, and the three of them needed her, too. "We can talk and catch up and—"

"You know, Grandma El," Jake cut in, with that affable grin of his, like it was all going to be okay any second now, "I think relaxing in front of the TV is a fabulous idea. In fact, let me carry your tea for you so you can put your feet up."

"Oh, thank you, Jake. You are such a sweetheart." She patted his cheek and gave him a smile as she shuffled off toward the living room. Yet the smile didn't linger on her lips, and the sadness seemed to hang over her like a cloud.

Gabby shot Jake a glare. What was he doing? Encouraging Grandma to wallow in her sadness? When they had this great news with the column to share?

Jake tucked the newspaper under his arm and picked

up the teacup. Seeing the delicate china in Jake's manly hands was such a juxtaposition that it sent a little flutter through her chest. Which was crazy. He was a man carrying a cup, for Pete's sake. Yet her body betrayed her with a flush of heat and a flurry of late-night thoughts.

That was not the way she thought of Jake, ever. Well, mostly not ever. Maybe it was because he reminded her of his cousin, but truth be told, sometimes she could barely remember Brad's name when she looked at Jake.

Allowing herself to imagine the two of them together was the last thing she needed right now. She had to focus on her family, her store, her own life. Until she got that all in order, she had no room—or right—to add someone else to the mix. Dating anyone, even Jake, would only make Gabby ignore important things even more.

Jake winked at Gabby. "Trust me," he whispered. At least he had the newspaper with him. She tamed her glare. For now.

"Why don't you tuck right into your favorite chair, Grandma," Jake was saying as he set the cup on the end table and picked up the afghan draped over the armchair. Grandma settled into the red velvet seat and propped her feet on the little footstool. Jake unfurled the pale-pink-and-gray blanket and draped it gently over Grandma's legs. "Hmm...I don't see your remote control. Here, why don't you hold this for me?" He handed over the pages. "And I'll take a look."

"It might be on the dining room table," Grandma said. "I listen to the news when I eat my lunch."

Jake gave her a nod and left the room, all Mr. Helpful and Chipper. Gabby stayed in the kitchen, pretending to assemble a plate of brownies but really just watching her grandmother out of the corner of her eye. For the longest time, Grandma just sat in her chair, staring at a lifeless television. Then she sighed, glanced down at the paper, and...

Began to read. Gabby held her breath. A long moment passed. Another. And then a smile curved across Grandma's face. "Well, I'll be," she whispered to herself.

Gabby hurried forward, the half-filled plate of dessert in her hand. "Did you say something, Grandma?"

"Oh, just this silly Dear Amelia column. It seems this week is a happy ending. For once," she added under her breath.

"Well, isn't that wonderful news? It's always nice to see someone's life working out." Gabby bent down and held out the plate. "I brought some of your favorite brownies from that bakery by my shop."

Grandma folded the paper and set it on the little table, the column tucked inside the fold. "No brownies for me, dear. You and Jake can share them. I'm still not quite myself today."

Jake ambled into the living room and handed the remote to Grandma. "Found it right where you said it was."

"Thank you, dear." She clicked the power button, and the TV came to life. In an instant, the logo for the History Channel filled the screen, and Grandma settled deeper into her chair.

Gabby frowned. She traipsed back to the kitchen and began returning the brownies to the box.

"What are you doing? Those are perfectly good brownies, Gabby Monroe."

"I don't feel like eating."

"Well, speak for yourself. There are starving bachelors

in this kitchen, you know." He grabbed the biggest brownie. Before he took a bite, he gave her a concerned look. "You okay?"

Gabby plopped into one of the maple kitchen chairs. In the other room, the low murmur of a documentary about jazz singers played on the television. "I thought she'd be so much happier if she read the column, you know?"

"It's only one letter. Give it time."

"I can't give it time, Jake. I can't sit around and just—"

"Let everyone figure out their own lives?"

She frowned. "I'm not controlling anyone. I'm just trying to keep my family together and happy."

"Have you ever considered that might not be your job?"

"Have you ever considered that might not be your business?" As soon as she said the words, she regretted them because they'd been too harsh. All Jake was doing was showing concern. Gabby reached out and touched Jake's hand. A warm rush ran up her arm and ignited all those thoughts all over again. "I'm sorry, Jake. You know I think you're part of this family, too."

"Yep. Just like a brother."

"Well . . . yeah." Except the longer she touched him, the less she thought of him as anything other than a very handsome man. Either way, the answers to any of those thoughts were far more than Gabby had room to deal with in her mind right now. She had sisters to stabilize and a grandmother to draw back into the world. And a business to somehow boost and revitalize. Jake deserved a woman who put her whole heart into their relationship, not one whose heart was already divided and who needed him more as a friend than as a boyfriend right now. "I have an idea."

Jake rolled his eyes. "Those words never end well."

She swatted at him, but he dodged the hit and shot her a grin. This was the Jake she liked, the one who seemed…well, just like a brother. No pressure, no flirting, none of these confusing thoughts that careened around her mind. "Just go along with what I say, and if you overhear anything weird, just keep quiet, okay?"

"Okay…although I'm already thinking this is a bad plan."

Gabby harrumphed, got to her feet, and headed into the living room again. "Grandma, what do you think about going to Bella Vita tomorrow night for dinner?"

"Oh, dear, I don't know. I'm not sure I want to go out." She flicked the remote, aimlessly scrolling through the channels, apparently giving up on the documentary about jazz, her favorite kind of music.

"They have such a great Bolognese sauce." Gabby's voice brightened into a cajoling, happy tone. "I know you love Italian food."

"I can order in. Don't they deliver, too? I'm simply… not up to being out and about. I'm feeling quite my age lately, Gabriella. Maybe it's time I slow down, take some time to…"

"To do what?" Gabby dropped into the opposite chair and wished she could erase the note of resignation in her grandmother's voice. Until the last few months, Grandma had a full, busy life and an optimistic outlook. Was it just the column bothering Grandma—or more?

Grandma sighed. "I don't know. I need to find something useful to occupy my time now that you girls are all gone and on your own." She settled on a quiz show for a moment, but then a second later went back to scrolling. "There's never anything on the television."

"How about you help me with Celebrate History in the Harbor? I could use some organizational help, especially with my bookkeeping, and I'm sure the event will bring in lots of business." Gabby laughed, if only to cover up the worry in her gut. She had her rent check written out but barely enough in the business account to cover it. She still needed to bring in some more spring inventory and get a new cash register to replace the one that kept dying, and build an e-commerce site. The to-dos didn't match her bank balance, and that left Gabby on the edge of panic pretty much every day.

"Sure. I can help." But Grandma didn't laugh or do much more than give a vague nod. "I swear, these networks put more and more drivel on the screen every day." *Click, click, click.*

As far as Gabby knew, Grandma wasn't much of a TV watcher. Her grandmother was active, always busy with the church or the bingo nights or helping out at a fundraiser. She was a big part of the Harbor Cove community, or had been until this little...funk—that's what Gabby would call it—had taken over.

Maybe Gabby needed to pull out some more desperate measures. Fib a little. Just enough to get Grandma to go along with her plan, especially if it involved one of the girls, since it seemed that missing her granddaughters being underfoot was part of the problem. A little white lie never hurt anyone, right?

Gabby leaned in close to her grandmother and lowered her voice to a whisper. Behind her back, Gabby sent Jake a wave that said *Trust me*, just as he had said to her a moment ago. "Here's the reason I asked you to go to Bella Vita. Jake asked me out to dinner, Grandma, and I think it would be weird to go alone. I was thinking maybe you could come, and I could introduce you to Frank Rossi, the owner. He's been divorced for quite a while and I'm sure he'd love a little companionship. Not a date, not really, just a nice night out with Jake and me."

A light sparked in Grandma's eyes. "He really asked you out? Oh my. That's wonderful. Especially after all that terrible Bradley boy put you through. You deserve a nice man, and if you ask me, Jake is the nicest man in town. But I don't want to be a damper on your date, dear, and I don't think Frank would be interested in me. I'm not really his type."

Out of the corner of her eye, Gabby could see Jake standing in the kitchen, mouthing, *What was that?* "This thing with Jake is not a date. Not…really. I just…you know he's like a brother to me, and I don't think I've quite gotten over Brad yet, to be honest." Except every time she was around Jake she forgot Brad ever existed because Jake felt less and less like a brother and more and more like…

Well, whatever it was, it wasn't a date.

"Jake is a lovely young man. But if you're nervous about going out alone, perhaps someone should go with you two, make it a double date. Just to make the conversation less awkward."

"Yes, exactly. Great idea, Grandma. I can pick you up—"

"Oh, not me, dear. I see the two of you almost every day. Why don't you invite that Sandy Williams along? She's lost her husband, oh, five years ago this month, and she was just saying at the garden club how she misses going out. Her kids all live in California, poor thing, and she just needs some company. In fact, I'll text her right now and tell her." Grandma tugged her cell phone out of her pocket, and, before Gabby could say a word, sent a message off to Sandy. "Besides, she thinks Jake is just the most darling thing. I think it's a match made in heaven."

"Sandy and Jake?"

"Silly dear, you and Jake. It's about time that boy noticed you as a girlfriend, especially now that you're single. I know that other Maddox boy broke your heart, but he was never really the right one for you, sweetheart." Grandma gave her a warm smile. "And not to mention, Sandy will be a perfect match for Frank. She loves Italian food."

Gabby let out a frustrated sigh. This was not going according to plan. At all. "Are you sure I can't talk you into it?"

"Maybe another time." Grandma clicked the remote again. "My show is on. And I'm tired. How about you and your sisters and Jake come over on Wednesday night, and I'll make us all a nice supper?"

Gabby could tell the subject was closed. If she pushed it too much, Grandma would grow suspicious. If she realized the girls were machinating behind the scenes to make the advice column end more happily, she'd undoubtedly feel even less useful. Gabby rose and pressed a kiss to her grandmother's cheek. There was nothing to do but give up on this battle and keep plugging forward with the war. "I love you, Grandma. I'll see you Wednesday."

She headed into the kitchen, glancing back every few feet. Grandma had her attention on the television, looking small and sad under her afghan. Worry knotted Gabby's stomach, twisting around the thoughts of her family. It was a fierce, protective instinct residing so deep inside her that it ran through her veins.

Her phone buzzed, and when Gabby pulled it out, she noticed two text messages from her father, wondering if she'd be interested in joining him and his new family— well, new as of twenty years ago—for his birthday dinner in April. She ignored them. She couldn't sit there and eat mashed potatoes and pretend she wasn't bothered by how quickly Dad had moved on. How close he'd been to Joanna right away, as if it were just that simple to replace their luminous mother.

Gabby had never told her sisters about the night she ran over to her old house, desperate to see her father, to be in that space that was so filled with memories of Momma. And there, in Momma's kitchen, was Joanna Cartwright, hugging Dad. Momma's pots and pans were simmering on the stove, and Joanna was wearing Momma's apron, as if she'd just slipped into their late mother's shoes. When Dad had announced several months later that he was dating Joanna, the only one who wasn't surprised was Gabby. She'd never warmed to Dad's second wife or to the romance that seemed have happened a split second after their mother's death.

"Well, well, Gabriella Monroe," Jake said, following Gabby through the kitchen door and out into the cool night. There was a comfort in his presence and the shared concern for her grandmother. Sometimes she was tempted to lean into that and let him carry half the burden, to tell him about how her father's betrayal made her wonder if real love existed at all. "Seems you and I have a hot date planned for tomorrow night. I just have one question for you."

"It's not a hot date. It was supposed to be a way to fix Grandma up with Frank, but she spoiled it by invit- ing Sandy instead." Gabby glanced up at the house and frowned. Why couldn't things just go the way she wanted them to? "Anyway, what's your question?"

"Windsor knot or open collar? I want to impress my date." He gave her a cheesy grin. "She is, after all, the most beautiful woman in Harbor Cove."

Gabby rolled her eyes. She didn't need him being flirty and cute right now, especially when she was feeling all kinds of confused. "Are you ever serious, Jake?"

"Every single day. You just don't see it, Bella-Ella." He held her gaze for a moment, a moment when the worry in her stomach untangled and became something else, something she didn't recognize or know what to do with. Before she could decide, he turned on his heel. "See you tomorrow night, girlfriend."

"I'm not your girlfriend!" But he was already too far down the walkway to hear her, and whistling to boot. The night had a chill in the air, but still Gabby lingered outside, wondering whether Jake meant what he said.

And why she cared so much.

SIX

After way too much internal debate, Jake had opted for a polo shirt. A tie would have been too formal, and a partially unbuttoned dress shirt seemed like he was trying too hard to be some kind of Romeo. Not to mention, he had about as much of a sense of style as a fence post. When he shopped, he usually bought the same shirt in two or three different colors and paired them with the same brand of jeans or khakis that he'd worn for at least five years. Fashion guru he was not.

Normally Jake didn't care what he wore or what anyone thought of what was in his closet. But tonight, as he walked up to the doors of Bella Vita, he found himself adjusting his shirt, checking his reflection in the plate glass window, and wishing he'd gone for the damned tie just to impress Gabby and maybe get her to see him as more than just the boy next door.

His phone rang, and as he fished it out of his pocket, he saw Brad's name light up the screen. Jake debated answering. Brad rarely called, so if he was trying to reach

Jake, there had to be a reason. Maybe something to do with Dad?

"Why don't you get in your car and come up here?" Brad said the second Jake answered. His voice was loud, his words a little slurred, and there was some kind of pounding music in the background. "New Hampshire is beautiful this time of year, and so are the girls at the casinos. Come on up and take your chance with Lady Luck, or any of the lucky and beautiful ladies at my side right now." There was the sound of giggling close by.

Jake scowled. "I don't work for the firm anymore, and I don't gamble, Brad."

"Not for work, Scrooge. For fun. One spin of the roulette wheel won't kill you. I've got three days left here and only one meeting on my agenda. What do you say we hang out, for old times' sake? Like when we were kids."

Irritation soured in Jake's gut. Years ago, he and Brad had been best friends, spending most of their school breaks and summers together. They'd grown up almost like brothers, especially after Jake's mother left, when Edward had relied on his brother and sister-in-law to pick up the slack with his seven-year-old.

But as the boys reached high school age, Brad began to spend more of his school breaks working in Edward's law office, Jake was at football practice or with the photography club or at Gabby's, and the boys started to drift apart. Two summers ago, Brad had asked Jake to bring "that girl he knew" along when they went downtown for a beer, and by the end of the first drink, Brad was turning the charm on Gabby and asking her out.

Ever since then, Jake had avoided his cousin, and avoided the conversation about how he'd hurt Gabby by dumping her in a text. There was no way Jake wanted to "hang out" with Brad. Not now. Not ever. "I have a job, Brad. I can't just leave."

His cousin snorted. "You mean that nowhere job with that nowhere paper in that nowhere town? Come on, Jake. We both know you working there is all about you showing your dad who's boss. Now that you've done that, come on back to the firm and make some real money. We are slowly cornering the New England personal injury market, and the bucks are just pouring in."

"I'm happy where I'm at," Jake said. Inside, he bristled at the way Brad talked about Jake's job and the town he loved, and how he equated the firm with an ambulance-chasing cash cow. "I mean it."

Brad scoffed. "Really? Because if you ask me, all you're doing is playing it safe. What are you, thirty now? Thirty-one? And you're still living in that town, driving the same piece-of-crap car, working for peanuts."

"Last I checked, it was my life to live, not yours." Jake raised his gaze to the night sky and muttered a curse under his breath. "Listen, I have to go. I'm meeting some people."

"Hot date?"

"Actually, I'm going to see Gabby." There was a moment of silence on Brad's end, and Jake knew he'd hit a nerve. Maybe it was petty of him—okay, it definitely was—but a part of Jake wanted Brad to know he'd treated someone incredible like garbage. "We're having dinner with some people we know."

Brad chuckled. "Yeah, right. Don't even try to make it sound like a date because we both know the truth. You had twenty-five years to ask that girl out, and you never did." There was a chorus of shouts in the background, and the music on the sound system shifted to something country. "Anyway, I gotta go. You ever want to get out of that Podunk town and have a real life, call me."

Jake hung up the phone and tucked it back in his pocket. He watched the cars pass through the intersection of Main and Washington and thought about why his cousin's words bothered him so much.

Maybe because there was a grain of truth in them. A grain that Jake had been ignoring for a hell of a long time.

"You clean up well, Jake Maddox."

He turned at the sound of Gabby's voice, and for a second couldn't remember how to form words because she was so beautiful she literally stole his breath away. She stood in the warm circle of light under the streetlamp, wearing a dark cranberry dress that accented every inch of her hourglass figure. She'd left her hair down, a waterfall of brown curls tumbling over her shoulders. "Uh...so do you."

"Gee, Jake, you really know how to make a woman's heart flutter with your charming words." She winked and gave him a jab in the arm. He winced, not because she'd hurt him but because she'd left him too flustered to come up with a better line.

"No, I'm serious. That's a gorgeous dress. Did you make it?" For as long as he could remember, Gabby had been making her own clothes or altering the ones she bought to fit her fondness for vintage styles.

"Thanks. It's one I made last summer. You really like it?" She spun in a little circle, and the skirt bloomed with the movement. "So, is Sandy here yet? Did you talk to her?"

"I was supposed to talk to her? And say what?"

"Jake, if you're going to be a part of this plan, you have to do your part." She put a fist on her hip. "I texted you yesterday. You were supposed to presell Sandy on Frank. If Grandma won't date him, we can at least try to create a happily-ever-after between him and Sandy."

"He's not a used Volvo, you know. I shouldn't have to sell his features and benefits to a prospective date."

A dark car pulled into the parking lot of Bella Vita, and Gabby nearly leaped with joy. "Oh, look, there's Sandy. Now remember, we're supposed to act like we're dating, but just to be clear, we're not really dating."

"I assume, Miss Bossypants, that you have rules for our not-dating evening?" He shifted closer to her, drawn by the sweet scent of her perfume and the intoxicating curve of her lips. "Because if we're to be a believable couple, I think we should..."

Her eyes met and held his, and her lips parted. A breath whispered between them, and for a second, Jake imagined her finishing his sentence with the word *kiss*. Instead, her face brightened, and she stepped to the side. "Hi, Sandy! So nice to see you!"

And Jake hid his disappointment behind a friendly grin that he didn't feel. "Good evening, Sandy."

The older woman pressed a hand to her short pale blond hair, a style that framed her face and green eyes. "Oh, I'm so nervous. I haven't been on a date since dinosaurs roamed the earth. Are you really sure that Frank wants to meet me?"

"Yup. He said he can't wait." Gabby stepped forward and brushed a piece of lint off the sleeve of Sandy's navy wool coat. "Now let's go in there and dazzle him with your beautiful smile."

Sandy giggled. "Thank you, Gabriella. And even if

this doesn't work out, thank you for giving this older woman—I refuse to call myself old—a lovely night out and a reminder that I've still got a little shimmy left in me." She gave Gabby a quick hug, and then the three of them walked inside Bella Vita.

The restaurant had an Old World Italy feel with its dark décor, stucco walls, and mural of the Italian coast. The hostess—a young woman Jake vaguely remembered from a photo shoot on town landmarks—recognized them and led them to a table at the back of the restaurant, tucked in a corner that was out of sight of the rest of the diners. Frank was already at the table with a bucket of wine chilling beside him. He got to his feet as they approached, his features hesitant and unsure. He gave Sandy a nervous smile and ran a hand through his gray hair. "I have to admit I have no idea what I'm doing here tonight."

Sandy leaned toward him. "Neither do I. But I think you and I can show these two young kids what a date used to be like, don't you?"

That was all it took to break the anxious lines in Frank's face. He chuckled, pulled out a chair for Sandy, and waved her toward it with a flourish. "My lady."

"Why, thank you, kind sir." She flashed him a smile, one that Jake swore made her look at least ten years younger. That was what joy did for a person, he thought. The kind of happiness that had eluded him for most of his life. The kind he'd seen in Gabby's eyes that first time he met her and that had kept drawing him back a million times over the years, hoping to see that light warm into something more.

You had twenty-five years to ask that girl out and you never did.

Because if he *had* asked her out, this would have been

a real date between them. They might have already been married and raising a couple of kids in a three-bedroom house. Or maybe they'd have broken up and gone their separate ways. Jake had no idea—because he'd never taken that chance, as Brad had so gleefully pointed out a few minutes ago.

Jake and Gabby took seats opposite Frank and Sandy, who were already chatting like old friends. Frank poured everyone a glass of wine and motioned to the waitress to bring over a basket of freshly baked rolls. "I'm a little out of practice," Frank said. "So forgive me if I stumble over my words or make a fool of myself."

"There's no such thing," Sandy said. "And there's no pressure whatsoever. To be honest, I'm just tickled to be out on the town tonight. Most nights, I'm home doing my crossword puzzle while I watch David Attenborough."

Frank's face perked up with interest. "He is brilliant, isn't he? The way he shows us a side of the world we never notice...just incredible."

"You like David Attenborough, too?"

"Love him. I've watched every episode of the *Life* series at least twice. Sometimes running the restaurant can be stressful, and a little David Attenborough at the end of the day is quite calming."

"I couldn't agree more. But have you seen *Wildlife on One*? It ran on the BBC—"

"From 1977 to 2005." Frank sat back in his chair and gave Sandy a smile. Admiration and interest shone in his eyes. "I received the boxed set as a Christmas present four years ago from my ex-wife." Then his face fell, and he cleared his throat.

Jake glanced at Gabby, who mouthed *Do something*, as if Jake had any experience in what to do to recover a first-date conversation that had already derailed. He could barely pick out a shirt to wear, for Pete's sake. "Uh, Frank, I was thinking about your ad campaign. Maybe we should change it up a bit."

Gabby nudged him under the table. "Ad campaigns? Isn't that kind of a boring topic for a dinner?"

"No, no, not at all," Frank said. "I could use some advice. To be honest, I never know what to write in those ads. I just don't have that knack for words. My...my ex used to do all that. I guess I should have paid better attention." He shrugged. "I'm just not good at that kind of thing."

Gabby's nudge turned into a kick. "Jake, I really think we should talk about something else. Don't you?"

"You could point out what a wonderful place this is for a romantic night on the town," Sandy said. "You have a lovely ambience here, Frank. Lovebirds in the spring and summer would just adore this restaurant. Valentine's Day isn't just for February."

He nodded. "That's a good idea, and a great line. I think I'll use that in my next ad. Thanks, Sandy."

She blushed. "I'm sorry. I'm not trying to tell you how to run your business, really. I just get these ideas and can barely keep them to myself," Sandy said as she reached out and touched Frank's hand, a light, brief tap. "But I was thinking you could even have some kind of date-night prix fixe menu. Include some wine, maybe a little chocolate dessert. Make it a spaghetti special and name it after that *Lady and the Tramp* movie."

"My grandson really loves that movie." Frank nodded again. "Excellent idea, Sandy. Wow. You are a brilliant woman."

Sandy dipped her head and the flush in her face

deepened. "You're a very nice man for saying that, Frank. Thank you."

This time, Jake nudged Gabby under the table, and when her attention darted to him, he whispered, "See? I was right."

"You got lucky," she muttered under her breath.

Considering they were only pretending to date, Jake wasn't going to call it lucky. A smart man, however, would take advantage of the moment and maybe, just maybe, if Gabby saw what a real date could be like, she'd see him as something other than a pesky extra sibling.

Sandy pivoted in her chair. "Oh my goodness, Frank and I got so caught up in talking about his advertising, I forgot to ask about you two. How long have you been together? And how did I not know that this handsome young man was your beau?"

Gabby sat there, mute, and he realized she had thought everything through in her plan—except the cover story for the two of them. Well, well. An opportunity for a little turnabout was something Jake simply couldn't pass up.

He draped his arm over Gabby's shoulders. Her skin was warm to the touch, and the lace of her dress whispered along his arm. "I count us as a pair ever since first grade. I knew Gabby was the cutest girl in the entire state of Massachusetts from the second I met her."

"Oh, that's so sweet," Sandy said. "Almost makes me choke up."

"Almost makes me choke," Gabby muttered. Then she turned to Jake, a bright, fake-as-Bigfoot smile on her face. "Jake, honey, you don't really need to talk about us. Let's just let Frank and Sandy get to know each other."

"Oh, please share," Sandy said. "Hearing about young love gives me hope for older love." Frank nodded his agreement. Gabby shifted so that her elbow was directly against his side, a position Jake knew from experience meant she was aiming to make a point in his ribs.

Sandy wagged a hand between them. "You two seem like you've been dating for a really long time. You're just so...in sync."

"Oh, we haven't been together that long, not really," Gabby said.

"Quite a while," Jake said at the same time. "I can't imagine her not in my life." That part was true. A life without Gabby or the Monroe family would feel empty and shallow. But really, how long was he going to sit in this town, pining after a woman who barely noticed he had testosterone in his veins? Maybe Leroy was right, and it was time Jake moved on from the paper. But with Gabby nestled against him, he couldn't think of a single other place in the world he wanted to be.

If it worked out, it would be the best thing ever. Of that, Jake was sure. And if it didn't—

Well, he was damned tired of living his life afraid of what-ifs. She was here, she was beside him, and he'd be a fool to turn down this chance to truly be with her, even if she was only pretending.

"Oh, that's so sweet," Sandy said. "How did you two go from friends to...well, loves?"

"We're not—"

"One day..." he said, interrupting Gabby's protest while he met her gaze. "One day, I looked at Gabby and realized I've been in love with her all my life. There was just something in that simple moment when we were on the rocks overlooking the cove where I just...well, fell head over heels." Jake's hand covered hers, and he gave her a smile. It was a lot easier speaking the truth and pretending it was a lie than pretending a lie was the truth. "She's amazing," he added softly.

Gabby's jaw dropped. She stared at him as if she'd just met a total stranger. He gave her shoulders a squeeze and dropped a kiss on top of her head. "Isn't that right, honey?"

"Uh... yeah." Gabby pressed her elbow into Jake's ribs, a clear *Quit with the hearts-and-flowers mumbo jumbo* message, as she turned toward Sandy. "So, Frank, tell us all about how you got the idea to start the restaurant. It's such a lovely place."

Frank beamed like a proud father. "Thank you. I'm so glad you like it." He started telling the story of how he'd loved to cook with his grandfather on the weekends and dreamed of owning a restaurant all his life. "Then I opened this place soon after I got married." He shook his head. "I'm sorry to keep mentioning her. I read somewhere, maybe it was that Dear Amelia column, that men shouldn't talk about exes when they first meet a new lady."

"That's all fine," Sandy said, covering his hand again and this time not moving away. "Your wife was a big part of your life for many years. Just because you got divorced doesn't erase all that."

Frank smiled at her, the two of them holding a soft, tender gaze for a long moment. Jake watched them and felt a curl of envy in his gut. What would it be like to have someone look at him like that? To have Gabby look at him like that?

As if she'd read his mind, Gabby shifted until her lips were close to his ear. "I think our work here is done," she whispered.

Not even close, he thought, thinking how much he

loved the feeling of her being this close, her breath warm against his cheek, her perfume in his nostrils. Of how he intended to see where this led, regardless of the outcome.

It was time. No, it was way past time.

SEVEN

An hour and a half later, Sandy and Frank were exchanging numbers and lingering under the awning of Bella Vita, saying good night and making plans for another date. Sandy's face was bright and animated, and Frank had a smile that looked like it was going to be permanent.

The whole thing had been successful. But Gabby had this unsettled feeling in her chest, partly because of the shift in the air between her and the man she had always classified firmly in the no-touch category. He was most assuredly touching her right now, and worse, she wasn't hating it. Jake's arm hung loosely around her waist. He was just playing the part of boyfriend, she told herself. Maybe a little too convincingly.

A side of Gabby wanted to bolt, but another side of her wanted to linger. Just because Jake was so warm, and there was a chill in the air. No other reason. Really.

There was no way he meant what he'd said about that day overlooking the cove. They'd been up there hundreds of times since childhood, and never once did Gabby get the feeling that Jake was in love with her. Every trip was the same—climb the rocks, have a snack, watch the water wash in and out. When they were teenagers, they'd snuck beers and nip bottles up there late at night, a little rule-breaking secret just between the two of them. Now there was less alcohol and more admiration of the beauty of the cove.

Definitely no lovey-dovey stuff. Or had she missed a cue along the way?

It was a fake date, she reminded herself. He was just playing a part with an Emmy-worthy performance. And she had no intentions of getting involved with anyone, especially not another Maddox man, while her family needed her. Her phone buzzed, and a quick glance showed a missed call from her father. She had yet to answer his text about dinner, and now he wanted to talk about it.

She'd needed her father when she was little, not now. She ignored the call, just as she'd ignored the texts.

"This was lovely," she said to Sandy and Frank, who couldn't look more over the moon if they were standing on the moon itself. "But I really should get home and . . . uh, get caught up on the books for my dress shop."

Sandy beamed at Gabby. She and Frank were holding hands now, and that weird unsettled feeling returned. Almost as if she craved what Sandy and Frank had in this moment.

Insanity. This was all to help Grandma feel better, nothing more.

"Thank you so much for introducing us, Gabby and Jake." Sandy leaned toward Gabby and lowered her voice almost to a whisper. "I'm kind of hopeful that Frank and I could end up as happy and in love as you two are."

"Me too," Jake said, hauling Gabby against his warm,

broad, and very strong chest. "It's wonderful to have that special person in your life."

"Uh, Jake, honey," Gabby said, faking a smile and pressing her hands to his chest, but he stayed solid against her. "I think I should go home now."

Before she got too used to him touching her. Before she read something into his embrace that wasn't there. Before she muddied her messy life even more with a relationship with Jake.

"Of course, sweetheart." He grinned. "Let me walk you to your car."

The *sweetheart* caused a little hiccup in her chest. Nice touch, she thought, to add a term of endearment. A bonus for his performance.

"Aww. Such a gentleman," Sandy said with a sigh. "You're such a lucky girl, Gabby. You'd better hold on to that one!"

But Gabby was tossing goodbyes over her shoulder and already walking away—hurrying, really—and trying her best to get out of that sappy rom-com movie scene. If she was truly honest with herself, she was trying more to get away from Jake and the way being in his arms had made her feel.

Hot. Bothered. Confused.

And oddly...loved. Which was weird. Maybe it was simply that Jake had known her forever, and sure, maybe loved her like he loved a sister or a friend. Or maybe it was just Sandy and Frank's instant infatuation rubbing off on the whole mood.

That had to be it. Not to mention, she'd been stressed about the business, and Grandma, and her sisters, and the fact that her father kept reaching out to her to have a conversation Gabby had done her best to avoid for years. She was running on high alert, nothing more.

Except all that sounded a lot more like excuses than truth.

"Honey," Jake said, taking one giant step forward and linking his arm with hers, "you really should slow down if you want me to walk you to your car."

Damn his long legs and his speed. When they'd been young, she could outrun Jake, but now that they were older—and how much did the man work out, anyway?—he could close the gap pretty quickly. "You don't have to. Our little charade is over, so you can go home now, Jake."

He tick-tocked a finger at her. "What if Sandy or Frank comes around the corner and sees us going in separate directions? Sandy thinks I'm a gentleman, after all."

"Well, Sandy is easily fooled." Gabby laughed and shook her head. She could tell by the set of his shoulders that Jake wasn't going to be easily dissuaded from playing the part of a gentleman for a few more minutes. It was all in fun, nothing serious. What was the harm in letting him? They'd have a good laugh about it all tomorrow. "All right, fine, Sir Lancelot. Walk me to my car."

He fell into step beside her, his arm still tucked inside of hers, which made their hips bump from time to time. It was all so...close. So intimate. So real. A rush of heat ran through Gabby. It had to be the glass of wine she'd had at dinner. Not the very close proximity of a man she had known most of her life.

They turned the corner of the building, into the shadows and out of the soft glow of the streetlights. The parking lot behind the two-story brick restaurant was darker than the sidewalk had been, more intimate, and

Gabby was suddenly very, very aware of Jake right next to her, even as traffic rumbled down the street and a siren sounded in the distance. The warmth of his body. The dark, woodsy scent of his cologne. The way she seemed to fit against his side so perfectly.

They stopped beside her little sedan, a twelve-year-old Honda desperately in need of a tune-up and new tires, but those things would have to wait until her business improved. She could ask Jake to fix the car for her, of course, but right now, asking anything of Jake seemed like a bad idea, given how this one favor had morphed into something…else.

Gabby dug her keys out of her pocket, but before she could press the unlock button, Jake's hand covered hers. "Don't leave yet, Bella-Ella."

There was something vulnerable and soft and enticing in his quiet voice, in the way the syllables of her nickname rolled off his tongue. She looked up at him, a man a full head taller than her, and broad and strong in a way that a woman could lean on. She'd leaned on him so many times in the years after her mother died, and every time, his arms had been there to comfort her.

But in this moment, in this darkened parking lot, she wanted to lean on him in a different way. Heat curled between them, and whispers of desire danced through her veins. She shifted closer to him, out of curiosity, she told herself, a burning need to know why her body was responding to Jake in a way it never had before.

"I enjoyed our date," he said.

"Our fake date," she corrected, more as a reminder to herself than to him. This was nothing more than a ruse to create another happy ending for Grandma's column. A ruse that felt like anything but. "Me too."

He put a hand on her car, close to her head, and then leaned in, narrowing the gap between them to inches. Her heart began to race, her pulse pounding so loud she was sure he could hear it. She stared at his face, his eyes, his lips, like she had never seen them before. "That sure seemed like a real date to me, Gabby," he said softly, his gaze dark and intent and sexy. "Because if it wasn't a real date…"

He paused, and her heart seemed to stutter in that space of silence. "If it wasn't a real date…" She gulped. "Then what?"

"I wouldn't want to kiss you as much as I want to kiss you right now."

"You…" She took a breath. Had she heard him right? Kiss her? Jake? She should tell him he was crazy, push him away, and get out of here. Instead she raised her gaze to his, the curiosity to know what it would feel like to kiss Jake so strong that she was sure it would engulf her. "You want to kiss me?" The question escaped on a squeak of breath.

"Only if…" He tipped her chin with his finger until her mouth was very, very, very close to his. "You want to kiss me, too."

"I…" And she had no other words, nothing that came to mind, nothing that could answer the riot of emotions and questions and thoughts in her gut. The way everything inside her was leaning toward him, like a plant desperate for sunlight and warmth. The pounding need in her veins that overrode every ounce of common sense and what she thought to be true.

She rose on her toes a fraction of an inch, and Jake closed the gap, and then he kissed her, slow and sweet.

And in that tender concert of his mouth against hers, he totally upended her world.

EIGHT

What the hell had he been thinking?

Jake sat at his desk the next morning, wondering if idiocy was a progressive disease. Because every minute that passed at dinner last night, he had been more and more of an idiot, finding any excuse to touch Gabby, to be close to her...

To kiss her.

He hadn't thought about it—well, he'd thought about kissing Gabby for the better part of his life, but he hadn't thought about the *consequences* of kissing her before he did it. Instead he'd reacted to this overwhelming sense that it was time. *Way past time* were the words he'd used in his head.

He knew he should feel a little disloyal to Brad, but Jake couldn't find an ounce of guilt in his conscience. He'd made a decision, somewhere between the appetizers and dinner, that he was tired of living on the sidelines of his own life. Tired of playing it safe. Tired of pretending he didn't feel half of what he felt.

Tired of denying himself the one woman he'd always been in love with. He'd taken a chance and kissed her, and then—

She left. She'd stuttered something about having to get home to check on her flowers—which made zero sense because as far as he knew she didn't own so much as a potted fern—and then peeled out of the parking lot so fast that her bronze sedan disappeared into the night like a cheetah.

"Maddox! You coming to the meeting?"

Leroy's booming voice jolted Jake out of his thoughts. He jerked to a standing position and headed down the hall to the conference room, getting all the way there before realizing that he'd forgotten his notepad. So he turned back, grabbed the legal pad, got to the conference room, and realized he'd forgotten a pen. Damn it.

Consequence #1: Distraction.

Leroy arched a brow when Jake snuck into the conference room and took the last seat among the half dozen assembled newspaper staff waiting for the morning editorial meeting and Jake, the late arrival. "You get lost? Took you three tries to get here."

"Sorry. Just have a lot on my mind." Like Gabby, and how perfectly she fit in his arms, and how kissing her was akin to tasting heaven. She'd let out this soft mewl in the middle of the kiss, and he'd wanted to sweep her off her feet and take her back home. He'd told himself for years that Gabby was out of his league, that they'd never have chemistry. And yet their kiss had been like lighting off a string of fireworks. Hot, powerful, and perfect.

Jake shook off the thoughts and tried to pay attention as Leroy started the meeting. But as the conversation drifted toward the upcoming stories and ads for the next issue, Jake's mind detoured back to Gabby.

Wondering what she was doing. If she was thinking about him. Or regretting the kiss. Or if he had completely tanked their friendship last night.

Consequence #2: Remorse.

As the staff was filing out of the conference room an hour later, Leroy tapped Jake's shoulder and stopped him. "You okay? You look like you lost your best friend. Or hit the lottery."

"I think I did both." Jake sighed. Maybe if he talked about it with Leroy, who was as much a friend as he was a boss, Jake could make some sense out of the whole thing. "I kissed Gabby last night."

"Really? About damned time." Leroy's chuckle said Jake's infatuation had been obvious to everyone except Gabby. And here he thought he'd done a good job keeping that under wraps. "I didn't even know you two were a thing. I thought she was dating your cousin."

"She was. They broke up last year." That meant Gabby was fair game, right? He wasn't breaking some blood-relative code by kissing her, was he? Did he even care if he was? Kissing Gabby had been amazing, and anything that incredible couldn't be wrong. "And we aren't a thing. Or we weren't. I don't know. It was a double date, but not really a date."

Leroy leaned in and sniffed the air around Jake's face. "Nope, not drunk. But you sure aren't making a lot of sense, my friend."

That was because his brain was a scrambled mess right now. All he could think about was the sound she had made and how she'd felt against his chest. Damn. "Gabby was trying to fix up Sandy Williams with Frank

Rossi. She thought it would be easier for them and less pressure if we did it as a double date, so we pretended to be a couple. Then I walked her back to her car and kissed her."

"And?"

"And I haven't heard from her yet." He felt like he was in middle school again, wondering if the girl he liked would pass him a note in the hall or ignore him in the library. The anticipation and anxiousness had his nerves dancing like a cat tiptoeing across a fence. "She could be mad. She could be—"

"You could be overthinking the whole damned thing." Leroy clapped him on the back. "Just go with your gut, man, and it'll all work out."

"My gut says I'm going to screw up our friendship if I date her." Jake ran a hand through his hair and let out a long breath. Last night, it had all seemed like such a good idea. Take a chance, see where it went, instead of wondering what if for the next fifty years. "I don't know. It could be the biggest mistake of my life."

Leroy leaned against the corner of the conference table and crossed his arms over his chest. He gave Jake a long, assessing glance. "I ever tell you how I met my wife?"

Jake searched his memory. He and Leroy had been friends for over a decade, meeting back when Jake used to work a part-time job at the paper while he went to college. That job was where Jake had fallen in love with the art of graphic design and made a life-long friend who'd been the voice of reason when Jake quit the law firm. He and Leroy had plenty of conversations over an impromptu hoops session or a couple of Coronas, but they mostly talked shop or sports, not women. "I think you met her after you got out of college, right?"

"Yup. She was tending bar at this little dive around the corner from my first apartment. I was working at a newspaper then, too, but in the warehouse, bundling the papers for morning deliveries. Not really going anywhere fast, as Rhonda says."

Jake chuckled. He'd met Leroy's spitfire of a wife. She was small in stature but big in personality. "I'm not surprised."

"Right? She's a strong woman, my Rhonda." Leroy smiled the kind of smile that meant he still loved his wife just as much as he had the day he married her, more than three decades ago. It softened his features, added a happy light to his dark eyes. "She told me she wasn't going to date a man who had no ambition. I gave her crap about being a bartender, and that's when she told me she owned that place. At twenty-six. Who does that?"

"Rhonda." Jake laughed again. "She's always been pretty driven, huh?"

"Man, my wife makes Bill Gates look like a slacker. I knew right then and there that she was the kind of woman a man needs to up his game for, or I was going to lose her. So I got my butt out of the warehouse and into the editorial department. Finally putting my degree to use, she said."

Jake didn't know the full background of Leroy's career but knew the editor had run another major newspaper, then a brief stint at a magazine, before he and Rhonda had decided to settle in a small town to raise their kids and he took over the *Gazette* chain. "Seems to have worked out well, though."

"I'm a happy man. I've got a lot to be thankful for.

Great wife at home, great kids, great job." Leroy leaned forward and gave Jake a hard stare. "My point is, the good women expect you to work hard and not sit here just thinking."

"So you're saying I should go after her?"

"You want her, right? And she's a good woman, right?" Leroy shrugged. "Then you have your answer, man."

"What if—" He couldn't even voice the thoughts. What if she was still in love with Brad? What if she didn't feel the same fireworks he had felt? What if he'd just screwed up everything?

Or what if this could be the most amazing thing ever? If daring to kiss Gabby and open the door to a relationship ended up with the kind of heaven most people dreamed of and never found?

"There's always gonna be a what-if, Jake," Leroy said. "If you keep focusing on what could possibly be down the road, you miss what's right in front of you." He pushed off from the table and headed out of the room.

For the next two hours, Jake tried to work and ended up scrapping and redoing two ads. When the clock rolled past noon, he gave up, grabbed his jacket, and told Leroy he was going out for lunch. When he reached the sidewalk, instead of turning toward Earl's, his usual lunch place, Jake veered left, toward the shops that lined Main Street. And to one familiar sherbet-colored awning.

As he walked inside, Lori glanced up from the magazine she was reading. There were no customers in the store, and despite the Muzak on the sound system, it had an empty-for-hours feel. Lori pointed to the back room. "She's busy pricing the new stock."

"How'd you know I was here to see Gabby?" he asked Lori.

She rolled her eyes and laughed. "When are you not? Anyway, she's kind of in a weird mood today. Stressed or something."

"Okay. Thanks." He ducked into the small room at the back of the shop and found Gabby surrounded by a pile of sweaters and a rack of dresses. She sat cross-legged on a small chair and hand-wrote price tags that dangled from twine matching the pastel colors of her awning. She had such a great artistic eye.

Her outfits were a reflection of that vision, and today was no different. She had on a white V-neck sweater with dark-wash jeans, an ordinary combo on anyone else, but Gabby had brought it to life with a bright coral scarf and matching flats. She had her hair up in a messy ponytail of curls, leaving several tantalizing tendrils dancing along her neck.

"I've always liked that you do that," Jake said. His chest tightened at the sight of her: the curve of her jaw, the twinkle in her eyes.

Consequence #3: Temptation to kiss her again.

Gabby looked up. "Jake. I didn't know you were here. I heard the bell and thought it was a customer."

"Nope. Just me. Lori told me you were in back." He reached for a bright yellow dress she had just tagged and hung it on the rolling rack. He noticed worry in her eyes and wondered if he was the cause of that, or if the empty store was. Either way, it didn't seem like the right time to ask, so he let it go for now. "I like that you hand-make the tags. It just seems so . . . small town, but in a good way."

"I'll take that as a compliment." She paused, and the silence between them, which had always been so comfortable and easy, stretched into uncomfortable territory. "Uh, so, what did you want?"

"Just wanted to know if you heard from Sandy." *Way to avoid the truth, Jake.* Not to mention the fact that the kiss had done exactly what he'd feared—changed things between them. He wanted to rewind, start over, get a mulligan. The distance between them was almost palpable.

"Oh." She fiddled with the tag. "You could have texted me."

Yeah, he could have. But then he wouldn't have seen her face or the look in her eyes, or heard the inflections in her voice. Should he push forward and see where this went, or cut his losses and preserve the friendship? He opted for somewhere in the middle.

"It's a nice day. I wanted to go on a walk for lunch." Liar, liar. He'd hoped and prayed the whole way here that Gabby had been thinking about that kiss as much as he had been. And she had—just not in the same way he had.

"It's thirty degrees out, Jake. Spring's apparently on vacation today. And you hate the cold."

"It's only cold if you aren't moving." The air had been brisk today, the wind running at a fast clip, icy under his jacket as he'd walked the two blocks from the *Gazette* offices to Ella Penny. He'd barely noticed the temperature because he'd been so intent on getting here and finally telling Gabby how he felt about her. But once he'd walked into the shop and seen her, his tongue seized, and he thought about how much it would suck to lose her as a friend. People didn't stay friends with exes. If he and Gabby dated and broke up, she'd be out of his life for good. And he'd lose not only her but her family, too. Better not to screw it up in the first place.

Except that kind of thinking was what had left a yawning hole in his life where Gabby should be. He'd always wanted more with her, and now that he had a chance at it, he was letting the familiar fears get in the way.

The little voice that whispered she'd never want the kid who had been different from everyone else grew louder, as it had a hundred times over the years when he was with Gabby. Why would she want him when men like Brad—smart, successful, handsome, and equipped with the kind of charm Jake had never mastered—were pursuing her?

Consequence #4: Self-doubt.

"So... are we going to talk about it?" Gabby said, plunking the elephant smack into the center of the room.

"That kiss? That was just part of the act." He kept his tone light, joking. Damn it. Was he really going to let all those voices keep him from what he truly wanted?

He'd never been in this place with Gabby. Except one time, when he'd tried—and fumbled—kissing her on the dance floor at the senior banquet. He'd pretended it was a mistake, brought on by some nips from a flask the other boys had snuck into the room, but the truth was Jake had been as sober as a judge and as nervous as a shiny fish in shark-infested waters.

"You sure had me convinced the kiss was real."

He took two steps closer, narrowing the gap until he could catch the floral notes of her perfume and see the errant strand of hair curling across her cheek. "And what if it was, Gabby?"

"Well, that would just screw up everything, Jake. Wouldn't it?" She shifted away from him, reaching for another sweater. "Anyway, thanks for agreeing to the double date and putting on the whole act. Sandy is over the moon and said Frank made plans with her for tonight and tomorrow night."

"Just part of my community service, ma'am." Jake tipped an imaginary hat in her direction. Again, light and breezy. The last thing he wanted to do was put pressure on her and do what he feared most—ruin the things that mattered in his life.

She laughed at his joke, and just like that, the friendship between them was restored. Jake could feel the relief rolling through him. Maybe this whole thing could work out after all.

Except, he was taking two steps back, going straight for the friend zone. No passing Go, no collecting two hundred dollars, and no more kisses.

That wasn't what he wanted, not at all. But of the two people in this room, it seemed only one was interested in anything more than the status quo.

"Are you coming to dinner tonight?" she asked, the conversation as normal as any they'd had before last night. Small talk, friendly chatting, no tension or flirting. "You know my grandmother will have a fit if her adopted grandson isn't there."

"Of course I will. I can't pass up an opportunity to see…" He cleared his throat before he said *you*. It was harder here, in the light of day, when she was so far away emotionally, to lay his heart bare and risk rejection. "I mean, pass up an opportunity to eat your grandmother's cooking."

"Just using me for the rib roast, aren't you?"

"You know it, Bella-Ella." He grinned, but the smile seemed to hurt his cheeks, and there was something empty in his chest, because things might seem like they were back to normal, but Gabby was still avoiding his gaze.

Consequence #5: Heartache.

"Anyway, I should grab a sandwich at Earl's and

get back to work. I'll see you later tonight. Unless you need a date for a wedding or a fake fiancé between now and then."

"I'm good. Thanks."

"Awesome," Jake said, and felt anything but that as he walked out of the shop.

NINE

"That man frustrates me more every day," Eleanor said to Gabby as they stood in her sunny kitchen early that evening while the rib roast baked and green beans simmered. Her granddaughters and bonus grandson would be here in a little while, which meant Eleanor's house would be filled with the sounds of a happy family very soon. If only that annoying wasp of a man next door would stop disturbing her days. "Why would he do such a thing?" She held up the offending item—a half-pint jar of raspberry jam that had been dropped on her doorstep that morning. How her neighbor thought that was a good idea, she'd never know.

Gabby laughed. "Grandma, Mr. Erlich is just being nice."

This was what Eleanor got for bringing over a batch of "welcome to the neighborhood" cookies when Harry Erlich had moved in next door a year ago. She was just being neighborly, and ever since, that man had been finding excuses to drop off little treats from time to time and worse, talk to her whenever they were both outside. He'd even gone and joined her walking group and spent more time trying to have a conversation with her than moving his feet. "I don't need him being nice. I can buy my own jam at the store."

She peeled back the kitchen curtain and peeked out at the tidy Cape-style house next door. His jam mission accomplished, Harry Erlich was heading across the lawn to his own house. A tall, thin man with a thick head of white hair and blue eyes that looked like mischief in a bottle, the man had the gall to turn back and grin when he saw her face in the window. She shut the curtains and jerked back. "He waved at me!"

"I think he likes you, Grandma." Gabby chuckled. "Would that be so bad? He's a widower. You're a widow. You're close in age. You both like to garden, and apparently eat raspberry jam. And you walk with him and that group of ladies almost every evening after dinner."

"That's just exercise. Not dating." Eleanor slipped a piece of bread into the toaster.

"Well, maybe Mr. Erlich sees it differently."

"I am too old for such foolishness. This is what happens when I make casual conversation about having tea in the afternoon and enjoying a piece of toast with jam with it. I swear, I will never talk to that man again." She shook her head and reached for the teakettle just as it started to whistle. She poured two cups of honey-lemon tea and handed them to Gabby. That was more than enough talk about Harry Erlich for the day. "Speaking of dating... What happened with Jake the other night? You know what they say about good friends making even better partners, right? Jake is also much more your type than his cousin was. This match might just be the one."

Her worrywart granddaughter needed to find a partner, if only so she would stop hovering over her family. Ever since Penny died, it seemed like Gabby had made it her personal responsibility to ensure everyone else's happiness. Sometimes, Eleanor suspected, at the cost of her own.

"Jake and I had a great time," Gabby said, "but it's not going to be a thing. It was just dinner."

"Why not? You two have known each other forever. Why, just a few days ago, you were chasing him around the yard like a cat going after a mouse." They'd always been great friends, but even a man on the moon could see that the two of them were attracted to each other.

"That's exercise," Gabby quipped. "Not dating."

Eleanor laughed. "Touché. But he did ask you out, so maybe it's time to see Jake as something other than the boy down the street."

"I think the tea has cooled off." Gabby picked up her mug and took a tentative sip, clearly trying to avoid a conversation she didn't want to have. "This tea is so good."

"You know darn well that tea is still hot and you're trying to change the subject." Eleanor's hand covered Gabby's. "I just want my granddaughters to be as happy as larks in the spring. I want to hear you girls laugh and see you smile."

"I'm happy, Grandma. I swear." Except anyone could see she wasn't. Gabby seemed stressed and anxious. Every time Eleanor tried to bring up things like the store, Gabby changed the subject. "The Celebrate History event is in less than two weeks, and I was hoping you could help me create a list of final tasks because you're so good at organizing and brainstorming, Grandma. So far, my list is comprised of making sure everyone has what they need for their booth, like electricity or lighting, and that we have enough volunteers lined up to set up signs and check in customers."

"Of course, dear. You know you can count on me. And we could—" She let out a gasp and shot to her feet. "There goes that man again. Why is he trimming the hedges? Jake does that for me."

"Maybe, Grandma, he's being a nice neighbor." Gabby bit back a laugh.

Eleanor harrumphed. The toaster popped, and she got to her feet to yank the toast out of the slot. She grabbed a clean knife from the dish drainer and unscrewed the jar of jam. Most days, Eleanor felt easygoing, relaxed. But today, that man next door had her so irritated that she could barely see straight.

"Grandma, do you like Harry Erlich?"

Gabby's question made Eleanor freeze. "Of course not. He's annoying and stubborn and keeps leaving me things I don't want."

"Oh, really? Then why are you slathering your toast with that delicious jam as we speak?"

Eleanor flushed and jammed the knife back into the tiny jar. "I just don't like to waste food. You know that."

"Uh, sure, Grandma."

Eleanor avoided her far-too-inquisitive granddaughter's gaze by stowing the jam in the refrigerator. "We should expand that historical display at the community center for the tricentennial event. Bring in the garden club and the knitting group and some people from the *Gazette* to exhibit historical pictures and facts. Sandy Williams is a veritable font of information about those things and has been talking about doing something like that for years now."

"I think that's a great idea. One of the people participating in the event is going to have a booth that specializes in repurposing old tools and furniture. She makes them into really interesting lamps and entertainment stands. It's like history given a new life."

"Perfect. You could set her booth up outside the community center, and it'll be a natural progression for people who appreciate old things." Eleanor took a bite of the jam-covered toast. "Darn him. He does make good jam."

Gabby drew her grandmother into a quick hug. "It's nice to see you back to your old self, Grandma. You've been so...down lately."

How could she explain to her granddaughters the hole their leaving had made in her life? How proud she was of them for growing up and being successful women in their own right, but how all of that had left her feeling like she had no purpose? And how the column that she'd written for so many years had started feeling just as useless as herself?

"You don't have to worry about me, dear. I'll be just fine. I'm...searching for my next phase, I guess you could say. With you girls grown and gone, I wonder if maybe I should do something new. Or move." She sighed and put the empty plate into the sink. Then she forced a smile to her face. "It'll all be fine. I'm just having a moment, as you girls would say."

"If you need help, just ask."

"What I need help with is setting the table." She handed her granddaughter the stack of plates and silverware and told herself that, once her family was all together at the dinner table, she'd be right as rain again.

Gabby set four places at the table, leaving the other head of the table empty. No one had sat there since Grandpa died, and likely no one ever would. Today, that seat seemed too empty. It had been almost thirty-two years since her grandfather passed away, and as far as Gabby knew, Grandma hadn't dated anyone.

Instead, her grandmother was far too focused on Gabby's love life, or lack of one. She'd hoped Grandma would forget about the date with Jake, since the whole thing had gone completely contrary to plan and left her feeling more confused than ever. When he'd come into the store the other day, she'd half hoped he would kiss her again, and then half worried he would. He'd seemed like he was going to say something, but instead she'd interrupted with what a bad idea that would be, which meant she never heard what he was there to say. Maybe because she was scared he would say that he regretted kissing her. And why was she so worried anyway? She had much bigger things to worry about. Like Grandma saying she might move.

The thought of Grandma not being here in this big, old house whenever Gabby came by was positively devastating. The Victorian was a lot for her to keep up, but the girls and Jake helped as much as they could, and last year, Gabby's father had started paying for a cleaning service to come once a week. Maybe there was more they could do or some other way to make life easier for Grandma.

As Gabby returned to the kitchen for napkins, she caught a glimpse of Harry Erlich standing on Grandma's side of the hedges, raking up the freshly cut branches and putting them in a plastic bucket. He worked quickly but meticulously, brushing the sides of the hedges to release the last bits, checking the cuts, evening up the spots that were a little messy.

Instead of getting the napkins, Gabby ducked out the side door and strode across the lawn. Harry looked up, a little startled, and a pile of branches tumbled to the ground. He hurried to scoop them up again. "Hello, Gabriella."

"Why are you doing that?" she asked, then caught herself. "Sorry. That sounds wrong and harsh, and I don't mean it that way at all. I'm just curious. Why are you giving my grandmother jam and doing her yardwork?"

He dusted off his hands and glanced at the house. Grandma was standing on the back porch now, watching Gabby and Harry, her face unreadable from this distance. "Because she's a nice woman, a good neighbor, and well, a lovely person."

"And..." Gabby leaned closer and studied Harry's features. "Do you like her?"

Harry laughed, and his cheeks pinked a little. "This sounds like sixth grade again. I guess I could say that yes, I like your grandmother. She's a refreshing dose of honesty and goodness in a world that well...isn't always."

"I know she can be a bit...bristly, but I think she likes you, too." Gabby picked off a leaf and twiddled it between her fingers. This whole thing with Harry might be an even better mood lifter than the Dear Amelia column idea. If Grandma could get back to normal, maybe Gabby's sisters would, too, and Gabby could stop worrying. Heck, who was she kidding? She'd done nothing but worry about her family since that day she'd forgotten Emma's backpack and they all paid a price no one wanted to pay.

Gabby shook off the memory. She couldn't go back and fix that, but she could fix what was happening today. She thumbed toward her grandmother, who was wiping her hands on a dishrag as she watched them. "Maybe you should ask Grandma to get coffee sometime. She'd like that, I'm sure."

"Didn't I read something like that in the paper the other day? A guy who wanted to date his wife or rekindle their love or some such thing, and that Amelia lady said to ask her to coffee."

"Well, Dear Amelia does give great advice. People should listen to it more often." Gabby grinned. Wouldn't it be hilarious if that one machination with Antonia and Luis spurred a whole bunch of happy endings over a cup of java? Like Frank and Sandy and Grandma and Harry and Jake and—

Not Jake and her. No, that coffee with him had been about advice, not a date. And the kiss? Well, that was an anomaly. A skip in the space-time continuum.

Gabby saw Emma pull into the driveway and park. Since Margaret wasn't coming, there was room for one more at the table, and one more meant another person between herself and all those questions about Jake. "Or even better, why don't you come over for dinner tonight, Harry? Grandma is making rib roast, and there's always more than enough."

He arched a brow. He had only a little pepper in his gray hair, giving him a distinguished air. "Does she know you're inviting me?"

"Oh yeah. She said you're welcome anytime, but she was afraid you'd turn her down if she asked you." Okay, so that was a complete lie, but how was she going to get Grandma out of her funk if she didn't nudge things along a little? Or rather, a lot. The voice in the back of her head whispered that all she was doing was avoiding the big subjects again. The tough conversations she didn't want to have, the stark realities about her business. That putting all of her attention on other people's lives left her own untended. "Grandma was just saying a minute ago that she should invite you for dinner to thank you for the jam and the yardwork."

Harry leaned on his rake and considered for a moment. "Will there be mashed potatoes?"

Gabby nodded. "And green beans she canned last year, plus a cherry pie."

"Sounds perfect." Harry brightened, and she swore his blue eyes were sparkling now. "Thank you, Gabriella. Should I bring something?"

"A sense of humor." Because chances were good that Grandma wasn't going to find this matchmaking attempt very funny. Jake's words about the dangers of meddling in her family's life echoed in Gabby's mind as she headed back into the house to grab an extra place setting.

Jake Maddox, that amazing kisser and troublesome man, could just mind his own business.

TEN

I n the end, he opted for flowers.

Nothing too fancy, nothing that screamed, *Hey, I screwed up and don't know if I can make this right.* Just a dozen bright yellow daisies and a half dozen calla lilies, along with a separate bouquet of white roses.

At five to six, Jake walked into Grandma El's house to a rising tide of female voices. The three of them—Gabby, Emma, and Eleanor—were in the kitchen, arguing about something. The rib roast sat on top of the oven, resting with a big pot of mashed potatoes beside it, waiting to be put into a bowl. Damn, that dinner looked good. And so, of course, did Gabby, with her hair in a clip and a few errant tendrils curling along her jaw. She had on jeans and a pale pink sweater that was a little big for her and kept slipping down one shoulder, exposing a thin white satin strap.

Damn. He was already distracted.

"Why would you do that?" Grandma was saying.

"It's the neighborly thing to do, Grandma," Gabby

replied. He recognized that innocent, pretending-this-wasn't-meddling tone in her voice, and he had to bite back a laugh at her obvious, but well-meaning, machinations. "I was just trying to help you thank him for the jam."

Emma laughed. "Gabby, you are in so much trouble," she said in a singsong voice while she wagged a chastising finger. Gabby shot her a glare.

He could see this going south quickly. The Monroe women loved each other fiercely, but that also meant that sometimes they had big arguments. The difference between the girls' and his own family's disagreements was that love was at the root of everything the Monroes said and was the bridge that brought them all back together again.

"Anyone need a mediator?" Jake said as he walked into the kitchen. "A mediator with gifts, I might add." He stepped forward, handed the roses to Grandma El, and gave her a quick hug. "For the best grandma ever, and for feeding me."

Eleanor laughed and hugged him back, giving him that little dose of familial love that kept him coming around day after day. A thousand bouquets of roses wouldn't be enough to express how much he loved this woman and her granddaughters. One in particular.

"You are a silly, wonderful boy, Jake," Eleanor said. "But thank you. And the other flowers are for... ?"

"For the most beautiful woman in the room." He grinned as he turned to Gabby and held out the second bouquet. Her eyes widened with surprise, and one side of her smile quirked up in amusement. Everything inside him skipped a little beat when he was close to her. She had this sweet and sassy way about her that had kept him hovering in her orbit for so long. "Daisies are your favorites, if I remember right. And some lilies, just because."

Just because they're perfect and sweet and remind me of you. Good lord. Next thing he'd be writing greeting cards.

"They are. I can't believe you remembered that." She inhaled the scent of the flowers and smiled, and he wished he'd bought more flowers. "But why?"

He couldn't say aloud, in this kitchen and in front of her family, that the flowers were because he wanted to make up for that kiss, for changing things between them, and for being too scared to tell her how he really felt about her. That was a little too much for a dozen daisies and a few lilies to do. "Because you've been working really hard on that tricentennial event, and I just thought you needed a little something that says…" He got lost in the depths of her big green eyes, the way she held his gaze so intently, and how all of that made something in his chest tighten.

"Says what?" Emma asked, in the same innocent tone Gabby had used earlier with her grandmother.

Jake was suddenly aware of the laser focus Grandma El and Emma had on Gabby and him. This was too big of a conversation to have here. So he drew himself up and cleared his throat. "Sorry. Just had something on my mind, and I got distracted." More than distracted. Derailed. "The flowers are a token of appreciation for all your work, Gabby."

"I didn't know you cared so much about the local artisans, or vintage dresses." Gabby grinned.

I don't. I care about you. "It's a big deal for the town. Leroy is running an article about tourism and how it's been down for a couple years. He interviewed several business owners, who stressed that the event is a way to jump-start sales for everyone. So many people sang your praises and said how grateful they were for the idea and the publicity it's been generating. The town...well, the town needs you." *I need you.* He cleared his throat again. "I mean, needs something like this."

"I have never seen you so tongue-tied, Jake Maddox." Grandma patted him on the back and gave him a teasing smile. One kiss, and yes, he was tongue-tied around her, like they were teenagers again and he was tangled up in his first crush.

Because that one kiss had opened a door to a possible future that Jake had never allowed himself to dream of having. A future with Gabby in his arms, every single day. That thought filled him with lightness and hope.

She could still be in love with another man or she could have no interest in dating Jake. The kiss could have been a moment of weakness that she regretted. He needed to pull back the hearts and roses in his head and be realistic. Just because he wanted something didn't mean it was going to come true.

He was saved from replying when Grandma El's phone rang. She picked up the cell and when she answered, she gave Gabby a glance. "Why hello, Davis."

Gabby got busy stirring the green beans. Emma sidled up beside Eleanor and leaned her head against her grandmother's, the two of them talking into the phone at the same time. "Hey, Dad. You should come to family dinner sometime."

A pause, and then Eleanor said, "Yes, of course, she's right here. Gabriella, come say hello to your father."

"I'm checking the green beans. I'll text him later."

Grandma El sighed. "She's busy, Davis. Yes, of course. I'll tell her. And thank you for the invitation. We'd love to be there. Is there anything I can bring?" A minute more of conversation and then Eleanor said goodbye and hung up. "What was that, Gabriella?"

Those green beans had to be the best stirred in the county, because Gabby had yet to turn away from the stove. "Nothing. I just didn't feel like chatting."

"Davis said he invited you to dinner and you haven't replied." Eleanor sighed again. "He is trying to have a relationship with you girls. The least you can do is try in return."

"He's too late," Gabby said. "And besides, after what he did—" She shook her head, and instead of finishing her sentence, she took the green beans off the stove and began pouring them into a serving dish.

"Besides what?" Eleanor asked.

"Nothing." Gabby soaked the pan and added a serving spoon to the dish. "I'll just put these on the table."

"Hey," Jake said softly as she passed him. "What's up?"

"Nothing I want to talk about."

"There used to be a time when we could tell each other anything," he said, and realized he'd missed the moment when that had stopped. "Are you sure you're okay?"

She just nodded and brushed past him. He watched her hurry into the dining room, drop off the casserole, and then head down the hall to the bathroom.

"She hasn't been herself lately," Grandma El said. "I think she's just stressed about that event she's been planning."

"I'm sure that's it," Jake said, but he didn't believe that was the source of whatever had Gabby so upset.

"If you're done watching over my granddaughter like a worried hen, could you carry the roast to the table for me?" She handed him the platter, along with a serving fork and carving knife.

"Of course." Keeping busy gave him a chance to tear his gaze away from Gabby as she returned to the kitchen, her expression calm and unbothered. "You good?" he whispered.

"I will be." She dipped her gaze and then gave his hand a slight squeeze. "Thanks for checking. You've always been a great friend, Jake."

"Nothing more?" he asked.

She glanced at the daisies, then back at him, and a rush of crimson showed in her cheeks. "Well, maybe something more."

The doorbell rang just then, and Grandma shot Gabby a little glare before heading down the hall to pull open the door. Hmm. This must have been what they were arguing about when he first came into the house. Jake wanted to stay in the kitchen and ask Gabby what she meant, but instead he dropped off the platter of rib roast on the table and craned his neck to look down the front hall. Harry Erlich stood on the porch with a bottle of wine and a look of uncertainty.

Jake glanced at Gabby. "*Harry* is coming to dinner?" he said. "And I take it you're the one who extended the invite?"

"Yup." Gabby shrugged, as if inviting a single, silver-haired male neighbor over for dinner were an everyday occurrence. "He likes Grandma, and she doesn't know it yet, but she likes him, too."

"You little matchmaker." Jake chuckled as he reached up and brushed a tendril of hair off her forehead. For a split second, her eyes fluttered shut and she leaned into the tender touch. It was a fleeting moment, but it was enough to tell him she'd been bluffing back in the shop. She was just as affected by his touch as he was by hers. "You know you are terrible at minding your own business, Gabby Monroe, right?"

"Shush. You have no idea what you're talking about. Just watch. It'll all work out beautifully."

So his girl—okay, maybe she wasn't his girl yet, but Jake wasn't giving up—was a romantic at heart. He liked that. A lot. "You want me to trust you that it'll all work out?"

"Yes, now shhh."

"Deal," he said. "But only if you promise to trust me, too." Gabby shot him a look of confusion, but Harry was stepping across the threshold and saved Jake from answering and adding, *Trust me that we are going to be great together.*

"Evening, Eleanor." Harry handed Grandma El the bottle of wine and gave her a smile. Jake could swear he saw the faintest blush in Eleanor's cheeks. "Thank you for the invitation to dinner."

"It was the least I could do after you dropped off the jam," Grandma said, or lied, rather, given what Jake had overheard a minute before. As she walked down the hall to the dining room, she glanced back at Harry. He'd worn a pale green button-down shirt and a tie along with pressed khaki pants and shiny brown dress shoes. Jake had seen the man several times over the year since he'd moved in and never seen him so dressed up. Given the way Eleanor was checking him out, it seemed that she hadn't, either.

I should have gone with the tie that night, Jake

thought. Maybe Gabby would be as tongue-tied around him as he was around her if he'd dressed up on their double date. Eleanor was clearly surprised by this other side of Harry, all handsome and clean-shaven. Would the same thing work on Gabby if Jake had a Windsor knot going for him? Hell, if that was the case, he'd break out a three-piece suit or even a damned tux.

Eleanor stopped by the table and counted the place settings. As always, the head of the table was blank, a space that had been there for as long as Jake had known the Monroe women and their grandmother. After her husband died, she'd never replaced that space with another person. "Well, seems we have a full table tonight. Except for Margaret." She shook her head and then clasped her hands together, a pose Jake knew meant a resolute decision was cementing in her mind. "Maybe you and I should deliver leftovers to her on Friday, Gabby, and check on your sister. Until then, the rest of us have a lovely dinner that's getting cold, so let's eat."

They all took their seats while Gabby retrieved the wine opener and a quintet of glasses from the glass-front hutch. Plates were passed, rolls were buttered, and the table fell into the easy conversational pattern that Jake loved so much. Sometimes he sat there and just listened to the sounds of a family, the warmth of their love, and the way they seemed to read each other's minds.

In his house, his father had been dictatorial, running things with an iron fist. Jake's mother was a meek woman who was bubbly and affectionate when it was just her son and herself but terrified to upset the dragon, as she'd once dubbed his father. Jake never understood why she'd moved back after two years struggling to get her alcoholism under control. Three stays in rehabs, then a halfway house before she returned to the grand, cold home around the corner from this warm Victorian.

For a long time, his relationship with his mother had been strained. Jake had been almost ten when she came back and tried to slip into a normal routine with a warm breakfast waiting for him every morning and a bedtime story at night. By then, he'd outgrown those kinds of things. He didn't believe in Santa anymore, and he didn't trust his mother not to leave again.

But she stayed, and they rebuilt their relationship piece by piece. She became a buffer between Jake and his hypercritical father, but he'd never found the kind of warmth and unconditional acceptance that he found in the Monroe family. As soon as Jake went to college, his mother filed for divorce and moved to Arizona. Now they talked once a week or so, and he flew out there for her birthday and Christmas. His entire childhood was sad, and frustrating, and the very model of what Jake didn't want in his future.

He wanted this—the squabbles and hugs and passing potatoes while they chatted about the day. The inside jokes and good-natured ribbing and well-intentioned meddling.

"So, Harry," Emma said as she drizzled gravy over her slice of roast, "are you retired? Dating anyone?"

"Emma Jean," Grandma El said. "That's too personal."

Harry leaned back in the chair and draped his arm over the edge. "I retired two years ago from a thirty-year career in engineering. Which means I can fix about anything, but I'm a bit fussy about it." He chuckled. "And no, I'm not dating anyone right now. It's been a few years since my wife died, and it took me a while to feel ready to date again. Plus my grandson was living with me until a month ago. Retiring, moving here were big steps I had to take first."

Gabby scooped up another helping of mashed potatoes. Emma read Gabby's mind and passed her the gravy. "Thanks, Em," Gabby said, adding a generous dollop of gravy to her plate. "Sounds like you have all your ducks in a row, and your squirrels in a tree, as Grandma would say."

He laughed, a hearty laugh that sounded like it came from deep inside his soul. Jake liked Harry. Liked him a lot. While he might not approve of all of Gabby's meddling, even Jake had to admit that this seemed like a good match. "Yes, I think I do," Harry said.

"So, Jake, tell us what's going on with you," Eleanor said. "A little birdie told me that you and Gabby had a date a few nights ago."

Emma choked back a laugh, mirth dancing in her eyes. Harry arched a brow. Gabby looked like she wanted to die.

"It wasn't technically a date," Gabby said.

"We did have a date of sorts, and if you ask me, it was a great night. Really great." He glanced at her across the table and was captivated all over again. Maybe it was the lighting in the room, or maybe the glass of wine he'd had was making him take another chance. Either way, Jake knew he didn't want to be his father's age or Harry's age and think *woulda coulda shoulda*. He wanted that two-kids-and-a-dog life for himself, and he wanted it with Gabby. The problem was getting Gabby to see him in that light. "Every moment I spend with Gabby is wonderful."

"Aww." Emma sighed. "I had no idea you were such a romantic, Jake."

"He's not one," Gabby said, and gave him a side-eye. Her brows rose, as if she was insisting he agree with her. "He's just hamming it up for the dinner crowd. Right, Jake?"

He would have believed her except there was still a touch of crimson in her cheeks and she wasn't her usual defiant, sassy self. Okay, then. He was going to push this envelope a little further and see where he ended up. If he wanted what he'd never had, he had to keep reaching for that brass ring or miss the opportunity forever and be left alone with his regrets.

Jake leaned across his plate, caught Gabby's deep green eyes, and said in his best Southern drawl, "Honey, I'm not acting at all."

ELEVEN

"Earth to Gabby," Emma whispered in a low, sharp voice. "You're supposed to be a tree, not a dog."

Gabby jerked her attention back to her yoga mat and the class of people who were standing with one foot resting on the opposite knee, their hands clasped in front of them, eyes closed. She sprang out of Downward Dog and into Tree Pose just as the instructor told them to do Warrior I, which put her another pose behind. *Distracted* didn't even begin to describe the cluster of butterflies flitting inside her brain.

It was late Thursday afternoon, and Gabby had finally managed to corral one of her sisters into doing yoga. Margaret had said she was too busy at work to come. When Gabby dashed into the studio two minutes before class started, she'd hoped the yoga and time with Emma would take her mind off Jake and that kiss and what on earth happened at dinner last night. But if anything, the nearly silent practice left her altogether too much room to think.

What had he meant by *Honey, I'm not acting at all*?

She'd never found out because she'd found a reason to excuse herself from the table early and go home, presumably to work on the event plans. In reality, she'd just sat on her couch while Netflix churned through *The Great British Baking Show*, trying to decide whether Jake was kidding. He'd texted her a few times, asking if she was okay, and she'd just ignored him because she didn't have an answer. Was she okay with him saying that? Okay with changing the status quo?

And then there was Dad, who was becoming more persistent in trying to get close to his daughter again. What was up with the men in her life?

"Catch me up on all the gossip and drama," Emma whispered as she stretched her fingertips and lifted one foot off the ground, moving seamlessly into Warrior III. "You've been quiet ever since you got here and barely texting the last couple days."

"If I tell you something, do you swear you won't tell anyone?" Gabby had to talk about what had happened with someone, if only to verbally dissect it and then deal with it. Every time she'd closed her eyes last night, she'd heard Jake calling her *honey* and thought of him kissing her.

Even though the kiss had been a few days ago, it was so vivid in her mind that she could almost feel his lips against hers, his hands on her face, the warmth of his body against her own. All of which meant a sleepless, restless night. She needed to get this little… blip in her relationship with Jake out of her system, and then everything would be okay.

Emma made a quick cross sign on her heart before she wobbled out of her pose. "You know your secret's safe with me."

"Jake and I…" Gabby drew her leg down, straightened, and followed the instructor through a sun salutation.

She curved up into a Baby Cobra Pose. "Well, we didn't just go on a fake date...We kind of kissed."

"Holy cow!" Emma's sharp exclamation earned her several shushes and dirty looks, along with an exasperated glare from the instructor. She lowered her voice and leaned toward Gabby. "You kissed him?"

"It was kind of a mutual thing. Sort of. I think." Gabby had, after all, been the one to rise up on her toes. It had been as much of an invitation as Jake's warm words against her cheek. All she could remember was a surge of want inside her chest, overriding any practical thoughts she might have had about the wisdom of kissing her best friend. "It was such a mistake."

"Why? Was he bad at it?"

"No. I wish he had been." She sighed as she dropped into a forward fold and gripped the backs of her ankles. A rush of blood went to her head. "He was...amazing."

"Ladies, this is a time of silence and reinvigoration," the instructor said. "Conversations are for *after* yoga."

Emma glanced at Gabby, a devilish gleam in her eyes. She mouthed, *Oh boy, we're in big trouble now*, which made Gabby giggle because it was just like their childhood days when they'd get caught sneaking cookies before dinner or coming in after curfew. Gabby clamped one hand over her mouth to keep the laughter from spilling into the room.

When class ended fifteen minutes later, Emma was asking questions before people even started rolling up their mats. "So, tell me everything. What happened? How did it happen? Do you like him...like that?"

"There's not much to tell." Gabby grabbed her mat and spiraled it back into a tight roll, avoiding her sister's gaze and answers she didn't even have for herself. She didn't know how she felt about Jake, or about the kiss. Even if her mind did revolve around both almost every minute of every day.

"You and Jake *kissed*. That's, like, breaking news. I really should alert the media." Emma grinned and tucked her mat into her canvas bag.

Gabby groaned. "It's not that big of a deal. And it was just part of our plan to get Frank to write a thank-you letter to Dear Amelia. Remember Grandma? She's what's most important now, not some silly date with Jake."

"True... but I disagree that what happened with Jake is nothing." Emma caught the annoyance in Gabby's features and raised her hands. "Okay, okay, I'll drop it."

"Thanks." Any other topic would be better than that one.

"So, what's up with you and Dad? Why haven't you RSVP'd to dinner at his and Joanna's house for his birthday?"

Okay, any topic but that one, too. Gabby sighed. "It's complicated, Emma."

"It's family, Gabs. What's complicated about it?" Emma rooted around in her bag, found her sunglasses, and then propped them on her head before digging in the bag again to find her keys. She juggled the bag, listening for the jingle, then yanked them out. "A-ha. Success! I don't get why you've always been so grumpy when it comes to Dad. When we were kids, you were the closest to him. He used to take you in to his office on Saturdays and let you work the adding machines, remember? I was so jealous I couldn't go."

"You were too little. And that was a million years ago." The days when she and her father had been close were light-years in the past. Whatever relationship she'd had with him when she was a child had disappeared the day she saw him with Joanna.

"And you've been avoiding him for years. How come? What crime has he committed besides getting married again less than two years after Momma died?" Emma asked.

"Along with never being here for us? Never mind. It's nothing, Em. He and I just don't get along." Gabby wasn't about to tell Emma the truth, that she knew Dad had moved on much earlier than two years after Momma died. That would only upset her sister, who was the one Monroe girl with a good relationship with him. "Anyway, did you notice that yesterday was the third time in a row Margaret and Michael didn't come to family dinner? And do you want to come with Grandma and me tomorrow to bring her leftovers, aka check on her?"

Emma shook her head. "Can't. I have a meeting with my boss to talk about the next wedding at the hotel. I doubt you'll find Margaret home, anyway. She'll probably be at work, like always. I tried reaching out to her a few times, but she's barely answering."

"She told me last week that business has been down, and maybe she's just frantically trying to build it back up." Gabby shrugged.

"Yeah, maybe." Emma trailed along behind Gabby as they headed out of the yoga studio. The day had warmed, another mercurial spring afternoon in Massachusetts, and now the temperature hovered in the low sixties. Traffic along Main Street ran at a steady pace, a good sign for the season to come, as the snowbirds started to return to Massachusetts, and people who had been cooped up during the long, gray winter started venturing out again. Soon Harbor Cove would be bustling with business and life.

"So, exactly how amazing was Jake?" Emma asked.

Gabby laughed. "You just won't let that go, will you?" She considered lying. She had, after all, been lying to herself about that kiss for days now. But then she closed her eyes, and she thought of the moment when his lips brushed hers and his hand came up to cup her cheek, and she sighed. "You know how you feel about the doughnuts at Marguerite's? Amazing like that."

Emma let out a low whistle. "Girl, you are in trouble. You might think you're not going to want to go back for more, but we both know I can't walk out of that place without at least a half dozen doughnuts. You'll be having seconds. I guarantee it." She gathered her older sister into a tight hug. "And for the record, I'm super happy for you."

"I'm not going back for more. Definitely not. I have bigger things to worry about. Like the vintage event and my store. And Grandma."

"Yeah, I get that. Grandma worries me, too. I was hoping she'd perk up after Antonia's date with Luis or maybe after that little stunt you pulled inviting Harry Erlich to dinner, but it doesn't seem like she did." Emma frowned. "I talked to her today, and she sounded kind of down again. Maybe Frank will write in about how awesome his date with Sandy was and Grandma will feel better."

"Maybe." Gabby fiddled with her keys. "Do you think we should see if we can drag Margaret out for drinks tonight?"

"It won't work. You and I both know that Margaret doesn't do things she doesn't want to do."

Gabby missed her sisters so much, even though they all lived in the same town. The gulf between them was painful, leaving an empty space in Gabby's heart. "I hate that the three of us are hardly together anymore. I'm so glad you came to yoga today and dinner last night. We need to do more of these kinds of things."

"Gabs, we're adults. We have separate lives now. We can't be little girls staying up past our bedtimes forever."

"Yeah, but maybe we could do a weekend getaway. Just the three of us." She could hear the rush in her voice, the desperate feeling that she was losing touch, losing them, and that the promise she'd so fervently made was falling apart at the seams. "We could turn off our phones and stay up way too late, laughing and eating."

Emma was already shaking her head. "That's not going to happen, Gabs. You know it. I think you have this image of the past that is a little more Hollywood than it really was." She gave her a quick one-armed hug before saying goodbye and heading for her car.

He was at it again, that frustrating man. Eleanor stared at the box on her doorstep on Friday morning and the little note tied to the top. A dozen doughnuts from Marguerite's, the bakery downtown—the bakery that Emma and Eleanor both loved. On Sundays, she stopped by after church and got one Bavarian cream doughnut, no more, because any more than that and the doughnuts would go straight to her hips.

> *I've seen you stop in at Marguerite's and thought you'd like these. Thank you for a lovely dinner. Next time, it's my treat. —Yours, Harry*

She stared at the words for a long time. *Next time. Yours.* That implied a future that Eleanor wasn't sure she was ready for. After all, she had the girls to worry about and—

Excuses. She knew it as well as anyone else. Excuses that had worked for decades to keep her from ever going through another heartache. After the loss of Russell and then Penny, it had been too much to think of getting close and opening her life to another. She simply couldn't bear one more loss, one more heartbreak. Best to keep her heart closed to anyone else and pour all her love into those girls, as she had for three decades now.

For a long time, it had been enough, but lately, she'd felt this odd...tug. An urge to shift directions or change or just...something.

At the same time as she started taking the box inside, a familiar car pulled into the driveway. The Lexus parked and shut off. A second passed, and then Davis Monroe stepped out of the car. Her son-in-law—despite Penny's death and Davis's remarriage, Eleanor still considered him her son-in-law—was a tall man who had gained a belly over the years he'd worked as a manager at the Harbor Cove Bank & Trust. His once-trim physique had gotten a little wider, but he still had the handsome face and square jawline that her daughter had fallen in love with. "Davis. What brings you by?"

"Just checking on you, El." He glanced around at the tidy lawn, the swept porch, the freshly painted house. "You doing okay? Need anything?"

"You ask me that a hundred times a year, and yes, I am. Why don't you come in and I'll put some coffee on? Gabby is due over any minute now, and maybe we can all have a visit."

"I don't think Gabby wants to visit with me. She's been very clear about that." He had one hand on the door still, as if he was about to climb back in his car and leave. Davis avoided confrontation like some people avoided cold germs. He loved his daughters, that much was clear, but it was as if he had no idea how to be a parent to a girl. Penny had been the one to braid the pigtails and bandage the skinned knees while Davis was in the garage, tightening training wheels. The death of the girls' mother had caused an earthquake among them, and as much as Eleanor had hoped her son-in-law would bridge that gap, he'd withdrawn instead.

"Davis Monroe, your daughters may be adults, but they still need you," Eleanor said. Honestly, why did no one listen to her advice? No one in the paper, no one in her real life. It all fell on deaf, stubborn ears. "You are going to have to work on those relationships someday, and what better day than this one?"

He shook his head and let out a long breath. "El, you don't understand. Gabby and I just don't see eye to eye. Em's fine, and Margaret, well, she's Margaret, but Gabby wants nothing to do with me."

"Maybe it's time you asked her why."

He shifted his weight from foot to foot. "Today? I don't know if that's a good idea."

"I have doughnuts." She hoisted the box. "They make any conversation easier."

He chuckled. "You always were a strong, persuasive woman. Have I thanked you for all you've done for my girls, and for me?"

"You have." Her smile softened. For all his faults, she loved Davis because he fiercely loved the most important girls in Eleanor's life. "And you've never needed to. I love them as much as I do Penny."

"Yeah. Me too. All right, I'll take your advice. But I

hope you have a cinnamon sugar doughnut, because that's the only kind worth that spin class my wife is making me take." Davis cleared his throat before entering the house and following Eleanor down to the kitchen. She put on a pot of coffee and set the doughnuts on a plate while they exchanged small talk about Davis's second wife and the sons she'd brought into the marriage, and the one they'd had together. When Davis had remarried, it had been hard news to take. Eleanor had sort of hoped he would pine away for Penny forever, but Davis was a young widower, and he deserved a second chance at happiness. So she'd bought the new couple a blender, and given them her best wishes, and missed her daughter in a way she hadn't missed her before.

Eleanor wasn't one to dwell on if-onlys, but the day she watched Davis pledge his love to another woman had been chock-full of what-ifs. How different all of their lives would have been if Penny hadn't been hit by that drunk driver.

Gabby came striding in the back door, sweaty and out of breath from her early-morning jog. She tugged out one of her headphones and stopped short. "Dad. What are you doing here?"

"Checking on your grandmother. And having doughnuts." He waved the cinnamon sugar doughnut he'd already bitten into. "Want to join us?"

She was shaking her head before he even finished the question. "I have things to do today. There's a lot left to plan for the event in like a week and—"

"Gabriella Monroe, have a doughnut. I swear, the two of you are a pair of brick walls." Eleanor pulled out a chair and motioned her granddaughter into it. "I'll fix you a cup of coffee while you exchange more than five words with your father."

Gabby shrugged. "Fine." Her reluctance came through in every inch of the word, like she was a teenager forced to attend a lecture about her curfew. She dropped into a chair, set her headphones on the table, and accepted the cup of coffee Eleanor had poured. "What's new, Dad?"

"I don't want to force you to talk to me, Gabby." Davis got to his feet and pushed the chair back. His expression was annoyed, pained, and frustrated. "I'll just leave you to your coffee."

Gabby dropped her gaze to the dark brew in the mug. "Yep, you do that, Dad. Just leave. Don't worry. I'll pick up the pieces behind you. I'm used to it."

He looked down at his daughter for a moment as if he was about to say something, but ultimately, Davis shook his head and headed down the hall. Eleanor called after him, but he was gone. Stubbornness was part and parcel of the Monroe DNA, that was for sure.

"You know he has trouble talking about things," she said as she returned to the kitchen. Eleanor refilled her coffee mug and sat down at the table. She had vowed she wouldn't eat a single one of those doughnuts from Harry Erlich, but that man had gone and put three Bavarian creams in the box. Besides, it was wrong to waste food, even if it came from someone who wanted something she couldn't give. And these doughnuts were amazingly tasty.

"And what, I'm supposed to do all the hard work for him?" Gabby said. "He's never here, Grandma. He's never been here. Heck, he barely took a breath before he moved on and started a new family. When the three of us were little, we needed him, and he was at work. He missed our soccer games and proms and first dates. You were the one who was here for all of that, not him."

"He had a really hard time after your momma died." *Hard time* was putting it mildly. Davis had become a veritable recluse, stuck behind the door of his office at work, spending sixty, eighty, sometimes a hundred hours a week at the bank. He'd walked around with shadows under his eyes and a slump in his shoulders, as if he had lost half of himself in that car accident. Maybe Eleanor had too much sympathy for Davis because she understood exactly how he had felt.

"Yeah, well, so did I." Tears filled Gabby's eyes, but she rubbed them away. "I don't want to talk about or with him right now. Dad has to learn to stay in one place long enough to have a hard conversation. Maybe then we can work things out."

"You're right, my dear wise one. I'll talk to him, although I daresay he's as stubborn as you and your sisters are." She patted Gabby's hand.

"Speaking of stubborn people, I'll be back after lunch, when Lori comes in, so we can head over to Margaret's together," Gabby said, deftly changing the subject and lowering the tension in the room. "She hasn't been going to yoga with me and Em, and she isn't coming to dinner here. She barely replies when I text or call her. I'm worried about her, Grandma."

Eleanor smiled. How she loved these girls, with their individual quirks and their big hearts. Penny would have been busting at the seams with pride if she could see how her daughters had turned out, so protective of each other. "You are such a shepherd, my dear granddaughter."

"As in I bring sheep over a mountain?" Gabby laughed and reached for a raspberry-filled sugar doughnut. The crumbs from Davis's half-eaten doughnut still sat on the plate.

"As in you are always corralling all of us, trying to get us to mend fences and be together." Eleanor paused. Gabby had a dot of raspberry jam on her chin and a dusting of sugar, just like when she was a little girl. Eleanor wiped it off and then cupped Gabby's cheek. "But you keep pushing your father out of the group."

"Grandma, if he wanted to be a part of the herd, he would have tried harder." She drew back and took another bite of the doughnut, maybe trying to hide the sadness in her eyes, the defeat.

Eleanor knew how much it pained Gabby, the one who was always trying to keep this family together, to have her father on the outskirts. She might not say it now, but surely she remembered the laughter and fun that had lived in the Monroe house. Davis might have been a busy, often disconnected dad, but when it counted, he was there with a hug or a kiss. When the girls were little, it had been as simple as that to connect with them. But now, there were old resentments to overcome.

"Maybe he doesn't know how," Eleanor said.

"He sure figured it out with Joanna and her boys. I saw him at the football stadium with their youngest son last week. Dad had his arm around him and was talking about what a good job Joey had done on the field." Tears welled in her eyes again, but this time she let them fall. She pushed the plate away and folded her hands on the table. "He didn't do that with us, not after she was gone. But he was there for Joanna, and for them. He was supposed to be our father, too. He was supposed to be here, Grandma. And he wasn't."

And there it was, the source of all the walls between Gabriella and her father. Eleanor could tell Gabby a million times that Davis loved his girls just as much, if not more, but the words fell on deaf ears if Davis's actions didn't say the same thing.

Oh, how she hated seeing these girls hurt. If she could have, she would have wrapped them in a bubble all their lives so they never felt pain or heartbreak. "You're a hundred percent right, Gabby. But unless you lose your partner, the person who knows you best in the world, you won't truly understand what your father went through when your mother died. I pray that never happens. I really do, because it leaves a gaping hole and an empty spot everywhere you turn."

Gabby scoffed. "Dad refilled his empty spot."

"He did." And seeing Davis beam love at another woman when Penny had such a brief window of that joy still pained Eleanor. She could see that it pained the girls who loved him, too. She covered Gabby's hand with her own and gave it a little squeeze. "He has a right to be happy again, Gabby. We can't go back and change the past. But we can't keep living in it, either. We need to move forward and look toward the horizon."

Gabby arched a brow over her sip of coffee. "Sounds like advice Dear Amelia would give."

Eleanor paused for a second and flicked a glance at Gabby. The off-the-cuff comment didn't mean Gabby knew anything, right? No, that was crazy. She was just being overly sensitive today. "Well, I think I've been spending far too much time reading that column. And far too little time eating doughnuts. Which one do you want to eat next?"

TWELVE

Jacob Theodore Maddox.

He typed in his name, the lines autopopulating after the many times he'd filled out the form, and this time he kept going, filling in his address, a little backstory about the photo, and then, finally, his credit card information. Then Jake took a deep breath, attached the picture, and hit *send*.

"About damned time," Leroy said from over his shoulder. Jake hadn't even heard him approach. "You entered, right?"

"Yup." Jake had been sitting here since early this morning, putting in extra hours on Friday because it was easier than tossing and turning, rerunning that dinner at Eleanor's in his head. *Something more.*

He'd taken a chance in kissing Gabby and pushing their relationship out of the friend zone. And it hadn't ended in disaster. If he was reading her right, she was just as shaken up by their kiss as he was.

Somewhere around five this morning, Jake had

decided that one risk could pave the way for another one, and he'd headed into the office to finally enter that competition. Leroy had come in a few minutes after Jake to finish up a couple of articles he'd had in the hopper.

Kissing Gabby had given Jake a literal taste of what he could have. What if they worked out and he had fifty years of happiness with her? What if he sent in the photo and won the contest and it spurred him to make his photography more of a full-time thing? All those what-ifs had dangled in the breeze for far too long, fueled by a critical father and a tough childhood.

"What changed your mind?" Leroy asked.

"I decided I'm going to start taking this photography thing more seriously. I've loved what I've done for the paper, but it's time to start branching out on my own," Jake said to Leroy. "Regardless of how it works out."

"Does that mean you're leaving me?"

"No. I love it here, you know that." And he did. He loved this town, the people in it, and the job he did. Helping the small businesses that he patronized and working with people he had known most of his life had become much more than just a nine-to-five. This town was his home, and he couldn't imagine living anywhere else. "I might end up working more Saturdays and nights, but I'm not going anywhere."

Besides, anywhere else wouldn't have a Gabby Monroe, and until he was done seeing where this went, either to happiness or heartbreak, Jake wasn't ready to leave Harbor Cove.

"Good, because I have an assignment for you." Leroy perched himself on the edge of Jake's desk. "You know how Gabby's store is going to have all that vintage-style inventory from local seamstresses? The dresses and purses and whatever knickknacks women buy."

"Yep. She's been curating all of it for weeks." That made him think of seeing her in the back room, tagging the items with her precise lettering. And wham, he missed her like he'd lost an arm.

"I thought it might be good to run a special extra edition with a photo spread previewing some of the items, alongside that piece on tourism and the articles on the history of Harbor Cove," Leroy said. "Give it all some depth and color. Do you think you could get someone to model some of those items and take some shots?"

"Sure. I'll go over and talk to Gabby today." Jake's pulse kicked up a notch at the thought. He hadn't seen her yesterday, and the world always seemed a little grayer when she wasn't around.

He'd given her space, because them kissing had been like throwing a grenade into the middle of their friendship. But now it was time to just go for it with Gabby. If it ended badly, he'd move to Timbuktu and spend the rest of his life forgetting her.

His phone buzzed, and his father's name appeared on the screen. *Need to talk to you*, the text said.

Whatever it was, Jake wasn't interested. Undoubtedly, Edward had some criticism over an ad, or another reminder that Jake had "thrown it all away" when he left the law firm. Jake flipped the phone over.

"Get me the photo spread by Monday, before the issue goes to press," Leroy said. "I'll save the inside pages for the full spread, and you'll have most of the space on the front page for a couple more photos. I'm going to get it out this week with some promo about the event and interviews with some of the other businesses involved and send it to all fourteen towns in our little family here. Hopefully that will drum up a lot of participation."

"Thanks, Leroy. Gabby is going to be thrilled to hear about all that promotion." Given how much of a hit Harbor Cove's tourism had taken over the last few years as Massachusetts endured long winters and too-short summers, this boost could be just the thing they needed to turn everyone's luck around. He thought of how slow the store had been every time he stopped by and wondered if maybe Gabby needed this extra promotion more than anyone realized.

"This town needs a little perking up, and I want to support anyone who's got the backs of the people who make Harbor Cove great. Even if'—he got to his feet and clapped Jake on the shoulder—"they eventually end up moving on to greener pastures."

"What, and make Frank work with a new ad designer? Never." Jake chuckled as his boss walked away. The old wooden floorboards creaked, and the sharp spring wind whistled between the cracks in the brick facade, but Jake loved this building, all the history in it, and the people he worked with. No, he wasn't moving on. Not quite yet.

Just after eleven, Jake grabbed his jacket and headed down Main Street. He debated stopping in the flower shop, then the bakery, and opted not to try too hard. Gabby, he'd learned over the years, was like a newborn colt. If you came at her with too much, too fast, she was liable to run. So he was going to take it nice and easy and coax her closer with a gentle touch.

He knew he hadn't imagined her being the one to rise toward him first or how she'd kissed him back with the same hungry fever he'd felt. Or the way she'd leaned into his touch the other night, and the flush in her cheeks. There was something there, and damned if he was going to let that get away again.

The shop was empty when he got there, save for Gabby dressing a mannequin in the center of the store with a bright green cable-knit sweater and a long multi-colored skirt. Gabby had her hair up in a messy bun and a set of glasses perched atop her head. She was wearing a pair of black pants that outlined her body perfectly and a blue V-neck shirt that set off her eyes.

Gorgeous. Absolutely gorgeous.

"Hi, Jake." She stepped down off the pedestal and put her hands on her hips. She gave him a wide smile, as familiar as his own hand. "Whatcha need?"

You. He wanted to kiss her right now but took a mental step back. *Slow down, cowboy.* "I came over to tell you that Leroy wants me to do a photo spread on some of the things you brought in for the show. He's going to run it in all the editions, along with a piece about the tricentennial and the businesses participating in the kickoff. It's going to be a lot of promo for you and the event."

"Really? That's so nice of him." She had relief in her voice, and her face brightened. "I was getting kind of worried that we wouldn't have the numbers we need. This is just...phew. A big help."

"Everything okay here, Gab?" Even as he asked the question, he could see it was anything but. It was a Friday, and normally, downtown Harbor Cove was bustling with people, especially commuters who took off early for the weekend and meandered through the quaint coastal towns of Massachusetts. Foot traffic on Main Street was a little light today, but that still should have brought some people into Gabby's shop.

"Yes, it's all great. Just great." But her smile wobbled, and he could see the worry in her eyes.

"You know I'm here to help you or support you?"

"That's what friends are for, right?" she said, and it was almost like she'd dropped an invisible wall between them. "Anyway, tell me more about this photo shoot thing."

"The bad news is my deadline is on Monday so I need to shoot it tonight, or tomorrow at the latest. I know it's short notice to figure out what you want to feature and find someone to model the clothes."

"I can ask Lori to do it. I mean, she knows the inventory well, and like you said, I don't think I can get anyone else on short notice. Emma's babysitting again for Antonia, and most of my friends work nights. But Lori is always looking for some extra cash. If she can't do it...well, maybe I could." Gabby started straightening a pile of T-shirts decorated with a rugged coastline and the words *Harbor Cove*. She folded with military precision, as if she needed something to do with her hands. "How about after we close tonight?"

"Perfect. I'll be back when you close. And Gabby..."

She glanced up. "Yeah?"

"I hope you're the model. Because you'd make everything look beautiful."

Her jaw dropped, and the usually loquacious Gabby was silent. Jake gave her a grin, said goodbye, and strode out of the shop. Oh yes, everything was going according to plan.

* * *

Margaret's house could have been a page torn out of
Architectural Digest: a two-story Georgian with white
columns and a wraparound porch that looked out over an
acre of lush frontage. Even the foyer, with its curved staircase and travertine floors, was impressive and elegant.
Margaret had hand-selected every piece in her house
and probably agonized over every chair, every vase, all
perfectly arranged in a soothing palette of blues and grays
and the occasional pop of coral or yellow.

To Gabby, the whole place felt as sterile and cold
as a mortuary. She wanted to come in and bake bread
on the kitchen counters so there'd be flour on the floor
or some crumbs by the toaster. She wanted to flop on
the couch and mess up those stacked pillows that looked
like soldiers marching down the leather. But most of
all, she wanted to get Margaret to loosen up a little,
enjoy her life, and stop working every spare minute
she had.

"Thank you for bringing this over," Margaret said to
Grandma and Gabby. She tucked the containers of leftovers into her fridge, storing them on shelves that had
apparently been divided into categories with neat square
glass containers and bins. "I'm sure it will be delicious.
And I'm sorry I can't visit, but I'm only home to grab
something and then I have to—"

"Get to work?" Gabby said. "Meggy, you never stay
for anything. I barely see you. Take five minutes to sit
down and chat with us."

"I agree with Gabriella. We all miss you, Margaret."
Grandma clasped Margaret's hand and gave it a squeeze.
"And you look like something is troubling you. Is every-
thing okay?"

Margaret smiled. "Of course. All good. Just busy

with work, like I said. It's nothing more than me being overwhelmed sometimes."

Except Margaret looked thinner than the last time Gabby had seen her. There were more shadows under her eyes and a gauntness to her face. Something was wrong, but whatever it was, Margaret clearly didn't want to share.

"And how's Mike?" Grandma asked. "He's not working from home today?"

Margaret's gaze shifted left, and she fiddled with the basket of lemons that added a perfect spark of color to the sky-blue and steel-gray kitchen. Gabby wasn't even sure the lemons were real. "He went golfing."

"Since when does Mike golf?" Gabby asked. "And on a weekday?"

"He has a hobby; is that okay?" Margaret shook her head. "Will you quit keeping track of our lives? Worry about your own."

Except the absence of Margaret and Mike had been so obvious that it was impossible to ignore. The last time Gabby had seen both of them together had been Christmas. That was several months ago. There'd been no real mention of Mike or social media posts tagging the two of them that Gabby could remember. Had they hit a road bump in their marriage? Or were they both just working too many hours?

But Gabby didn't say anything because she could sense that the personal questions were making Margaret bristle. She'd never been the most open person, and when things bothered her, she generally kept it all to herself. Maybe it was better to change the subject and ease the tension in the room.

"So, Meggy, I wanted to talk to you about the

Celebrate History event. I was wondering if you were going to have a booth because I didn't see you on the list, but you've been on the committee all along. Not that you went to any of the meetings—" Gabby caught herself midcriticism. "Sorry. I'm just asking about the booth. Do you plan on having one?"

"Yes," Margaret said, and relief washed over her face at the conversational shift. "I forgot to send in the paperwork, but I promise I'll drop it off first thing Monday morning. I have two jewelry designers who want to exhibit their spring lines. One of them has been doing great things with a locally mined quartz, and the other does a lot of ocean-themed pieces with shells he collects from the coastline. They both have a nice selection and wide price range, which should fit the audience of the event, plus have that local tie that tourists love."

Sounded like a marketing pitch more than an update from her sister. Whatever was bothering Margaret was making her distance herself, emotionally and mentally. And as for organized, meticulous Margaret forgetting a task? That was highly unusual. Maybe she was that busy, but something in her voice said there was more to the story.

Gabby wished she could throw out a line and tow both of her sisters back into the tight-knit circle they'd once had. Except...how tight had it really been?

I think you have this image of the past that is a little more Hollywood than it really was.

Emma's words came back to her. Margaret had said something similar that day in the attic. Maybe her sisters were right, but Gabby would rather go down with the S.S. *Unrealistic Memories* than lose the bonds that had helped her survive a tough childhood. Or lose either of them.

She hadn't been responsible the day Momma died and hadn't watched Emma as closely as she should have. That oversight had sent Momma out in the rain, late at night, to retrieve Emma's backpack. Gabby had forgotten what school project had been so important in Emma's bag, but she had not forgotten the storm and the sight of her sisters, broken and shocked when Dad sat them down.

That was a mistake Gabby couldn't undo, but she could protect and watch over her sisters every single day after that and try her best to keep this family together.

"So...Meggy, I was talking to Em, and we were thinking that the three of us should do a girls' weekend away." Okay, so that was a white lie, too, and Gabby was undoubtedly going to be struck by lightning at any moment, but it would be worth it if she could erase the shadows under Margaret's eyes and give the girls a chance to unplug, unwind, and reconnect. "Maybe just shoot down to Newport, grab an Airbnb, and get away from it all. It would be fun, like the old days when we stayed up late and ate cookies in my bed."

"I did vacuum up a lot of crumbs from your bedrooms," Grandma said with a little laugh. "But I loved the sounds of you three having fun."

"I'm too busy, Gabby. I'm sorry." Margaret grabbed a sponge out of the sink and began wiping a countertop that was already clean. Her body was tense, her gaze averted. "Anyway, guys, thanks for the food, but I have to get to work."

In other words, conversation over. Gabby dragged Meggy into a tight hug, but her sister remained stiff and unyielding. "Love you," she said.

"Love you, too." Margaret tossed the sponge in the sink and then swung her tote over her shoulder and snatched up her keys. "Hate to kick you guys out, but I have to go."

All in all, their visit had lasted six minutes. With no other way to extend their time here or pry any more information out of Margaret, Gabby and Grandma headed toward the foyer. Just as she turned the handle of the door, Gabby noticed something out of the corner of her eye. "Meggy, why is there a suitcase on the floor?"

"Oh, that. I...I just forgot to put it away after I cleaned out the closet." She followed them out to the porch and clicked the remote to unlock her car. "I'll come to family dinner soon."

"Promise?" Grandma asked.

"I promise." But there was no weight in Margaret's words, and as Gabby and Grandma got into Gabby's car and left, the image of the suitcase was one that Gabby couldn't shake.

THIRTEEN

His father's office smelled like leather and high expectations. Jake paced the expansive lobby while he waited for his father's receptionist to usher him in for what would surely be the latest lecture about disappointment or missed opportunities or some other way that Jake had not lived up to all his father dreamed of when his only child was born. He'd tried over and over to please his father, to mold himself into what Edward wanted.

So Jake had put in the effort, gotten the degree, passed the bar, and even practiced for a couple of years before realizing he'd rather walk across a football field of broken glass than sit in this office for one more day, and that his father's standards were impossible to meet.

Now Jake had been summoned, as he liked to say, just after lunch on Friday, with a cryptic text message: *Come to my office at one. I need to discuss something with you.*

This text had been more direct than the one he'd ignored this morning. Much more of an order, too.

Jake had debated not going. Debated that right up until he reached the lobby and greeted the receptionist—what was her name again? Florence? Francis? His father fired as many people as he hired, so it was tough to keep track. She'd picked up a phone, murmured something into the receiver, and then gone back to her near-silent work on the computer.

Muzak played on the sound system, some kind of soft jazz that bordered on white noise. If he hadn't had three cups of coffee this morning, he'd fall asleep standing up. Time ticked by on the wooden clock on the wall, and Jake's irritation rose. He turned, about to say screw it and leave, when the receptionist looked up from her workstation. "He'll see you now, Mr. Maddox."

"Thank you." Though he wasn't sure if it was good etiquette to thank someone for sending a man to the slaughter. Undoubtedly, whatever his father wanted was something that involved Jake and bad news.

Since Jake had quit working at the firm, he'd barely seen his father. Perfunctory visits on holidays and a short phone call on Jake's birthday, but other than that, Dad did what he always did—spent time with Brad. His nephew could have been a reprint of Dad, so much so that sometimes Jake wondered if the cousins had been switched at birth. Brad was two years older, ten million times more driven, and had risen quickly at Maddox & Maddox. The day Jake quit and packed up his desk, Brad had moved into the office before Jake's chair had a chance to get cold.

He didn't hate his cousin, but there was no love lost between them, especially after what happened with Gabby. As far as Jake knew from the social media for the firm, Brad was off at yet another ribbon cutting for the ever-expanding and busy company. Thank goodness for small favors. That was one conversation he was happy to avoid.

His father was seated in an oversize leather chair with a partial view of the Boston skyline in the far distance, along with a whole lot of Atlantic Ocean between Harbor Cove and the state capital. A massive mahogany desk held a slim black laptop and a neat stack of files. The phone that had announced Jake's arrival was flanked by a leather box holding a few pens and a stack of heavy white cardstock notes. Everything in its place and serving its perfect purpose.

"Sit down, Jake." His father gestured toward one of the two visitor chairs.

"I'd rather stand."

"Suit yourself." His father cleared his throat. Edward was shorter than Jake by a couple of inches but trim and precise in everything from his haircut to his mustache. "I think it's time, Jacob."

"Time? For what?"

"For you to give up these foolish notions that you were hell-bent on exploring and rejoin the firm." His father waved at the air, as if he could erase Jake's job and every choice he'd ever made. "All I've done is try to give you opportunities that you wouldn't have had otherwise, and you have turned your nose up at them. It's time you grew up, Jacob."

Jake bristled. Exactly what he'd expected. Another dressing-down, as if he were ten years old and forgot to take out the trash or flunked an algebra quiz. "That I wouldn't have had otherwise? What is that supposed to mean?"

His father's gaze dropped to the floor. "You know what I mean."

"You can say the words, Dad. Because I wasn't born perfect. Because all those surgeries put me a year behind the other kids in school. Because I was shy and quiet. You have a million reasons why I wasn't enough." Jake leaned forward, putting his hands on the desk. "Here's the thing, Dad. There was nothing so wrong with me that I couldn't get into BU on my own. I didn't need anything from you."

"You think you didn't. But you needed me more than you realized."

The words hung in the air as Jake made the connections. Yes, he'd had good grades, and high SAT scores, and thought he'd nailed the interview. But maybe it hadn't been enough after all. "Are you kidding me? What did you do? Donate to the school just to get me in? Did you really think I didn't have enough smarts to do it on my own? Or were you just that desperate to have your son follow in your footsteps?"

"You were never motivated. You were always off day-dreaming or taking pictures or whatever foolish notion was in your head. You needed a nudge in the right direction," his father said. "So I helped pave the way for you a little. That's all."

"For a path I didn't want or ask for. I never wanted to be a lawyer, Dad. That was your idea, not mine." So much his father's idea that he'd gone and renamed the firm Maddox & Maddox while Jake was still in law school. Jake had tried to make it work but hated every day he spent here.

His cousin, however, had taken to law like a duck to water, much to the delight and pride of Edward Maddox. The two of them had been a world unto themselves, with Jake in the background, unable to match their fondness for golf and travel and fishing. Or heck, anything.

Brad had been the son that Edward truly wanted— the high school quarterback who took his team to the state finals, the valedictorian who'd earned a scholarship to Harvard, and most of all, the lawyer who had built Edward's firm into a multistate operation concentrating on lucrative personal injury cases. Brad loved the law, loved the challenge of it, and, Jake suspected, loved the billboards and ads with his face on them.

"I gave you almost three years to pursue this foolish photography, graphic design thing, or whatever you call it. And where did you end up? Designing ads for dog groomers and aerobics instructors?" His father shook his head. "You are too smart for that."

"Has it ever occurred to you that I like working in the ad department? That I enjoy my job? That I might want a totally different life than the one you planned out for me?"

"What are you making? Not enough, I'm sure." Edward's tone ranked Jake's salary on par with dumpster diving. "I didn't raise you to work for practically minimum wage in some drafty building in an industry that is going under more and more every year. Hell, the whole world is going digital, and in a second, you and your precious paper will be a distant memory."

Jake considered arguing with him but knew it was pointless. He could tell his father all about how he was spearheading the paper's move into creating a digital advertising hub, customized to each of the small towns in their reading audience. Or how one of his ads had won the paper an award, and two more had received honorable mentions. But what would be the point? Jake knew from experience that his father would sneer at anything less than Edward's version of achievement.

An image that Brad had fit perfectly since his birth.

Jake couldn't compete with that. He didn't even want to. What he wanted was to get the hell out of this office as soon as possible.

"Is this what I'm here for?" Jake shifted his weight. "To rehash an argument we have had a hundred times in the last thirty-one years? Yet another disappointment from the son who was born imperfect?"

"No." His father interlaced his fingers and stared at his hands for a moment. The only sound in the room was the soft whir of the air system circulating. "I'm taking some time off, Jacob."

Jake laughed. "You must be sick or something, because you never take a day off."

"I am." The quiet whirring continued, like a whisper in the background, but neither of them said a word for a long time. Jake thought maybe he'd heard his father wrong. Edward Maddox never got sick, never betrayed a weakness, and never, ever asked for help.

"You're serious?"

His father nodded. "I've got a little cardiac thing going on, and my doctor thinks it would be a good idea for me to have some time off."

The years of disagreements and tension between them became a distant thought. Jake's gut clenched, and he shifted into one of the leather visitor chairs while the shock settled in his system. His father was sick? Truly sick? Jake leaned forward, studying Edward's stoic face. For a second, he looked exactly the same. Then there was a flicker of vulnerability, no, of...fear in his eyes. "*Little* cardiac thing?"

"It's nothing. I have to have some tests done on Monday and then maybe get a stent or a bypass. In the meantime, the damned doctors want me to take it easy because they think I'm too stressed. But really, it's nothing to worry about."

A bypass? Jake was no doctor, but even he knew that was a big deal. "Sounds like something I should definitely worry about."

Edward shrugged. "I'll be fine. What I need, however, is for you to help your cousin out. He can't run this firm alone, not with the expansion rate we have going. Six offices in two years, Jake, with two hundred attorneys on staff. *Two hundred.* Brad is going to need someone he can trust to run things when he's checking on the new locations. They've just opened, and they still need a fair amount of hand holding."

"Dad, I barely practiced law. I can't run a law office."

"You can sit behind this desk when he can't be here, can't you? Anyone could do that."

"Like a figurehead? The heir and the spare?" Jake shook his head. Just when he started feeling sorry for his father…Jake sighed. "Dad, I don't have time for this discussion. It's pointless anyway. I have a job. I can't just leave it."

"I'll pay you three times what you make at that pissant paper." Edward tugged on the drawer of the desk, pulled out a checkbook, and reached for a pen. "How much do you make a week? I'll triple it right now."

"It's not about the money, Dad. It's—" Jake ran a hand through his hair and got to his feet. What was the point in arguing? His father had never seen anything other than his own viewpoint. "Forget it. I'm arguing with a wall."

He started to leave, frustrated that, once again, the two of them had hit an impasse. For two men who shared a lot of DNA, they had never had much in common.

Jake was creative, artistic, and outdoorsy. His father was driven, logical, and worldly. For years, Jake had tried to fit into a mold cast by his father, and he'd been desperately unhappy. What would it do to him to try to fit that mold again, even on a short-term basis?

"Your family needs you, Jake." Then his father lowered his voice and in a sound that was nearly a whisper, said, "I need you."

Those were words Jake had waited his whole life to hear. Jake had existed in his cousin's shadow, desperate to make the father who'd sired him proud. A father who had always seen him as lesser than, from the minute he was born with one imperfect foot, as if that somehow diminished the Maddox family line. But now, his father was asking Jake to be here because he needed him. As a son. "I...I don't know what to say."

His father made a sour face. "I had hoped I could count on you to help your family for a couple of weeks. It seems I can't."

Disappointment. That was the overriding note Jake heard. What was his father asking of him, really? It was, after all, only a couple of weeks out of his life, not a ten-year contract. He could work at the paper after hours, and yeah, juggle a lot at one time, but he could manage both. *I need you.* "Of course you can. I'll do it."

His father gave him a quick, short nod. The matter was settled, and the split second of emotion was gone. "Brad's plane gets in this evening at ten. I'll tell him you're picking him up so that you two can talk details on the ride."

"I have plans this evening." Plans he definitely didn't want to cancel, because they involved Gabby. The photo shoot for the tricentennial event could easily take a few hours, depending on how much he ended up shooting. With a Monday deadline, there was no way to reschedule or there'd be an empty space on the front page of the *Gazette*. What's more, he'd let Gabby and all the businesses involved down. That was a choice he couldn't make.

"Plans that are more important than the future of this company?"

And there was the guilt trip, served up on a nice little platter. "Dad, Brad can take an Uber or something, and I can catch up with him over the weekend. It'll be fine."

"We have a very important meeting with investors Monday morning. One that... well, needs to go right, and believe me, if I could be there, I would, but the damned doctors are insisting on running these tests and the investors are not available again until next month. Brad says we need to jump on this opportunity."

"It can wait, Dad, if you're sick."

"Brad thinks the time is right to move into these new markets. Honestly, I've been so busy running the law side, I've barely looked at the expansion plans. I trust he knows what he's doing."

Brad says. Brad thinks. Jake bit back his irritation. His father was a brilliant lawyer who had amazing instincts for when to negotiate and when to pounce. Brad, the schmoozer, definitely fit the role of meeting with investors and contractors. It seemed, however, that in the past two years, his father had put an awful lot of trust in Jake's cousin. "I don't know anything about the expansion plans."

"When you pick Brad up at the airport, he will brief you. As part of the interim team, I would expect you to be at the meeting, to represent me, and you can't be there if you aren't up to speed." His father's dark gaze narrowed. "You said you would help. Are you already backing out?"

"You're springing this on me pretty suddenly. I have a job and commitments to that job that I have to fulfill. I can't just drop everything in an instant."

His father waved a hand, as if Jake's objections were a pesky fly in the room. "I've already spoken with Leroy. He's agreed, given the circumstances, for you to take a leave of absence."

Here was the controlling father he'd known all his life. The man who moved the pieces on the chess board to get where he wanted to go, whether or not his opponent agreed. It was part of what had made him and Brad so successful in the personal injury industry. But that didn't make it right or any less infuriating. "You went over my head, talked to my boss, and arranged this whole thing without asking me first? Or even knowing if I'd agree to this plan?"

"I have never before asked you for anything, Jacob. Not a single thing. I need you now, need you to step up and be a part of the company that housed you and fed you and paid for your college." His father's stern face softened, a temporary wash of something that could have been classified as hurt in his eyes. "You and your cousin work well together, which will make for a much easier transition during my absence and when I return. You're my son. I trust you. I don't want the company that I worked so hard to build in the hands of a stranger during such a critical time. I want it to stay in the family. Our family."

Edward knew exactly which words to use to override any objections Jake might have. *Our family*. He might be long past the age of Boy Scouts and camping trips, but he still wanted his father to be proud of him and to know he loved him. And most of all, to feel like his father's first connection was to the son who shared his DNA.

"Okay," Jake said, wondering if he was making a choice he'd regret. "You can count on me, Dad."

The closer the clock got to seven, the faster Gabby paced and stressed. It was a photo shoot. Nothing more. She'd been alone with Jake hundreds of times. This was no different. So what if he seemed a little flirty earlier and the other night at dinner? If they got too close again tonight, she'd just remind him that she had no interest in or time for a relationship. No desire to have her heart broken again. And definitely no desire to fall in love with a man who could move on in a blink, as if she'd been no more memorable than a turkey sandwich.

Lori had picked up a shift at the bar where she worked part-time, which left Gabby as the model for tonight. Gabby knew her inventory inside and out and had been the creative vision behind Celebrate History in the Harbor, so it made sense for her to be the face of both.

Yet a nervous tickle persisted inside her all day. Something had shifted between Jake and her after that kiss, and it had tipped her entire world to one side. Now they were going to be alone, at night, for hours. Pre-kiss, she'd never give something like that a second thought. Now she was having third and fourth and fortieth thoughts about whether this was a good idea.

Just as she flipped the sign on the door to CLOSED, she saw Jake striding up the sidewalk, a backpack slung over one shoulder and a tripod in one hand. The streetlights bounced off his dark hair, his rangy build, his strong stride. She watched him for a moment, wondering when he got so tall and ... well, handsome.

The answer was easy. All those changes had happened when she hadn't been paying attention. When he'd been nothing more than the sometimes-annoying boy next door. When she'd been dating his cousin, and getting her heart broken, and investing all her energy into her family and her shop.

"Hey," she said as she pulled open the door and let him and a gust of cool spring air into the building. "Thanks for being on time." Because that meant she'd be done sooner and less tempted to make another mistake.

Was it a mistake if she had enjoyed it so much? If her ears were attuned to his every word, hoping for another endearment? If she looked at those daisies and lilies in the vase she'd set on her countertop and missed him in a way she never had before? Or maybe she was just a hopeless romantic like Momma had been.

"Thanks for doing this." He glanced around the store. "So is Lori here or . . . ?"

"She couldn't make it. So . . . it will just be you and me." When she said those words aloud, it sounded way more intimate than she had meant it to. He was just so tall, and so *there*, and she couldn't stop wondering if he would kiss her again.

Did she want him to kiss her again?

No. Definitely, positively no . . . ish.

"Uh, why don't you get set up?" She backed up, stumbling over her own feet and nearly running into a rack of clothes. "I'm just going to try on the first outfit and, well, you can do your magic."

She scurried off to the fitting room, drew the curtain closed, and stood there for a solid two minutes, completely forgetting what dress she had planned to wear first, what shoes she'd wanted to pair with it, and basically everything but her own name. *This is Jake*, she told herself. *Get a grip.*

She should be focused on her shop and the event coming up in a week. Her bank account sat at an alarmingly low number, especially after barely making her rent payment, and yet her mind kept circling back to kissing Jake.

Gabby changed into a dark maroon maxi dress, a little more of a bohemian style than she would normally wear but with a nice seventies vibe that some of her clientele loved, and paired it with gold gladiator sandals. She unpinned her hair, releasing the curls until they ran down her back. Outside the fitting room, she could hear Jake cursing under his breath as he wrestled with the light stands. Maybe she wasn't the only one freaking out about this whole thing.

It's just Jake, she told herself one more time before opening the curtain and stepping back into the shop.

In the few minutes she'd been changing, he'd transformed a corner of the room, shifting around the few pieces of furniture she had. A white wicker chair, her potted plants, and a bookcase she had filled with jewelry and clutches had been combined into a spring oasis. Several lights ringed the space, casting it in a bright, sunshiny glow. It was as if he had peeked inside her brain and dropped her vision into this five-by-five area.

She stepped into the vignette. "This is brilliant, Jake. I can already see it on the page."

"Wow, that dress looks great on you. It's so different from what you normally wear." He shifted closer to her and reached out, as if he was about to touch her. "You look...wild and free."

Her breath caught, and her heart hammered in her

chest. Jake had complimented her before, surely he had. Why was this time different? Why did this one make her feel shy and demure? And leave her at a loss for how to say thank you for a few kind words? Instead, she avoided replying to his compliment altogether. "So, uh, where should I be? Sitting in the chair or standing or...?"

Great strategy, Gabs. Ignore everything.

"Let's try sitting in the chair. Pretend you're reading a book on a warm summer day, sitting under a tree in your backyard or in the park. Let's get people to envision their lives in these great dresses, which will, of course, make everything in here a must-buy. Here, try this." He dug in his backpack and handed her a hardback book. The familiar dark brown leather edges were well worn, the pages faded and dog-eared in multiple places.

She glanced up at him. "You kept it." It wasn't a question, just a statement of surprise to see a gift she'd given him almost twelve years ago. A little flicker of emotion squeezed in her chest.

He shrugged, as if holding on to her gift was no big deal. "When the girl you...uh, know, gives you a copy of Tennyson's poetry because you mentioned once that you love his work, you keep it."

"And read it," she said, flipping through the pages. "You must have read it a dozen times."

"A hundred," he said so softly that she almost didn't hear him.

She'd never realized Jake was sentimental and romantic. Her mind skipped over their history, past the holidays and birthdays and the things she'd given him. The shelves of his downtown apartment were filled with mementos from their past. All this time, she'd thought it had been because the things he'd kept—the tiny stuffed animal she'd given him as a joke, the empty glass from sharing a drink at the fair, the picture of them making a goofy pose at the senior banquet—had been accidental. Things he tucked on a shelf and forgot about.

Was there more to all of that? Was he holding on to pieces of *their* history, not just his own?

Before she could ask, Jake raised his camera, and the moment was broken. "We should get to work."

"I agree. I'm sure you have something else to do tonight, so I don't want to waste too much of your time." Good lord, was she fishing for information? Asking if he had a date after this?

"Actually, I do have to be somewhere later." He checked the settings on the camera and raised it again. The sentimental moment was erased, and they were back to all business again. "Okay, so pretend you're lost in thought on a summer day. The sun is warm on your face, the book is engrossing, and you don't have a care in the world."

Somewhere to be later? With another woman? What else could he be doing late on a Friday night?

Well, there were a dozen things Jake could be doing, and it was none of her business if any of those things included a date. None. Of. Her. Business.

Gabby stared down at the book, but her body remained stiff, acutely attuned to the man clicking his camera a few feet away. Every time she looked at the pages before her, she remembered the day she gave him the book and the sweet gratitude on his face.

You remembered, he'd said. *I mentioned that poem in freshman year. And you paid attention. No one has ever done something like this for me before.*

I didn't know what to get you for graduation. She'd

acted as if the thoughtfulness of the gift was a coincidence but really, because the look in Jake's eyes was so deep, so intense, she didn't know how to explain the impulse that had led her to search three used bookstores in a twenty-mile radius until she found a first edition collection of Tennyson that included one of the poet's longer, less popular narrative poems, "Maud."

Thank you, Gabby. Then he'd given her the trademark Jake grin, flicked the tassel on her cap, and teased her about her gown being too long. She could almost convince herself she had imagined that moment of vulnerability with him, that peek inside the parts of Jake that he usually kept hidden.

She'd known his childhood was difficult, if not horrible. She'd heard his father yelling, seen Jake being punished for some small infraction and having to weed for hours or wash the windows or wax the car over and over again until it shone. Those years when it was just his father and Jake had been the worst, almost as if Edward was punishing his son for the absence of Jake's mother. From the very first time Gabby ran into Jake's father, she'd thought Edward was a stern, cold man, the complete opposite of the son who looked exactly like him.

"Can I..." Jake reached over and captured a lock of her hair, lifting it and letting it fall over her shoulder. "I just think it will look better in the pictures."

His hand was centimeters away from her face, and she had the strangest urge to grab his palm and press it to her lips. To feel his warmth against her, to tell him she remembered the book, too, and all he had gone through. Her breath caught, and she had to force herself to let it out.

" 'My life has crept so long on a broken wing,' " she

said, reciting the snippets that she could remember. Jake's features softened with surprise. " 'Thro' cells of madness, haunts of horror and fear, that I...' "

" 'That I come to be grateful at last for a little thing,' " he finished. The tendril of hair slid through his fingers. "My favorite poem," he said as he stepped back.

"I know." *I know more about you than you think*, she thought. She knew he liked peanut butter cookies more than chocolate chip, that he hated geometry but loved algebra, that he rooted for the Bucs instead of the Pats. Surface things, Gabby realized. None of the really deep things, like what Jake dreamed of for the future. Or what on earth he was thinking right now. She cleared her throat and shifted over. "So are we all good? We should probably move on to the next outfit soon."

"You're right." He stepped back and started snapping pictures again, cool and professional. "I think I got some good ones of this dress. Why don't you try on something else? Maybe something a little different in style or time period?"

For the next two hours, she tried on outfit after outfit while Jake posed her and touched her and the temperature in the room climbed. Every time he brushed away a lock of hair or nudged her a few inches to the side, she had to fight this overwhelming need to turn into his arms, curve against his chest, and raise her lips to his again. He made no moves that were unprofessional, didn't betray so much as a single flicker of desire. Maybe that other kiss had been an accident. Maybe she was blowing all of it up bigger in her mind than it was in reality.

He bent over the small screen on the digital camera, clicking through the images. Even from where she stood, she could see the bright, clear, crisp pictures Jake had captured. "I think I got a lot of great ones," he said, "but I think we need something fun. Something personal to you. Just to give the story that necessary connection to you and your store."

"I don't have anything that's personal. Except…" Her gaze went to the window display. "There's my mother's wedding dress. Betsy Josephs made it ages ago, and it has a connection to me, and this town."

"Perfect." Then he paused and studied her face. "If you're okay with wearing it?"

She nodded. "I've worn it a million times. I used to sneak up to the attic and put it on all the time when I was a little girl because I missed her so much." This would be just like those times, wouldn't it? No different just because Jake was here and she was having all these romantic thoughts. No different at all.

Gabby climbed into the window, weaving her way past the other mannequins, and carefully set the veil aside before she undid the delicate fabric-covered buttons at the top, and then the finicky zipper, before lifting the dress over the mannequin. She cradled the dress in her arms, setting the veil atop the organza and satin, and turned to get out of the window display.

Jake was there, as he had always been, with his hand already out to catch her. "Let me help you."

"Thank you." She slipped her palm into his, and he helped her over the step and down into the shop. He held her hand just a second too long—or too short, depending on how a person looked at it—before releasing her. She swallowed hard. "I'll, uh, just put this on."

"Mind if I rearrange the setting? This dress takes us in an entirely different direction, so it needs an entirely different backdrop."

"Not at all. Use whatever you need." Oh heck yes, this was taking them in an entirely different direction. Already she was imagining wearing the dress to walk down the aisle. To meet her groom and pledge forever. To see Jake—

No. She had no intentions of marrying Jake. The kiss had been good—well, more than good, fantastic—but that didn't mean she heard wedding bells ringing. Plus, she had already seen how a storybook marriage worked out, how quickly her father had found someone else to write a happily-ever-after with.

Inside the dressing room, Gabby laid Momma's dress on the small bench before she stepped out of the svelte jumpsuit she'd had on for the last pictures. Outside the room, she could hear the sounds of furniture being moved as Jake rearranged.

Gabby slid Momma's dress over her head. The fabric settled along her chest, her waist, her hips, with a soft rustle. The train puddled at her feet, a river of silky satin just waiting to be unfurled. She nestled the veil among her curls, using the small combs attached to the sides to keep it from moving.

When Gabby looked up, her heart stuttered. In the reflection, she could see Momma, almost like seeing a ghost. It was the mother she remembered, young and vibrant. The same dark hair, light eyes, high cheekbones. Emma may have been a carbon copy of Momma, but Gabby's features were a close second. If her hair were a few inches shorter and she were a couple of inches taller, she'd be Momma, standing in the vestry of the church, full of breathless anticipation, waiting to marry the man who made her smile and laugh every day of her too-short life.

She settled the delicate blusher over her face. The image went hazy, blurred by the tulle. When she inhaled, she swore she could catch the floral fragrance of Momma's perfume, the one that had been in that emerald-green bottle with the tasseled sprayer.

Gabby closed her eyes and imagined she was waiting at the entrance to the church, one arm tucked into Grandpa's, a bouquet of daisies in the other hand. The organist began playing, the music swelling to fill the space, reaching up to the rafters, the belfry, the very air outside the church. The double doors opened, and Momma took the first step toward the rest of her life. It was a moment of sunshine and flowers, of hope and joy.

All of it over almost before it began.

A tidal wave rushed up Gabby's throat, full of grief and regret. She couldn't breathe. Couldn't see. Couldn't move.

Tears trickled down her cheeks, and a soft, choked sob escaped her. Thirty-odd years ago, Momma had put on this dress, expecting to spend the rest of her life with the man she loved, raising children and building a home. She'd been full of hope and promise, blind to what was coming around the corner in a few short years. Everything she could have been, everything she could have dreamed, had been cut short, demolished in the impact of that crash.

If only wasn't a strong enough pair of words to describe the sorrow in Gabby's heart. The desperate wish for a do-over, a way to change the destiny that had impacted every single one of them.

I'm sorry, Momma. I'm so sorry.

But her mother would never hear those words. All that was left of the beautiful, magical woman who had been the center of their world was an empty shell of a dress. A dress that Gabby could fit into, but shoes she could never fill.

"Gabby?" And then Jake was there, his hands on her shoulders, his broad, solid chest behind her.

She turned into him and pressed her face against the warmth and strength of his shirt. "I…I miss her so much."

He held her tight and whispered against her hair. "I know you do."

"I…I never should have…" She couldn't finish the sentence, couldn't bring herself to tell Jake that she was the reason Momma had been driving in the rain that night.

He lifted the blusher and then tipped her chin until she was looking at him. "There is nothing you could have done that made this happen, Gabby. Accidents are just that. Accidents."

Gabby cried in a way she hadn't cried in years, and Jake held her and stroked her hair and whispered that it was all going to be okay, just as he had years ago. She didn't know how long she stood there, wrapped in the comfort of his familiar strength.

She drew back and swiped at her cheeks. "I'm sorry. Putting on the dress made me miss her."

"It's okay. Really. And you don't have to wear it. It was a silly idea."

"No, I want to. It's like a way of saying she's still here. Let me just clean my face." Jake was staring at her, and a flush of embarrassment hit her, so she averted her gaze. "I'm sure I look like a wreck."

"You? Gabby, you are the most breathtaking woman I have ever met." He tipped her chin up until her eyes were lost in his. "Breathtaking." He drew out the word on a whisper, and something deep inside her began to long for more—more of his words, more of his touch, more of him.

"Jake, I...I can't date you." Was she telling him or telling herself? Because in this tiny dressing room with him so close, she couldn't quite remember why it was a bad idea.

"Of course you can't." His mouth curved into a grin. "That would be a crazy thought."

"We would be terrible together."

"You're right. We're just friends, aren't we?" His hands dropped to her waist, and she found her body shifting closer against the objections of her sensible side. "Absolutely terrible. Worst couple ever."

"Then why do I want you to kiss me again right now?" The truth was a whisper on her lips, a rush of words that croaked out of her throat. And she did want that, more than she could remember wanting anything in a long, long time.

"Because you're just as crazy as me." His arms went around her, pressing into the small of her back, drawing her to him, into the space she had been craving for days. Then he leaned down and brushed his lips against hers.

Finally.

A hot surge of desire rocketed through her, just with that one simple touch. His mouth danced against hers, his lips strong but teasing, tasting of coffee and something that she could only call the flavor of home. Her arms went around him, and as his touch tightened, she felt the ripple of the muscles of his back.

Never before had she been kissed with such tender care, such attention. It was intoxicating, and all she wanted was more of Jake. Much more.

No, no, no. She couldn't fall for him. She had other things that needed her attention and her emotions. She didn't have any to spare for a man who would only break her heart in the end. She knew where romantic dreams ended and couldn't bear to watch that happen in her own life.

She stumbled back, breaking the kiss, nearly hitting the mirror. "Uh, we have to finish the photo shoot." She spun toward the mirror, and in the reflection, she saw a woman who had just been thoroughly, wonderfully kissed. Red lips, flushed face, mussed hair, a chest rising and falling with unspent want.

"You're right, Gabby," he said. Then he paused, his hands settling against her waist. "But let me just get this for you before I go." The only sound in the tiny space of the dressing room was the soft snick of Jake sliding the zipper into place. Gabby held her breath, sure that if she did anything other than stand still, she'd end up back in his arms. Jake brought his face beside hers, the two of them looking into the shiny finish of the mirror. "See? Breathtaking."

Then he slipped out of the tiny space and went back into the shop. Gabby stood in the dressing room, but no matter how hard she tried, she couldn't calm her racing heart. *Breathtaking*. Oh yeah, that was exactly how she'd describe what just happened.

FOURTEEN

Gabby couldn't carry a tune if someone paid her a million dollars. That didn't stop her from singing almost from the minute she woke up on Saturday, especially when she was happy. And today she was insanely happy.

She kept thinking about what had happened Friday night. The way Jake had kissed her and held her. The touch of his hand on her face, along her neck, heck, pretty much anywhere. He'd made everything better simply by being there, as he always had. But when he kissed her...

He sent her thoughts flying to another stratosphere. When she'd gone home after the photo shoot, she'd lain awake in bed for a couple of hours, replaying the kiss, thinking about what it meant for their relationship—and what kind of relationship they had right now exactly. They were more than friends, but no one had put the "dating" label on whatever this was.

Was she even ready for that label? Quite possibly... well, maybe.

Except her experiences with men had been anything but happy. There'd been a few guys in high school and college, but no one she'd been all that excited about, not until Brad. The callous way he'd treated her heart had made her wary of ever dating again. And then there was Dad, the poster child for what Gabby didn't want. She had a hundred reasons why she shouldn't date anyone, never mind Jake, but every time she thought about his kiss, those reasons weakened.

Business at the store had been relatively brisk this morning, probably due to the sale she had advertised in the *Gazette* and on her social media platforms. The weather had been gloomy again this weekend—which rescheduled Jake's paint job on Grandma's house a second time—but not so rainy that it kept people home. There'd been several customers who asked if Gabby was going to get in more vintage stock, and she promised she would before the tricentennial event.

"But will you have anything original?" one woman asked. "Like something one-of-a-kind?"

Gabby had told her that most of the inventory she carried was unique to the area, but it apparently wasn't the answer the woman was looking for. She left without purchasing anything, and Gabby tried not to take it personally.

Still, with money in the cash register, an upcoming front-page spread in the *Gazette*, and a maybe-relationship, Gabby felt like she could take a breath. Even Grandma sounded more chipper this morning and said she was excited that Sandy had such a good time with Frank.

Everything was finally on the right path. Maybe that rough patch was behind Gabby for good. Maybe.

"So, are we all set for the event?" Gabby asked the

assembled table of people on the Harbor Cove Tricentennial committee: a half dozen local business owners, including, to Gabby's surprise, Margaret, who had walked in a second ago. Even though her oldest sister had joined the committee months ago, she hadn't come to a single meeting until today. There were shadows under her eyes, and she seemed tired. Gabby vowed to get Margaret to sit down for lunch or come to a family dinner soon. The image of that suitcase lingered in her mind, a little yellow flag that Gabby couldn't ignore. Something was going on, but whatever it was, Margaret wasn't sharing.

"I love the dress you put in the window," Renata Andrews said, drawing Gabby's attention back to the oval walnut table. "It's like something Jackie O. would have gotten married in."

"It was our mother's," Gabby said, with a nod in Margaret's direction. "And it's an original Betsy Josephs. My customers have raved about it, too. They like the unique vintage vibe. At least that's what one woman said yesterday."

"Well, everything you have is unique," Renata said. "Even what you wear. I sure wish I had your sense of style."

"You can buy it, twenty-five percent off, this weekend." Gabby laughed. "Just kidding. But thank you. I love my mother's dress. It was the inspiration behind the shop and the vintage theme."

Stanley Garrison, who owned a bar on the corner of Main and Oak, leaned forward. "An original Betsy Josephs? We should create postcards or posters or something that link the dress to the display that's going to be here at the community center. There's so much history in this town. Why, my little pub has an original Old

Bushmills Irish Whiskey mirror that my great-grandfather brought over when he immigrated to the United States. Tourists love it." He brightened. "Hey, how about I run a special on Bushmills cocktails to combine the two things? Maybe print out some coupons for people to use at my place and others?"

"That sounds like a great idea," Margaret said. "But ineffective. This is the age of digital advertising, and if Harbor Cove doesn't get on that wagon, we are all going to be left in the dust."

Gabby could see a few of the other business owners begin to bristle. Margaret was smart as hell, but not the most tactful person in the world. "I think Margaret makes a good point. The world is going more and more digital every day. In fact, I'm working on an e-commerce site for my own store. Digital postcards would cost a lot less to produce and be something all of us can share on our social media, as well as on the Harbor Cove community page, right, George?" Harbor Cove's longest-serving selectman nodded in response. "And," she continued before anyone voiced an objection, "if they're digital, it's really easy to include specials that encourage people to do things like visit Stanley's bar and see the mirror in person."

George nodded and thought for a second. He was the kind of man who loved a good cigar and an even better glass of pinot noir, and most of all, he was fair and conscientious. He'd done a good job during his tenure on the board of selectmen. "All right. Let's go with Gabby's modern version of postcards. Might do us all good, as Margaret said, to get with the digital age."

"We still need someone to design them," Stanley cut in. "My graphic design skills are at toddler level."

"What about Jake Maddox?" George said. He shifted

toward the head of the table. "You know him well, right, Gabby?"

Did she know him well? Oh, hell yes. And knew him in a whole new way ever since he kissed her. The memory was at the edge of every thought she had and made her jump every time her phone dinged. She half hoped it was a text from him and at the same time was half-terrified it would be, because that would mean that he'd been thinking about her as often as she'd been thinking about him.

Which was way too often.

There was no way she was going to fall for Jake. It would be insanity of the highest degree.

She'd been using the excuse of Brad and the bad track record of Maddox men, but in truth, she was scared of falling in love like Momma had and ending up with a husband whose love could evaporate in a moment.

That was the real reason behind why she resisted Jake. If she found out his emotions were just as mercurial as Dad's...

Well, it would break her. Better to not even take the risk than to end up disillusioned and heartbroken.

"I do have some bad news," Nathan Legrand, owner of the Harbor Cove bookstore, said, interrupting Gabby's thoughts. He was an energetic millennial with a pair of red-framed glasses perched on his nose. "I talked to a lot of the Airbnbs and hotels in the area. Reservations are down compared to last year."

"Down? Are you sure?" Last year, Gabby had barely squeaked by and spent the "extra" profits from the busier spring and summer season by midwinter. She couldn't afford to have business be even slower than before. Saturday morning had been so busy that surely things were on the upswing. "But we did that social media campaign, and the *Gazette* has run stories on the event and—"

"Down." He frowned. "Believe me, I'm no happier than anyone else at this table. We have to prepare for the fact that this event won't bring us the numbers we were hoping for."

"What was your sample size?" Margaret craned her head around George and gave Nathan a sharp, assessing look. "Ten people? Twenty? Because that's not representative."

Nathan consulted a sheaf of papers before him, flipping between several pages before getting to the one he wanted. His lips moved as he silently did the math. "Uh, sixty-five. I think."

"Last I checked, we had more than three hundred Airbnbs in this county. Seven hotels. Ten motels. Twelve bed and breakfasts. Your sample size is too small to be indicative of what will truly happen." Margaret scoffed. "We can't make decisions based on inaccurate information that accounts for less than twenty percent of the reservation capacity."

"I have to disagree. I think twenty percent is a good indicator."

Margaret laid her hands flat on the table. Everything about her was strung tight, from her shoulders to the lines around her mouth. But her words were controlled, even. "Every one of us is here because we need a boost in business and because we want to help each other increase profit margins. I don't think coming from a negative place—"

"It's not negative," Nathan cut in. "It's fact."

"Is productive," she finished. "What do you expect us all to do, Nathan? Give up on something we worked so hard to create just because we hit a *projected* road bump? Walk away from what we all built because you all got scared by a bit of bad news? People who are committed stay. They don't run."

Gabby glanced over at Margaret. What the hell was that? It sure seemed like Margaret was worked up about more than just Nathan's numbers. Was she talking about Mike? The image of that suitcase came back to her mind.

"Well, either way, all we can do is keep moving forward," Gabby said. "I'll shoot off an email to Jake today about the digital postcards and then update all of you. Please keep sharing on your social media, and if you need help setting up an event or a page on any of those sites, give me a call and I'll walk you through it." She looked at each of the people at the table in turn, praying no other arguments broke out. Margaret was right—they were all here to support each other—and arguing would undermine everything the committee had worked to build. "If there's nothing else, we can adjourn."

The committee members began getting to their feet and exchanging small talk. Gabby sent a quick email to Jake, then saw out of the corner of her eye as Margaret gathered her bag and her papers and headed straight for the door. Gabby hurried after her and touched the sleeve of her severe dark burgundy suit. "Hey, what was that?"

"What was what?"

"All that stuff about commitment and road bumps." She drew in a deep breath and lowered her voice. "I saw the suitcase. Is something going on, Meggy?"

Margaret cut her gaze to the door. Her grip on her handbag tightened. "Nothing you'd understand."

Did "nothing" have something to do with Mike's

scarcity at family events over the last few months? The continual stress in Margaret's shoulders and sadness in her eyes? "What's that supposed to mean?"

"That you're not married and you don't get it." Margaret's mouth thinned into a tight line. "I'd rather write to Dear Amelia than get advice from someone who has no idea what my life is like."

"Ouch." Gabby reeled back and put up her hands. "All I was doing was making sure my sister was okay."

"You can stop hovering over all of us, Gabby. It's not your job anymore. It never really was." Then she pushed on the metal bar, opening the heavy door which let out a creaking and protesting groan, and stepped out into the brisk spring sunshine.

The door swung shut. Gabby stood there a second longer, but Margaret didn't turn around.

The happy mood Gabby had walked in with had evaporated, replaced by a deep worry, the sting of hurt, and a sense of failure.

Her cell phone chimed, and the message she'd been hoping for popped up on her screen. *Want to grab some breakfast?* Jake had written. *It seems like forever since I saw you.*

It was as if he'd read her mind and knew she needed a little lightness right this second. Between the disagreement at the meeting and Margaret's hostility, Gabby could use a shoulder to lean on.

It's been like eleven hours, LOL, she wrote back.

Yeah, but you're my favorite person to talk to. So what do you say? French toast and bacon at Earl's in fifteen minutes?

Her stomach rumbled. *You're not playing fair. Earl's French toast is irresistible.*

So are you. He added a winky face.

Did the winky face cancel out the implication that she was irresistible to him? Say that he was joking? Ugh. The emotional context of texts was so indecipherable. *You're a dork*, she wrote back. *See you at Earl's.*

Jake replied with a thumbs-up. A surge of giddy anticipation filled Gabby as she hustled down the sidewalk to the shop. Lori arrived at the same time, and the two them ducked inside. Gabby dug in her bag for a compact, paused in front of one of the mirrors, and checked her makeup. She wiped away a smudge of eyeliner with her thumb, dotted on some more foundation, then unearthed a dark pink lipstick and swiped some across her lips. "Lori, sorry to ditch you right when we open, but I have to run out. I'll be back in, like, an hour." The breeze had made Gabby's hair a riot of curls, and she did her best to smooth them into obedience. "I have to meet someone."

"Someone special?" Lori grinned. "Because you sure seem to be unusually interested in your hair and makeup for just anyone."

"Someone who...might become special." Gabby did one last check before shoving the lipstick and compact back into her bag. "Are you good to hold down the fort until I get back?"

"Absolutely. Have fun."

Gabby arrived at Earl's Diner seven minutes after Jake's text, and as soon as she walked inside realized how being early was clear evidence that she was anxious to see him. But he was already at a booth, maybe equally anxious to see her, which made something in her chest do a little leap. She made her way past the diners seated on the stools at the counter and the waitresses bustling back and forth with breakfast orders and over to the table. "You're early."

"So are you." He grinned, as if he could read every secret she held. Maybe he could. Jake knew her pretty darn well, and Gabby wasn't so sure that was a good thing, especially when she was still trying to figure out what this was.

"I, uh, didn't have far to walk. And I was…hungry." Better to say that than admit that she couldn't wait to see him. To see that familiar smile and hear the voice she'd known for most of her life.

"Me too." He reached across the table and took both her hands in his. His long fingers covered hers, warm and comfortable. "Your hands are freezing."

"The wind is cold. Spring in Massachusetts, you know?" She laughed, trying to make light of how his touch made her want to lean across the table and kiss him again. Before she could do something foolish like act on these crazy impulses that seemed to pop up every five minutes, Gabby withdrew her hands from his grasp and grabbed the menu. "Any good specials today?"

"We've been coming here for ten years, Bella-Ella. You always get the same thing."

"Maybe I'm in the mood for something different." A different life. A different relationship. A different future. She was, after all, already going down a different road with Jake, one she'd never really imagined before.

"Hi, Gabby. Hi, Jake," said Renee Simpson, taking a pen and a pad out of her apron. Renee, a tall redhead, had been a year or two behind Gabby in high school, and was still as skinny as she had been the day she won the hundred-meter dash at the state championship. "What can I get you?"

"Coffee, French toast, and extra bacon," Gabby said, the order as automatic as her own name. She grinned at Jake. "Okay, so maybe I like things that are familiar."

"So do I." He held her gaze for a second and then ordered the same thing. Renee tucked the pad back into her apron before hustling across to the coffee station and returning a minute later with a pot of steaming brew. Renee flipped over the thick white mugs and filled them each to the brim.

The interruption gave Gabby a second to gather her thoughts—or more like, rein them in. She'd been going down mental paths that involved a future with Jake ever since that night inside the shop. Maybe it had been the wedding dress or the intimacy of the setting or her emotional vulnerability, but something had shifted in Gabby, opening her heart to the possibility that maybe, just maybe…

Jake could be something other than a friend.

"So…" He let out a nervous chuckle. "Here we are again."

"It's kinda awkward, isn't it?" She busied herself with dumping sugar and creamer into her mug, until the rich, dark coffee was a light vanilla color, about five shades too pale. She just needed something to do so she wouldn't stare at him and try to read what he was thinking.

"A little," he admitted, a bemused expression on his face. "But we're grown-ups. If we can get past that day at camp, we can get past this."

She laughed. Thank God he'd steered the conversation toward more familiar ground. "Oh, I can't believe you remember that. I was so embarrassed."

He took a sip of coffee, watching her over the rim,

his eyes full of mirth. "Well, it's not every day you split your shorts and fall into the lake."

They'd been twelve or thirteen, at that weird age when nothing went right, and she was all elbows and clumsiness. She and Jake had been paired up for the boating excursion, really just a spin around the lake in a small dinghy with a motor. As they were coming back to shore, Jake asked Gabby to hop out and grab the rope to help bring the boat into its spot along the dock. She'd put one foot on the pier but hesitated in pushing off the deck with the other. The boat drifted left, Gabby's other foot stayed on the pier, and... the next thing she knew, she was in the middle of the most embarrassing moment of her life. She heard the sound of cotton tearing just before she dropped into the lake, and Jake started laughing his butt off. "I fell into the water like a lead balloon. It was like a cartoon in slow motion. I was such an idiot."

"Nah. Blame the driver of the boat. He should have been better at his job."

That was so typical of Jake, to try to ease the embarrassment and shoulder the blame. "You were great, Jake. After all, you were the one who rescued me." In seconds, Jake had flipped off the boat's engine, hopped into the water fully clothed, and hoisted her onto the pier. Once they were on shore, he darted ahead to get a beach towel from the boathouse. Then he draped it over her shoulders and tucked it tight around her body, a burrito of terrycloth. He held her to his chest until she stopped shivering, ignoring her worries that he was cold, too. *I'll be fine*, he said. *Let's get you warmed up*.

She'd leaned into his strength and protection, and for the first time noticed how tall he was getting, the way his shoulders had broadened. At some point that summer, he'd stopped being a gangly, awkward boy and become a strong, confident young man.

She'd never really looked at those moments with Jake, the times when he had given her his jacket in the rain or carried her schoolbooks or kept her warm, as anything other than him being a friend. But as she thought back over the other guys she had dated, she realized no one had been as protective and considerate as Jake was.

No one.

"You were there," she said now, "as you always are."

"I'll always be there to rescue you, Bella-Ella." He met her gaze and held it. Her heart skipped a beat, and everything inside her seemed to warm. If there hadn't been two feet of table separating them, she would have leaned into him, into whatever was in his eyes. "No matter what happens."

"Even if..." She couldn't put words to whatever this was between them, this confusing mix of friendship and attraction and kisses, never mind where it all might end up. Already she felt a little panic at the thought of losing Jake. He was her biggest annoyance and, frankly, her best friend. She couldn't picture a day that didn't have him in it, and she didn't want to.

"Even if."

She smiled and sipped her coffee. It was too sweet and too light, but the mug was warm, and it gave her a second to calm her racing pulse.

He cocked his head and studied her. "You look pretty lost in thought. Are you thinking about last night? About the future? About me? About pizza?"

Gabby was saved from responding by Renee, who slid two plates loaded with French toast onto the table. "Extra bacon," the waitress said, "and a lot of maple syrup." She set a pitcher in the center of the table. "Let me know if you guys need anything else."

"This is all great. Thanks, Renee." Gabby drizzled warm syrup all over the bread and bacon and then cut off a slice of the crisp French toast and popped it in her mouth. Eating gave her an excuse to create some distance between them, something else to do with her hands and her attention. She wasn't ready for more and wasn't sure she even wanted that because all she'd ever seen was unhappy endings and broken hearts. She should just tell Jake—

"So I was thinking we should go on a real date," Jake said.

She stopped, the next bite halfway to her mouth. Apparently she was the only one thinking slower was better. "A real date?"

"Just you and me, no ulterior motives for the Dear Amelia column or anything else." He bit off a piece of bacon. The *crunch-crunch* seemed to be the loudest thing in the room because all she could focus on was him and the way his mouth had just formed words she'd never imagined Jake Maddox saying.

A real date. Maybe with candles and flowers and...kisses. Something more? She'd just decided she didn't want more, right? Heck, she was barely able to deal with the kisses.

But oh how sweet they had been. And addicting.

"I don't know, Jake. Is this a good idea?" she said. "If we break up, it would ruin our friendship."

"We'll deal with that when we get there, if it happens." Jake shoved his half-empty plate to the side. He reached across the table and took one of her hands in his own. His touch was warm and familiar, and so, so tempting. "I'm tired of being afraid to take risks, Gabby, of worrying about what other people will think or what I might lose. You were right. I've been sitting too long in my comfort zone, and if I stay there for one more minute, I'm afraid I'll be stuck there forever."

There was something to be said for comfort zones, she thought. For knowing where you will be tomorrow and the next day and every day after that. There were no hidden detours or dark tunnels that led to misery when you were the one in control.

"Except...I'm one of those 'do as I say, not as I do' people. I give advice I don't take myself." She sighed. "And when I do act without thinking, it never ends well." Like choosing to stop at the candy store with Emma instead of going straight home after school. Like opening a shop with no real plan for success. Like kissing her best friend and adding a strange new dynamic to the most stable relationship she had.

"What is it they say? Difficult roads often lead to beautiful destinations. Let's take that difficult road, Gabby. Let's see where we end up."

"We could end up alone and never speaking to each other again."

"I'm willing to take that chance." The rest of the diner, with its clatter of dishes and murmur of conversation, disappeared. For a second, it was just the two of them and the question hanging between them. "Are you?"

"I...I don't know."

"Well, I do know. I love having you in my life, Gabby. I love being with you. And I want to be sitting here in this diner ten years from now, watching you drown your French toast in syrup and listening to you laugh."

The words softened her, opening a fissure in her armor. "Ten years is a long time, Jake."

"If you ask me, it's not long enough." He grinned at her, that lopsided smile that was half tease, half fun, and the tension at the table ebbed. "By the way, I entered that photography contest and...I did one other thing." He reached into his pocket, pulled out a slim piece of paper, and slid it across the table.

"Business cards?" The front of the white linen stock was inscribed with MADDOX PHOTOGRAPHY, along with Jake's email address and phone number. On the back of the card, he'd used one of the landscapes he'd shot, one of her favorites. A wide shot of the rocky cliffs along the cove with a storm rumbling offshore. Gabby was a dot on the right, her back to him while the wind whipped her hair into a wild frenzy. She remembered that day, and that image, and dashing back to the car with Jake when the skies opened up. They'd turned up the heat and belted out Usher as he drove through the storm. "I've always loved this picture," she said. "We were drenched and cold, and it was still one of the best days of my life."

He smiled, a kind of shy, surprised smile. "Me too. That's why it's on my business card."

She flipped it back to the front and ran a finger across his name. "You're opening a photography business?"

"Part-time." He chuckled. "Actually, very part-time. I have some...other projects that are taking a lot of my hours right now, but I figured it wouldn't hurt to start getting the word out. There's so many great things to capture in this area."

"That's awesome. Maybe you should get a booth at the event. Show off some of those amazing photos hanging on your wall."

"Maybe I will. If you promise to stop by and be my biggest fan."

She laughed. "Of course I will. I'll be there for you, Jake. Always." Her eyes met his and held for a moment.

"I've got your back, and you've got mine," he said quietly.

"Even if?" She couldn't help but ask one more time, because all this was new territory, dangerous ground.

"Even if."

FIFTEEN

The man was infuriating.

Eleanor picked up the teapot filled with flowers that Harry Erlich had left for her on the small table by her front door. A little note hung from the handle. *Thank you for a lovely dinner. Let me return the favor by taking you out Friday night. Yours, Harold.*

Maybe the teacup roses and baby mums were adorable, especially in a blush of pale pastel colors that were a perfect complement to the soft-green-and-white teapot. And yes, maybe he had remembered that she'd mentioned loving tea. But giving her doughnuts and flowers simply for serving him some rib roast and mashed potatoes, why, it was simply too much.

She had no space in her mind for another person, not right now. Gabby seemed troubled about something, and Margaret's marriage was clearly in a rough spot. Eleanor made a mental note to call her granddaughters later today and check in with them, especially Margaret. Every marriage had its roller coaster times, and maybe Eleanor could be a voice of wisdom and understanding.

As she turned to go inside, she saw Harry getting into his dark gray sedan. He paused and waved at her. She waved back. "Thank you!" There. She'd been polite. Maybe he would quit after this.

"You're welcome! So, what's your answer?" he called back. "I heard you love Italian food."

"I think I'm busy. Thanks!" Then she scurried inside before he could belabor the question. Eleanor closed the front door and leaned against it, clutching the teapot to her chest. Her heart was hammering, her pulse rushing. She almost felt seventeen again.

Which was exactly why she couldn't go to dinner with him. She remembered the all-consuming love she'd had for her late husband when she'd first met him, the way he became her center of everything.

"Grandma, you look like you just went running." Emma came around the corner, a dishrag in her hands. Eleanor's youngest granddaughter had stopped by on Sunday morning after Eleanor got home from church. She'd stayed to visit and have waffles.

Eleanor was always glad to see any of the three girls, but it seemed like they'd been at the house more often lately. They were becoming little worrywarts, hovering over everything that Eleanor did, when in fact she should be the one worrying about *them*. "I'm fine. It's cold as a freezer in Alaska out there; that's why my cheeks are flushed."

"It's almost sixty degrees. I don't think that's cold." Emma nodded toward the teapot. "Did someone send you flowers?"

"It's nothing. That frustrating neighbor of mine felt compelled to thank me again for dinner. A dinner, I might add, that I didn't even invite him to."

"Yet you talked to him more than us that night, and he lingered over coffee and dessert. When I went home, he was still here." Emma grinned. "You didn't seem to be too frustrated with him then."

Well, yes, maybe Harry had stayed for an hour after dinner while they shared cups of tea and talked about their children and their gardens and their town. It had been a nice conversation, easy and sweet, and yes, she might have enjoyed it quite a bit. But that didn't mean she wanted to date him or do anything more than exchange the occasional neighborly wave. "I pitied him. He's a lonely widower who doesn't have three granddaughters like I do."

"You know, Grandma, it is okay to date again," Emma said. "To fall in love. Maybe even get married a second time."

"Once was enough for me, thank you very much." She glanced at the portrait of Russell sitting on the hall table. A layer of dust covered the glass over his handsome face, and Eleanor felt guilty for not noticing sooner. "I would feel disloyal to your grandfather if I dated again. He was my one and only love."

"I think we all get more than one and only. I mean, how sad would it be to live the rest of your life alone because you lost your soul mate?"

Eleanor cocked her head and studied Emma. Of the three girls, she was the least likely to end up in the white-picket-fence life. She was as wild as a leopard set loose on city streets, and even less likely to stay contained in this little town. "Are you becoming a romantic, youngest granddaughter?"

Emma laughed. "Heck, no. I'm never doing any of that. I don't want to settle down, and I don't want to get married. I want to travel the world. And I swear, I'm going to do that at the end of the summer."

"Why then?"

"We have this huge wedding that's going to take place at the hotel, and my manager asked me to stay on until that nightmare is done, because it's one of those all-hands-on deck kinds of things. The bride is a total bridezilla, and she's marrying some senator's son, so it's been a lot of work." Emma rolled her eyes. "As soon as that bride and groom are on their way to Bora-Bora for their honeymoon, I am dusting off my passport."

Eleanor set the teapot on the windowsill in the kitchen. She had to admit that the flowers added a nice pop of color to the sunshine-yellow room. She'd also noticed today that Harry had a nice smile and a friendly face. Always good traits in a neighbor, but as for more . . . Well, that was something that would have to wait. "I'll miss you terribly, Emma. Why can't the three of you just go back to being little girls who were here all the time?"

"Because we'd cramp your style, Grandma. You have a hot widower who wants to sweep you off your feet. Might as well give him a whirl on the dance floor, or in the bedroom." Emma waggled her eyebrows.

"Emma Jean. That is not going to happen, and I can't believe you just said that."

"Life is for living, Grandma. Someone wise told me that once. I believe it was you." She grinned and pressed a kiss to Eleanor's cheek. "And I intend to live the hell out of it as much as I can. You should do the same."

The flowers sitting on her windowsill and the jar of jam in her refrigerator probably agreed. But Eleanor knew herself and knew she was happy just as she was.

SIXTEEN

Go on a date with Jake? The question hung at the edge of every thought as Gabby walked out of the diner and back toward Ella Penny.

No, not when she had a store that was struggling. A sister with a suitcase in the hall. A grandmother who still wasn't quite herself.

Her phone rang, and when she pulled it out of her back pocket, she saw her dad's face on the screen. She could have let it go to voice mail, but Grandma's words echoed in her mind. *We can't go back and change the past. But we can't keep living in it, either.*

Easier said than done, Gabby thought as she pressed the button. "Hi, Dad."

"Gabby. Glad you answered. Listen, it would really mean a lot to Joanna if you came to dinner for my birthday. She's got a whole thing planned."

Of course he'd put it that way—that it would mean something to Joanna, not to him. "I...I might have plans."

There was a pause. "Listen, if you don't want to come, just say so. I'm trying to get a head count for Joanna." Her father let out a long breath. "What is it, Gabby? Is it me? Jo?"

"I don't want to talk about it." The last thing she wanted to do was to get into this conversation, one she should have had years ago, while she was walking down Main Street. Even now, the memory stung, seeing Joanna in her mother's house, among her mother's things, hugging her father.

"We can't be a family if we don't talk," Dad said.

"You should have thought of that before you started seeing her, Dad." The retort came sharp and fresh, rushing in on the heels of the memory.

"Jo? Gabby, I didn't start dating her until—"

"I saw you. With her. At the house. Mom was barely dead, Dad."

A long silence, so long that Gabby was sure he'd hung up. "That wasn't what you think, Gabby. I—"

"I don't need to hear it, Dad. I really don't. I gotta go." Then she clicked off her phone and tucked it back in her pocket. Here was the exact reason she didn't want to get serious with anyone and why she wasn't interested in dating Jake and having him break her heart, too. There had been enough of that to go around already.

She was so lost in her thoughts that she barely looked up as she turned the corner of Pine and onto Main. Out of the corner of her eye, she noticed a familiar tall figure coming in the opposite direction. For a second, she thought she was seeing a ghost—or a nightmare. Gabby stuttered to a stop. "Brad?"

"Gabriella. What a pleasant surprise." Jake's cousin had on a dark suit with a crimson tie, topped with a long gray wool coat. His dark hair, shorter and a deeper brown than Jake's, had been tamed to one side. The two-day scruff he'd had when she dated him was gone, replaced with the clean-shaven look she'd seen in the ads and billboards with his face. Nothing like a forty-eight-foot-wide image of the man who broke your heart hanging over the highway to brighten a girl's day.

"You're back in town?" she said. And why hadn't Jake mentioned it? "I thought you were running one of the branches in New Hampshire."

"I'm actually floating between all of the new locations." He straightened his tie and flashed her his trademark smile. "I have a meeting in Harbor Cove on Monday, and came back early to brief Jake on the meeting with the investors. We didn't get a chance to cover everything last night."

She blinked. Had she just heard him right? "Jake? As in your cousin Jake?"

"Is there another one?" Brad laughed. She couldn't be positive, but the tone seemed condescending. "Surely he told you he's working with us now."

"He quit the paper?" She literally just saw him. He would have told her if he had quit, wouldn't he?

"That job was going nowhere fast. Jake has ambition, finally. He saw the sense of coming back on board with his father and me. Took him a while, but I think it's all going to work out great. We might need to add a third Maddox to the masthead. Assuming, that is, that my cousin has the sense to see where his real career lies." Brad laughed again. "So, what are you up to these days? You look...gorgeous."

She was windblown and stunned, not gorgeous, but she didn't argue with him. Now that she was over a year away from the relationship, she could see Brad's compliments for what they were—empty words designed to further whatever agenda he had. Apparently, today's agenda was to turn her against Jake.

Was the meeting with Brad where Jake went last night after the photo shoot at the store? Why wouldn't he have told her he was meeting his cousin? Did he think she would pump him for information? Or was he trying to keep her from finding out he had quit working at the *Gazette*? And if that was so, why was he doing a photo shoot at her store?

Had the whole thing been a ruse to be alone with her? No, that was impossible. Jake was smart, but he'd never been sneaky or underhanded, not like his cousin.

Then the little voice in her head reminded her of seeing her father holding Joanna. *Maybe I don't know Jake as well as I thought I did.*

"I saw that event you set up for the town's tricentennial," Brad said. "I bet every woman in a hundred-mile radius is coming here. You have such a great eye, Gabriella, and I'm sure that store is going gangbusters now that you've got a solid year under you."

"Oh yeah. Total gangbusters." She hated it when he called her by her full name. Brad had never given her a nickname, never even called her by an endearment. He'd wined and dined her, but it had always felt a little ... empty. As if he were trying to win the biggest stuffed animal at the fair, not actually get into her heart.

Brad shifted closer. She could catch the faint scent of his cologne, a spicy blend that had once intoxicated her and now turned her stomach. "What do you say we go get a drink or some coffee? For old times' sake."

He seriously thought she would go out with him

again? "You ghosted me, Brad. Broke up with me by *text*. That's a crappy thing to do to anyone. Those old times weren't as great as you think."

"I was an idiot. I mean it. I was so wrapped up in my career that I didn't realize what a great thing I was giving up." He moved another inch or two closer and took her hand in his. "I miss you, Gabriella. All I could think about when I came back to Harbor Cove was seeing you again."

When Brad talked to someone, his gaze was intent, his attention seeming undivided. When she'd first fallen for him, he'd made her feel like she was the only woman in the room. Then she'd realized she was nothing more than a goal he wanted to attain, another checkmark on some mental list.

"One drink," he said. "We'll catch up and…see where it goes from there. If that's nowhere, well, it's my loss, without a doubt."

She drew her hand out of his. If there was one thing she knew about Brad, it was that all he wanted to do was win, whether it was a game of pool or the eligible girl in his cousin's life. "I'm not interested. Not anymore."

"Well, if you reconsider, you have my number." He leaned in and pressed a kiss to her cheek. "I really do miss you, Gabriella," he whispered, then gave her a smile and continued down the sidewalk.

What just happened? Had the world turned upside down? Since when did Jake work for his father? And on what planet did Brad come back and try to woo her again?

It had to be a mistake. Jake would have told her about such a monumental change in his life. He'd had business cards printed up for his photography company, for Pete's sake. Just to be sure, she fished the card out of her pocket, and yep, it still had his name and business printed across the front.

Was Jake just as much of a liar as his cousin had been? A man with a secret like her father? Or was she the fool to fall for another Maddox man's empty words?

Jake was in a foul mood from the minute he woke up on Monday morning. As he walked into the offices of Maddox & Maddox, in a suit and tie instead of the usual polo and jeans he wore to the *Gazette*'s offices, he already felt constrained. Strangled, even.

It was going to be a long two weeks.

He did have one bright spot, at least. Dinner with Gabby tonight, an impromptu plan they'd made when they were walking out of Earl's the other morning. Instead of a restaurant date, he'd asked her to come to his place. He had one dish he could make well, a pasta combo with mushrooms and freshly grated Parmesan. He'd add a salad, some candles, and a little Michael Bublé to the mix.

Their breakfast had been flirty, fun, and for the first time in a long time, Jake had hope that maybe he and Gabby could be a thing. Then she'd gone oddly quiet on texts after breakfast. Maybe it was just that the shop was busy or the last-minute details for the Celebrate History event were consuming her time. Either way, he'd ask her about it tonight and see if he could help lighten her load. Not that he had time to add one more job to his plate, but if it was for Gabby, another hour or two in his day was worth it.

He'd arrived at the office before anyone else, partly to get settled in and not feel like a fish completely out of water and partly because he'd barely slept last night. He'd submitted the photo spread to Leroy late and stayed up until two in the morning to get a head start on the ads for this week's issue. If he could get out of the law office early enough, he'd be able to put in a couple more hours on things for the *Gazette* before Gabby came over. Sleep was going to be a precious commodity in the weeks ahead.

Jake let himself into his father's empty office. The room that had seemed so imposing just a few days ago seemed to echo without Edward's large, intimidating presence. Jake sank into the deep leather chair and booted up the computer. His father had left detailed instructions on the desk. Jake was unsurprised but also a little grateful to have a sense of where to go and what to do with his days besides sit here and try to look commanding.

He was just finishing up pulling the list of financial reports for the 10:00 a.m. meeting with the investors when Brad poked his head in. "You look right at home."

Jake scowled. "This is a temporary gig."

"Yeah, yeah. Sure it is." Brad laughed and gave him a knowing wink. "The law is a seductress, Jake. She's going to suck you right back in."

"Not going to happen." Jake spun toward the credenza and grabbed a pile of papers from the printer tray. "My dad left me a list of financial reports we needed for the meeting, so I pulled them and looked them over. I wanted to be up to speed. But . . ." He hesitated.

"But what?" Brad glanced at the heavy gold watch on his wrist. "It's nine forty-five, Jake."

"When I was in the accounting program, I thought I noticed something amiss." Even as he said the words, he wondered if he should be mentioning it. After all, he'd only been here for a couple of hours.

"Nothing's amiss," Brad said. "It's all fine."

"The receivables seem a little...low and the expenditures pretty high." Jake had given the books a cursory glance and could very well be reading the data wrong. But something in his gut said otherwise. "Dad said the company was doing great."

"It is. We've had a couple rough months, but that's because we've had so much growth lately. Nothing to worry about."

"Okay. If you say so." This was his cousin, after all. There was no reason for Brad to lie or cover up anything. Plus, Jake had been away from these offices for more than two years. What did he know about the inner workings of Maddox & Maddox?

But the nagging doubts persisted throughout the day. The meeting with the investors, a man and a woman who worked for a venture capitalist looking to expand his investments in New England, had been strained from the start. They were surprised to see Jake at the head of the table instead of Edward. Brad, in his typical smooth-talking style, jumped in to assure them that Edward was merely out sick for a couple of days and it was all business as usual.

"We're growing by leaps and bounds," Brad said. "We have three more locations targeted for opening by the end of the year. It's a perfect investment for you. Here, let me show you the numbers." He'd wiggled two fingers in Jake's direction, taken the financials that Jake was planning to present, and basically commandeered the meeting.

At the end of the meeting, the investors left without promising anything one way or the other. Brad stopped Jake on his way back to his office. "You did great in there."

"I barely talked. You did everything, including present the financials. My father said I was—"

"Yeah, yeah, but you don't know the company like I do. Your old man was just trying to get you more involved, but you wouldn't know the profits from the losses if they slapped you across the face." Brad laughed. "No offense."

"Yeah. None taken." The words tasted like sandpaper in his mouth.

Brad took off after lunch, saying he had a meeting to get to, but when Jake asked him with who, Brad just smiled. "Nothing for you to worry about."

Jake puttered around the office, checking things off his father's list but feeling more like a trophy wife than an actual part of the company. He supposed that was justified, given that he'd left. By three o'clock, he ended up logging into his *Gazette* account and spending a couple of hours getting caught up there.

"Hi, Francine," Jake said to the receptionist when he finished. He'd looked up her name when he was going over the payroll earlier. "If you want to go home early, that's fine with me."

"Oh, thank you, Mr. Maddox, but I really have a lot to get done. I'll go home at six, my regular time."

"Yeah, uh, great." Even the receptionist had more purpose here than Jake did. Why on earth had his father insisted that he come into this office and warm the seat? Was this some kind of backward way of getting Jake to want to join the firm? *Hey, son, here's a job so boring you can't resist it*?

On the way home, he called Gabby. She didn't answer—odd, but he figured she was busy with the store—so he left a voice mail reminding her to come over for pasta at 6:30. At 6:40, he had a simmering pot of white sauce on the stove and a half pound of noodles draining in the sink.

And not a word from Gabby.

He called again, but the call went straight to voice mail. *What's up?* he texted.

I should ask you that.

He stared at his phone, confused. Had he missed a step somewhere? *What are you talking about?*

Three dots appeared and then disappeared.

Hey, talk to me, he wrote.

Three dots appeared again. Jake waited, but once again, they disappeared, and Gabby didn't answer. He paced the small space of his kitchen, running through their last few conversations, looking for what would suddenly make her so distant.

Have a good night, Jake, she finally texted, and an insane amount of relief ran through him. *I'll talk to you tomorrow.*

She'd been busy, that was all. Everything was fine, nothing to worry about. But when he went to bed, the nagging doubt in the back of his mind became a disquieting rumble that kept Jake awake for hours.

SEVENTEEN

9 11.

Emma's text came in around closing time on Tuesday, a group text with all three sisters. Gabby had sent Lori home early since business was slow, just as it had been Monday, and after a second day of steady rain and brisk winds, there was little chance of anyone trekking downtown. The weather was predicted to stay dreary for the next three days, and that sure wasn't going to help Gabby's bottom-line situation. She prayed for good weather this coming weekend or the entire tricentennial event would be ruined, which would hurt more than her own profits.

Gabby dug through her accounting program and budget, searching for a little bit of money to put toward her e-commerce site design. Nothing, even after the great sales on Saturday. Her bills had eaten up the profits again. Then her phone pinged.

Sisters' meeting at the Nightcap. Margaret, this is NOT optional. Be there or be square, Emma wrote.

She added a series of exclamation points. *See you at seven.*

Gabby sighed and shut down her computer. Maybe she'd get lucky and her bank account would breed dollar bills while she was out. She'd invested a lot of hope and money into Celebrate History in the Harbor, and if it didn't work as everyone prayed, she was seriously going to have to consider shutting down Ella Penny next month. Already, she'd cut Lori's hours to fifteen and would have cut her further, but she knew the young girl loved her job and needed the money to pay her own bills. Even if the income were there, Gabby doubted she could build and launch an e-commerce site in time to save the store.

What on earth was she going to do?

A little before seven, Gabby switched the sign to CLOSED, locked the shop, and walked the two blocks to the Nightcap bar. Jake texted her—again—and asked her if she was okay. She told him the same thing she had this morning: *I'm busy but great.*

Yeah, maybe that was avoiding a conversation she didn't want to have, and it was most definitely a cowardly move. Tomorrow, she vowed. Tomorrow, she would talk to Jake and clear up this whole thing about him working at the firm again. Maybe Brad had been mistaken, because Gabby couldn't think of a single reason why Jake would keep something like that from her. Especially if the two of them were...

Well, whatever they were. Yet another thing she was avoiding talking or thinking about. Kissing him—twice—had made her feel things she never imagined she'd feel for Jake, things she didn't have time to feel. This whole mess with Jake was going to go on a mental shelf tucked far out of sight.

Emma was waiting at a four-person high-top table inside the bar. Only a handful of people were sitting in the booths of the Nightcap, which made Gabby feel a little better. She wasn't the only one with sparse business tonight. She nodded toward Stanley Garrison, the owner of the bar, and then crossed to Emma's table.

Her younger sister had a glass of white wine before her, a second one waiting on the right, and a glass of red on her left. Gabby slid into the seat on Emma's right. "Must be some kind of emergency," Gabby said with a knowing grin, "considering you already have a glass of chardonnay waiting for me."

"It is. Thanks for coming." Emma touched the sleeve of Gabby's dress and gave an approving nod at the deep sapphire fabric, accented by razor-thin gold thread embroidery around the hem. "Wow. I love this dress. Where did you get it and do you have more in the store?"

"No, it's my own creation." Gabby glanced down at the dress, a retro pencil skirt with a sweetheart neckline, darted bodice, and wide waistband that gave the appearance of a slimmer silhouette. "I found this great print at the fabric store months and months ago and had no idea what I wanted to do with it, only that I couldn't pass up such gorgeous material. Then I was watching *The Marvelous Mrs. Maisel*, and I saw that crimson dress she wore. I loved it but wanted a different silhouette than the swing skirt she had. I just love everything Rachel Brosnahan wears on that show."

Emma shook her head. "I have no idea how you do that, or what half the words you said mean. You just make it up and then sew it, and have it look so fabulous. It's like an art form, it really is." She gave Gabby another once-over. "You should make more of these dresses and sell them in your store. I bet women would love them, especially given how popular that show has been. Plus it fits your retro vibe at Ella Penny. I'd buy one for sure, especially if you did it in other patterns."

"I just sew for a hobby. I started when I was little because it was something to do with Momma." Gabby shrugged. "I didn't go to school for it or anything." Not to mention, she was barely breaking even at the store and adding inventory would be silly. She needed to invest in e-commerce, not one-of-a-kind designs. And if that didn't perk up the store's sales, well...

Ugh. The whole thought of her future and the idea of starting over *again* depressed Gabby to no end.

"You have great instincts, and you should definitely—" Emma perked up and pointed toward the door. "Hey, she came."

Their oldest sister walked into the Nightcap, pausing while her eyes adjusted to the dim interior. Gabby pressed a hand to her heart in mock amazement. "Miracles never cease."

Margaret caught the gesture as she crossed to the table and gave Gabby a frown. "Hey, I come to stuff. Sometimes. Anyway, I only have a minute, Emma. So what is it?" She perched on the stool but didn't take off her coat or sip her wine.

"No, Meggy, what is it with *you*?" Emma asked. "You've been avoiding us for weeks. Now you're ready to leave before the door has finished shutting behind you. What's going on?"

"This better not be some kind of Margaret intervention just because I missed a couple family dinners," she said. "Just tell me what the big emergency is and then I can get out of here. I have—"

"Let me guess," Gabby said. "Work to do?"

Margaret was silent for a moment, as if weighing her words. She glanced at each of her sisters, and then, maybe because she was tired or feeling weak, something seemed to crack in Margaret's careful facade. She let out a long breath. "No, not work. More like a conversation I need to have with Mike." She put up her hands, warding off the questions Gabby and Emma were already forming. "And no, I don't want to talk about it."

"You can't just drop a bomb in the middle of the room and walk away," Emma said. "What's going on?"

Margaret took off her coat and then sat back down. She slid her wineglass closer. "We've hit a little snag in our relationship, that's all. It happens to everyone. We'll be fine after we talk." Margaret took a long sip of her wine, and when she spoke again, the words were so soft that it was almost as if she was talking to herself. "We'll be just fine."

Everything about Margaret, from the slump in her shoulders to the way she was clutching the glass of wine like it was a lifeline, said there was something deeper going on at home.

"Are you sure that's all it is?" Emma asked.

Margaret twirled the glass and watched the last dregs of wine swirl up the sides. "Yeah. I'm sure."

Gabby gave Margaret a dubious look but didn't say anything because she knew from experience that pushing Margaret would make her clam up and leave. So she opted not to bring up the suitcase again, or the fact that Mike was suddenly playing golf, a sport he hated.

It was enough that all of the sisters were here. Margaret had opened a tiny door into what was bothering her, and that was more than she'd done in months. "So what's the big emergency, Em?" The change of subject immediately lightened the air at the table. Gabby could almost feel Margaret's relief.

"It's a two-parter. First, Harry Erlich," Emma said.

"Grandma's neighbor?" Margaret said as she scanned the bar for a waiter. "What about him?"

Emma sipped at her wine. Unlike Margaret's glass, Emma's was still full. "He's dating Grandma. Or rather, he wants to, but Grandma isn't cooperating."

"Since when?"

"Since you didn't show up for family dinner, Meggy," Gabby put in. "Hey, we had to fill your seat somehow. Those mashed potatoes weren't going to eat themselves."

Emma laughed. "Gabby's right. There was an empty seat, and Gabby invited him because he's been giving Grandma little gifts. Like jam and doughnuts. And on Sunday, he gave her"—Emma leaned forward and lowered her voice—"*flowers.*"

"Oh, the scandal will rock Harbor Cove for decades." Margaret rolled her eyes. "Is that it? I really need to go."

"For Pete's sake, Margaret, will you just be part of your family for five minutes?" Gabby said, her voice rising in frustration. Almost as quickly, she tempered her tone. "Things have been going on, things you don't know about, because you are barely here, and even when you are, you're always halfway out the door."

Margaret bit her lower lip and clutched the stem of the wineglass. "I have my own things going on, Gabby."

"I know you do." Gabby put a hand on her sister's. "Just let us help you."

"I appreciate it, but this is something I have to decide on my own." Margaret took the last sip of wine and then signaled the waiter for another glass. "Back to Harry Erlich. What can we do about him and Grandma?"

Emma tucked a strand of long, straight hair behind her ear. Tonight she had on jeans and a loose coral sweater that made her blue eyes look almost like an ocean. "I think we need to talk to Grandma about moving on. Grandpa's been gone for decades, and she deserves to fall in love again."

"We can't make anyone fall in love with another person, or make them rekindle a love that has died," Margaret said, and once again, Gabby got the feeling that Meggy meant something other than the subject at hand. "That emotion is something that's either there or…not."

"Grandma still seems a little down, despite everything we've done with the column," Gabby said. "Maybe a new love in her life will be just the ticket to bring her some joy again."

"Okay, I'm in," Margaret said. "Anything for Grandma. Plus, it'll be nice to think about something other than my own stuff."

Gabby covered her sister's hand. "If you ever need to talk, Meggy…"

"I know."

A moment passed. "I volunteer to talk to Harry," Gabby said, "and encourage him not to give up."

"Good idea. Okay, now that we've settled that, the second part of the emergency is this." Emma dug in her purse and pulled out a piece of paper. She unfolded it and laid it in the center of the table. "This is the letter that's going to go to Dear Amelia tomorrow. It came into her inbox at the paper just an hour ago."

Gabby glanced at her little sister. The printout was

time-stamped today, just a few minutes before the 911 text went out. "How did you get it so early?"

Emma shrugged. "I asked Jake."

"You saw him?" Gabby tried to keep the surprise out of her voice and the tiny bit of envy that Emma had seen the man who had been swirling around Gabby's mind for days. "Was he working in the *Gazette* office?"

"Of course he was." Emma gave Gabby a confused look. "That's where his job is, silly. Anyway, I had texted him about the hotel's ad for this week, and he said to drop by the art department after six today. He said he was working late on some extra project."

The only extra project Gabby knew about was the photo shoot and layout, but that was coming out in the extra edition for the paper, a special release in time for people to make plans to attend the tricentennial event. His deadline for that had been yesterday. What other project could he have to do?

Unless...Brad was telling the truth, and Jake had gone back to work for his father.

She was more likely to believe Brad was lying. The man had, after all, broken up with her by text and disappeared from her life as if she'd never mattered. Maybe he was trying to get under her skin, driving a wedge between her and Jake. From the first date, it seemed like Brad had been jealous of her friendship with Jake. Maybe he still was. Either way, something wasn't adding up.

"Anyway," Emma went on, "Jake said the newest letter had just come into the Dear Amelia inbox, and he asked me if I wanted to see it. As soon as I read it, I knew I needed to get it to you guys." Emma pointed to the first full paragraph. "We need to do something about this one."

Dear Amelia,

> *I'm writing to ask for advice about my relationship with my grandson. Six months ago, he moved in with me after he lost his job in the city. He just moved out last month after getting a great job at a hotel. He and his father had a big argument several years ago, and they stopped talking. It breaks my heart to see them estranged.*
>
> *My grandson recently told me that he is gay and had me meet his partner, a wonderful man who is clearly in love with my wonderful grandson. I was raised in a different era, but I was also raised by a family that taught me love is love. I'm happy to see my grandson happy and told him so. He's afraid that, if he tells his father the truth, their estrangement will only get wider. It's a small town, and we're a small family. I just want us all to be together again.*
>
> *How do I mend these familial fences? I miss my son and my grandson terribly and am not sure how to handle this.*
>
> *Signed,*
> *Concerned Grandpa*

"Do you think that's Harry Erlich? Didn't he mention his grandson used to live with him?" Gabby asked. "I don't remember specifics, but I definitely think he said something."

"Wait, do you mean Roger Erlich's father, Harry? The guy who works for me?" Margaret asked. "When was this?"

"Margaret, you really need to start coming to family dinners again. It was last Wednesday at Grandma's." Emma shook her head. "Keep up, will you?"

"How can I when the two of you are moving at lightning speed, trying to meddle in other people's lives?" Margaret glanced at her sisters. "I'm sorry. Maybe that was a bit harsh."

"It's okay, Meggy."

Margaret rolled her eyes at the nickname. "I am not a child anymore."

Gabby grinned. Teasing Margaret was one of her favorite things to do, and one of the few things that got her uptight sister to relax a little. "Too bad. I'm going to call you that until you're a hundred and five. Face it. It's what sisters do."

"Ugh," Margaret said. "I want a new family."

Gabby dragged her sister into a tight side hug. "You're stuck with us. Sorry."

Margaret pulled away, but she was smiling as she did it. The waiter dropped off a second glass of wine, and this time, Margaret let it sit instead of guzzling it. "You all aren't too bad to be stuck with, I guess."

The three of them laughed. For a few minutes, they traded stories about childhood trips to the lake and late-night Monopoly games and the tabby cat they'd rescued from a drainpipe. The air in the room warmed, and the wine slowly disappeared as their memories drew the three of them closer.

"So what do you all think we should do?" Emma said. "How do we help Harry?"

"We just leave it in Grandma's capable hands," Margaret said. "I'm sure she's going to have a great piece of advice."

"*If* she responds to this letter. She's not talking to Harry right now, and it's not like she needs a degree in rocket science to realize this could be from him. She knows his son Roger because he works in Meggy's jewelry store, and she met his grandson, Chad, more than once when he lived next door with his grandfather." Emma sighed. "What if she doesn't feature his letter in her column? Plus, there's a full week of a time delay between it coming into the paper's office and her response. We all know lots can happen in a family in a week, and just like that, someone's gone." Emma's face colored. "I'm sorry."

Even all these years later, the memory of Momma dying had a tendency to hit like a left hook, hard and fast. Gabby's heart still ached with a bone-deep longing for the woman who should have been here to braid Gabby's hair and hear about her first date and watch her get married. The woman who should have been the voice of wisdom in her ear and the one to hug her when she had a bad day. The one to tell Margaret it would all be okay and give Emma a kiss on the forehead for her concern about her family. Maybe then they wouldn't be so fractured, and Dad would never have deserted one family for another.

Margaret cleared her throat and broke the silence. "So what exactly are you proposing, Emma?"

"A two-pronged approach. We work up some Harry sympathy first. Then we let Grandma see the letter. Jake said he can pull it out of the inbox for a day or two, then put it back. Grandma's column isn't due until the end of the day Friday, so if we can get her to feel sorry for Harry—"

"We can catch two birds with one net, encourage her to like him, maybe date him, and in the process, find a happy ending for Amelia herself. Then Amelia will gladly give good advice to someone she cares about." Gabby put up her hands in a victory gesture. "All problems solved."

Margaret shook her head and pushed the letter toward her sisters. "This is going too far, you guys. Way. Too. Far. You can't fix up people like they're two lonely pandas at the zoo. Grandma is a grown-up. She can make her own dating choices."

"The problem is she's not making any," Emma said. "After Grandpa died and we lost Momma, Grandma poured all her energy into raising us, instead of her own life. Now that we're all grown up—except you, Margaret—" Margaret stuck out her tongue, and Emma laughed. "She needs to focus on what makes her happy. And I think Harry could be the one to do that for her."

"She did talk to him until really late on Wednesday." Emma fiddled with the letter. "I think we need to solve Harry's problem at the same time we're working on softening Grandma's stance. That way, when she writes her advice, it'll already be in the process of working."

"How do you know what advice she would give him?" Margaret said.

"Easy." Gabby shrugged. "We just think of what she'd tell us." After all, they had piles of letters filled with their grandmother's advice, as well as years of listening to her guide them through dating and school and living on their own. The three of them were a treasure trove of Grandma's wisdom. Surely they could execute this just as she would.

"And what would she tell us to do?"

At the same time, Emma and Gabby said, "Bring over some cookies, brew some coffee, and sit down at the kitchen table to talk about it."

An amused smile crossed Margaret's face. "So what are you guys going to do? Show up on Harry's doorstep in your old Girl Scout uniforms and get him to buy some Samoas?"

"Well..." Emma looked at Gabby and then back at Margaret. "I was thinking all three of us could get involved in this one."

"How am I supposed to..." Margaret's gaze narrowed. "No. Absolutely not. Roger is my only designer on staff. I can't afford to lose him because I dragged him into some family drama thing."

"You won't lose him just by getting him to talk to his father, especially if you don't make it obvious," Emma said. "I know Harry's grandson because he works in the hotel kitchen. He's one of the sous chefs, and he's doing a fantastic job, so believe me, I don't want to lose him, either. Plus, he's in charge of the samplings for the brides, and he handles it so well, especially with the bridezillas who drive my boss and me crazy. Anyway, we'll handle this carefully, and without anyone being the wiser. Gabby, you'll be in charge of Harry." She drummed her fingers on the table. "Now we just have to figure out an occasion to get them all together in the same place at the same time."

Gabby had the answer right away. "The Celebrate History event. It's perfect. No pressure, a social outing, lots of other people around. Roger is working your booth, right, Meggy? And Em, why don't you get his son to work the event? The hotel was going to do samples from the restaurant, right? Put Meggy's booth on his route, and I'll invite Harry as my guest so we can just happen to stop by your booth all at the same time."

Margaret shook her head. "This sounds like a really,

really bad plan. Do you know how many ways that could go wrong?"

"Well, short of breaking into Roger's phone and sending out some conciliatory texts, do you have a better idea?" Gabby took a sip of chardonnay. Talking to her sisters and concocting a plan was a lot better than worrying about her store, her future, and that annoyingly handsome Jake Maddox.

"How about you both let people be grown-ups and figure out their own stuff?" Margaret shot a glance at Gabby, then Emma. "Ugh. You two are a pain in my butt, you know that, right? If this goes sideways, I'm blaming you guys."

"Are you in, Meggy? The Monroe Musketeers together again?" Gabby grabbed her sister's hand. Her solitaire, a two-carat round stone, dug into Gabby's palm. "It'll be the three of us hatching a plan, like we used to when we were kids. I miss that."

"Gabby, that was before…" Margaret tugged her hand out of Gabby's and got to her feet. She grabbed her coat. "We can't go back in time. We just can't. Good luck with your plan. I'm out." She shoved her arms into the burgundy velvet.

"Meggy, come on."

Margaret fished in her purse for a few bills and tossed them on the table beside her half-empty glass. "I've got enough going on in my own life. I don't need to mess with someone else's."

"But if I can't make this right with Grandma—"

"That's the problem, Gabby," Margaret said. She gripped the back of the stool with one hand, almost as if she was using it as a barrier between herself and her sisters. "You think there's actually something to make right. There isn't. People make mistakes. People get hurt. People die. You can't rearrange the pieces to make everything come out the way you want it to. That's not how life works."

"But—"

Margaret sighed. "Stop beating yourself up for something that happened more than twenty years ago. I have."

"Have you, Meggy?" Gabby asked. But her older sister just shook her head, grabbed her keys off the table, and headed out the door.

"What's up with her?" Emma asked.

Gabby sighed. She watched the door swing shut, hoping for a second Margaret would change her mind, but her stubborn sister didn't return. "I think things with Mike are worse than she's saying. When we were at the committee meeting, she said something about me not understanding marriage and wouldn't really talk about it. All she does is stuff things down and not deal with them."

"I think we all do a fair amount of that," Emma said as she picked up the menu and gave it a cursory glance. "So what was that comment about Margaret still beating herself up? Were you talking about when Momma died?"

Damn it. If there was one thing Gabby didn't want Emma to remember about that day, it was the backpack and the entire reason their mother had been driving late at night in the rain. Emma had been so little that the details of what had happened—and why—had blurred in her memory. The guilt that Gabby had carried for more than two decades wasn't something she would wish on anyone, most especially her baby sister. As for Margaret, the load she carried was entirely misplaced. She'd been at Girl Scouts when Gabby was supposed to be collecting Emma and all her things and walking both of them home from school. Gabby was the one responsible, not Margaret. "I think all three of us have lots of what-ifs about the past. That's all."

"Okay." Emma flashed a quick, suspicious glance at Gabby before focusing again on the menu. "Want to get some wings? Or maybe a flatbread? I'm starving."

"Sure. Whatever you want." Anything to change the subject. When the waiter came by, Emma and Gabby opted for a buffalo chicken flatbread and another round.

"So, I think our plan with Grandma is going well," Emma said after the waiter left. "At least the Dear Amelia part."

"Two success stories." Gabby finished her first glass and set it to the side. Her head was a little woozy, and she realized she'd barely eaten today. Stress had filled her gut most of the day. That flatbread was arriving just in time. "If we can just get this thing with Harry to work out…"

"We will." Emma unwrapped her silverware and spread the black cotton napkin across her lap. "This has been nice, Gabs."

"The wine?" She laughed. "Because I have to agree with that."

"No. Us being together. You were right, that day in the attic, when you said you missed having us all be a team. I didn't realize how much I missed it, too, until this whole thing with the letters came along."

Gabby draped an arm over Emma and pulled her close. "You have no idea how happy it makes me to hear you say that."

"Sisters to the end, right?" She grinned and plopped her chin in her hands. "So, tell me all about you and Jake. Are you guys making things official yet?"

This was definitely not a subject change Gabby

wanted. The whole thing with Jake was…complicated. "Emma, we haven't even been on a real date. And we're not anything. Plus…"

"Uh-oh. I know that tone. Plus what?"

Gabby thanked the waiter for delivering the second glass of wine and took a sip before answering. "Brad is back. I ran into him downtown. He said he regrets breaking up with me and wants to go out again. If there's a reminder of why I don't want to be in a relationship, it's right there."

Emma scoffed. "Brad broke your heart. He doesn't deserve to see the back end of your car leaving him in the dust."

Gabby laughed. "Either way, Brad being back in town just makes things with Jake even messier. Plus, I don't think there are a whole lot of happy endings in the world."

"What about Momma and Dad?" Emma asked. "They were like a storybook."

"Yeah, a real novel there." Fiction, at least on Dad's side. Gabby shook her head. "Doesn't matter. I don't want to get involved with anyone, especially a Maddox man. Besides, I really need to concentrate on my shop."

"I hear an implied *and* in that sentence." Emma cocked her head and studied Gabby. "I'm your sister. I know you better than you think. So come on, spill. You can't ask Meggy to do it and then clam up yourself. What's bugging you? Besides the whole mixed-feelings-on-Jake thing."

The weight on Gabby's shoulders—the worries about rent and paychecks and inventory—was heavy. Emma was smart, creative, and knew Gabby better than anyone. Maybe her little sister had a point about Gabby shouldering more than she should, and maybe Emma could be the sounding board Gabby needed.

"Honestly? Business has been slow," she said. "Like, really slow. And I'm...bored. Isn't that awful? This was supposed to be my dream. To open a shop that was part Momma's vision and part mine. I thought it would be awesome, but to be honest, I feel like I'm just watching a clock half the time."

Emma's brow furrowed, as it always did when she was thinking about something. "Hmm. Maybe you can...I don't know, tweak your approach? I mean, what makes you happy?"

"Paying the rent, for one."

"That makes your landlord happy." Emma pointed a finger at her sister's chest. "What makes *you* happy?"

"I don't know. I mean, I thought I knew, but I was wrong." Gabby shrugged. "The only creative boost I get during the day is designing the window dressings. I think that's why I create my own things after hours. It's an artsy outlet."

"Well, if you aren't feeling joy inside yourself, how do you expect your shop to bring joy to others?"

Gabby rolled her eyes. "If this is some yoga lesson or a recommendation to meditate, Em, I'm—"

"It's a recommendation to listen to your heart. When I went on that five-day silent retreat in the Catskills—"

"Which I would have paid good money to see." Her chatty sister being quiet for more than an hour? Gabby couldn't imagine it. Every so often, Emma read about something like that—a meditation weekend, a meeting with a Buddhist monk, a tour of old temples—and she cashed in her vacation days and headed out on a whim. With no boyfriend or kids to tie her down, she traveled as much as possible. There would come a day, Gabby knew, when Emma was going to leave Harbor Cove in a quest to see more of the world. Gabby hoped that day was far in the future.

"Well, there's a yoga retreat in Nevada in a couple weeks, and you're welcome to come with me. I already put in for the time off to go. Those days of silence really helped me listen to my inner voice," Emma went on. "Maybe you should try just sitting still and being silent for a bit. Listening to yourself and whatever is in your head."

"I don't have time for that, Emma. I have Grandma and you guys and the store and the tricentennial event and Jake and—"

"Where are you in that equation?" Emma put up her hands in a don't-shoot-the-messenger gesture. "I'm just saying, that's a long list, and you aren't anywhere on it. And Gabs, if anyone deserves to be a top priority, it's you."

By Thursday, Jake had no doubt that something was up. He had gone over the books a hundred times and discovered that Maddox & Maddox looked better on paper and in Brad's reports to investors than it did in reality. The deeper Jake dug into the accounting program, the deeper the mystery became—and the less the numbers added up, so he'd left early and headed across town.

When Brad came on board, Edward had handed over the financial side of the business. Brad's bachelor's degree in business administration and management, earned before he went to law school, had made him the perfect candidate to oversee the company's growth. When he'd first started working at the firm, he'd made an enthusiastic pitch for taking charge. Edward hated the financial end and gladly let his nephew take the reins. Jake had seen it as just one more way Brad made himself indispensable to the firm and to Edward. But now, Jake was thinking there was more to the offer than just a little brown-nosing.

Winter's last gasping effort to hold on made for a brisk wind that afternoon, and a handful of snow flurries that flitted through Harbor Cove but didn't stick. Hopefully, the weather warmed before the Celebrate History event on Saturday, particularly for Gabby's sake.

Jake parked in the hospital lot and headed up to the third floor. He had a folder tucked under his arm, and hundreds of second thoughts running through his head as he made his way to his father's room. Was he doing the right thing? Was he reading everything wrong? Maybe he'd misinterpreted the numbers.

No. Jake was no accountant, but even he knew something was up. At the rate of growth and investment Maddox & Maddox had been enjoying for the past couple years, the firm should be much deeper in the black, instead of teetering in the red.

When Jake knocked and entered the room, he saw his father sitting up in the bed, wearing a hospital gown and a frown. An IV snaked along his arm while the heart monitor above the bed showed a steady rhythm. Edward's reading glasses were perched on his nose, and he was going through a pile of case files sitting beside him. There was a sag in Edward's shoulders, though, and he looked paler and frailer than the last time Jake had seen him.

"Hey, Dad," Jake said as he swung around the bed to drop into the visitor's chair. "How are you feeling?"

"Just fine. Just fine. The damned hospital is making me stay another day to keep an eye on me." He scowled. "I have work to do. I can't waste hours in this bed."

Stubbornness ran heavy in his father's veins. Part of why he was so successful in court—and a pain in the butt everywhere else. "That's exactly why the hospital is making you stay. Because you're not listening."

"I'm not a take-it-easy guy. I can't stand just sitting here or on the couch, doing...what do they call it? Bingeing that Net movie thing?" He said it as if the mere words disgusted him. For as long as Jake could remember, his father rarely watched anything other than CNBC on TV, and even that was only for a few minutes in the morning.

"It's called Netflix, and a few days of bingeing won't hurt you. It could actually help you recover, because you'd have to stay in the same place for more than ten seconds." Jake shook his head. He was arguing with a brick wall. "You just had a medical procedure. On your *heart*. Don't you think a few days of recovery is good?"

Edward ignored the question. He set the folders on the small table beside the bed and clasped his hands in his lap. "Catch me up on the office. How did the meeting with the investors go? Brad needs to pull the trigger on that Hartford location or we're going to lose our option on the building."

"The meeting went pretty well." That was a lie, but one that would reduce his father's stress. "Brad can talk the paint right off a wall and convinced them we're a good investment. I think they're interested in partnering on the Portland office as well."

"Excellent, excellent. I knew he'd pull that off." The pride in Edward's face caused a twinge of envy in Jake's gut. What would it take for his father to look at his own son that way?

"Yeah, Brad's great." Jake fiddled with the folder in his lap. Maybe this wasn't the right time to bring up his concerns. Dad was, after all, still recovering from his stent procedure, and even though it was a relatively straight-forward medical treatment without a lot of complications, it probably wasn't a good idea to tell a man with heart problems that his nephew might not be on the up-and-up. "How you feeling, Dad?"

"You already asked me that." His father took off his reading glasses and leaned in Jake's direction. "Spit it out, whatever it is that you've come here to tell me."

Jake drew in a breath. If he left without saying any-thing, his father would just fret. That was stress Edward didn't need. And if Brad was skimming as much as Jake suspected, Edward couldn't afford to sit on this, which meant Jake had to break the news to his father. "The numbers aren't looking right to me."

"What numbers?"

"The ones in the company ledger. I've been going through the accounting program and—"

"Who told you to look at the company ledger? Brad handles all of that."

"I know. But I wanted to be prepared for the investor meeting, so I ran the financial reports the other day. I thought I'd save Brad some time and get acquainted with what you two were working on. What I saw raised a little warning flag in my head, so I went in and did a deeper dive this week." Jake tapped the folder in his lap. "Some-thing's not adding up, Dad."

"Bah. Impossible. You're bad at math or something."

Edward snorted. "I own that company. You think I wouldn't notice if things were wrong?"

"You handed off the financial side to Brad a few years ago. How much have you overseen it since then?"

His father bristled at the implication. "Brad is the one with the accounting degree and also the one in charge of expansion. It only makes sense for him to know what we're working with for operating capital." Edward grabbed the files on his bedside table and flipped open the top one, ignoring Jake. Case dismissed. "You have no idea what's going on at Maddox & Maddox. You abandoned the ship years ago."

"I did; that's true." Jake gritted his teeth to keep from saying much more and possibly driving another wedge between himself and his father. It was only the instinct that something wasn't right that kept him in that chair and having this conversation. "But that doesn't mean I can't read a general ledger or make sense of accounts."

"You draw pictures all day. You have no idea how accounting works."

Jake sucked in a deep breath and willed himself to remain calm, to not take the bait. "That's not quite what I do, and you forget that I did take a semester of business accounting as part of my degree."

"Fat lot of good that did you. You're still working at that stupid paper."

"I am not retreading that ground with you, Dad." Jake cursed under his breath and got to his feet. This was a pointless argument. It was always going to come back to the same thing—Jake was the disappointment and Brad was the one who could do no wrong. "Forget it. I never should have brought this up."

"You're right about that, at least," Edward said. "And

you never should have dug your nose into the company's business. We were doing just fine without you."

"Really?" Had they wiped his father's memory when he went in for that procedure? That wasn't the conversation they'd had just a few days ago. "Because I distinctly remember you saying that you brought me in because you can trust me."

"Words. Just words." Edward slipped his reading glasses back on and dropped his attention to the documents on his lap. "I wanted you to have a more meaningful job than that worthless one you have now. I figured if you could get back in the fray, you'd see how much you loved law."

"I don't love law. I love puzzles. I love figuring out how to make something unique and productive. That's what's great about advertising. I'm always trying to reinvent the wheel and get better results. Same with photography. It lets me help people see the world in a different way, and part of the excitement is figuring out the angle that gives them a perspective unlike any other. In fact, I have this one photo that I entered in a contest that—"

Edward shook his head, cutting off Jake's words. "Are you done? I have work that needs my attention. If I can get a hold of my damned doctor, I can tell him I need to get released later today."

Why had he thought he could change anything? His father was always going to side with Brad, and see his own son as a failure. Edward had no interest in what Jake did or what Jake loved, and never would. Better to abandon the argument before it went any farther south. "Do you need a ride home?"

"Brad will be here. I already worked that out with him."

"The bonus son, stepping right into my shoes." Jake swallowed a bite of envy and tried unsuccessfully to keep the bitterness out of his voice. "I'm glad you're so pleased with his performance."

"I'd be more pleased if my own flesh and blood was the one stepping up. But you're just here to complain."

"No, Dad. I'm here to warn you." He'd try one more time to get through to his intractable father, and if that didn't work, well, he'd done his best. "There's something going on here, and you're too blinded by your admiration or hero worship or whatever the hell it is that you have for my cousin to see the truth." Jake tossed the folder onto his father's bed. Spreadsheets spilled out and scattered across the thick white blanket. All the proof Edward needed, right there, but his father didn't even spare the paperwork a glance. "You know, you didn't have to have me come in to cover for you. You already know there's no way I'm going back into law, so it didn't make sense to ask me. You want to know what I think?"

"You're going to tell me whether I do or not, aren't you?"

"I think you had me sit in your office chair on purpose. You have good instincts, Dad, or you wouldn't be as successful as you are. Your Spidey sense has been tingling, and you wanted an outside perspective from someone who has always had your back. Whether you believe it or not."

"You're wrong, you know." Edward's sharp eyes met Jake's. "About your cousin."

"Facts don't lie, and these numbers are facts that could hold up in court. You taught me that, Dad." Jake gave his father a nod. "Let me know if you need anything. I'll check on you again tomorrow."

"Don't bother. No matter what those doctors say, I'm going back to work tomorrow. So I won't need you anymore." His father shuffled the spreadsheets to one side and then dropped his gaze to his own files, effectively shutting Jake out.

The dismissal stung, but still Jake stood there, wishing his father would look up, would actually see his son, and realize that Jake wasn't going to abandon his father that easily, or leave him with all that stress on his shoulders. "Whether you believe me or not, I care about what happens to you and to the firm," Jake said quietly. "Whatever you need, I'm here to help you."

"You've done quite enough, Jake," Edward said, never once looking up from the work before him. "Don't you think?"

EIGHTEEN

Gabby should have been tossing confetti and popping champagne. The Celebrate History in the Harbor event was a bigger success than anyone had expected. The weather was warm and sunny, perfect for enticing people who had been housebound for the long winter months into an outdoor event. Gabby had more traffic in her shop and at the sidewalk sale she'd set up than she'd had since she opened her doors. Sales were triple what they had been the spring before.

Any other day, she would have been overjoyed. But yesterday she had stopped by the *Gazette*'s offices to drop off her ad for the next edition, only to find out from Leroy that Jake wasn't working there during the day anymore. "He's...uh, working on an extra project," Leroy said. "Something with his dad."

And there it was, the proof she had needed to know that Jake had lied to her, just like Brad had and her father had. How many times did she need to learn this lesson before it sank in?

As she made the rounds, every single vendor told her or texted her throughout the day that they were excited about the turnout and the boost in business. Their social media numbers climbed, and the soft *cha-ching* of cash registers rang all over Harbor Cove.

"This was a great day, wasn't it?" Harry said as he strolled alongside Gabby. She'd invited him to walk the event at the end of the day under the guise of wanting an outside opinion on the setup. It was a flimsy excuse but enough to get Harry here. "Thank you for inviting me. It was nice to get out of the house."

"I'm glad you had a good time." She liked Harry. He was affable and easygoing and friendly with every person he met. She couldn't imagine Harry not being trustworthy. But then again, she hadn't imagined Jake wouldn't be, either.

Right now, though, Harry seemed perfect for Grandma. Even if they didn't have a romantic relationship, it would be nice for her to get out more and have someone bring her flowers. Harry could do that, if nothing else.

But every time Gabby had tried to bring up Harry's name over the last few days, Grandma had shut her down, calling him a "nuisance." At the same time, Gabby caught Grandma peeking at Harry when he was in his driveway or working on his landscaping. And she'd gone along on the evening walks with the neighborhood group, staying on the opposite side of the other walkers as Harry but engaging in chitchat with her neighbor from time to time. Grandma said she was merely being polite, but to Gabby, that spelled interest, whether Grandma wanted to acknowledge it or not.

"I also had some great pretzels from Earl's," Harry

said. "I don't know if you've tried them, but they're fantastic." He scanned the people filling the town square, which had been set up with dozens of white tents for vendors. The green-space commons served as a sort of wagon wheel center, leading to the shops that lined Main Street in either direction. "I don't see your grandmother. Did she come today?"

"She said she was feeling under the weather." Maybe…if she couldn't work on bringing Grandma around, she could work on Harry and get him to see that Eleanor Whitmore was worth the effort.

"Eleanor has been saying the same thing about why she's leaving our evening constitutionals with the neighbors after the first loop. Yet I've seen her walking with Sandy Williams on many an afternoon, so she's clearly not sick." Harry stopped walking and faced Gabby. "Is she avoiding me? Did I do something to offend her?"

She could lie, but Gabby was tired of hiding the truth. It had become such an exhausting exercise and one that did nothing but weigh on her conscience. So many secrets in this little town, and in her family. Maybe it was time to stop holding all of them.

"Yes, she's avoiding you," Gabby said finally. "I'm sorry, Harry. If it helps, it's not personal. She says that dating someone else would be disloyal to my grandfather."

"But he's been gone for more than three decades."

"I know that, and Grandma knows that." Gabby leaned toward Harry's ear and lowered her voice as they passed by a group of people Gabby knew. "If you ask me, she's scared of getting her heart broken."

"Well, I can certainly understand that." Harry stopped walking and faced Gabby, his face serious as a stone. "I hope you know I have nothing but the best intentions with your grandmother."

Gabby laughed. What a sweet thing for Harry to say. So old-fashioned and considerate. Grandma was crazy if she didn't fall for this man. "You don't have to ask me for her hand in marriage or anything. I'm sure you're a nice guy. I've seen you with your grandson, and he looks like he loves you as much as we love our grandmother."

"Thanks. We are pretty close. Especially since his father…" Harry cleared his throat. "Well, that's neither here nor there. Speaking of my grandson, I think he said he was going to be distributing desserts from the hotel's kitchen at this event. He promised to give me an extra sample."

If Emma had done her part, then Harry's grandson would be on his way toward Margaret's shop right this very minute. Gabby tugged out her phone and checked her texts. *Operation Concerned Grandpa is in motion,* Emma had written a few minutes ago. *Get Harry in position.* "Hey, I have an idea. Let's walk down Main Street and see if we can catch up with your grandson. I'd hate for the hotel to run out of dessert before you get some."

"I like your way of thinking, Gabriella. You're smart like your grandmother." Harry chuckled.

At the end of History Alley, as the committee had dubbed the path that led customers from one business to another, sat Margaret's jewelry store, tucked in a storefront on the far side of a long, boxy, seventeenth-century building that had been painted a dark gray and accented by red trim. It had a decidedly Pilgrim feel to it, a perfect accompaniment to the harbor full of boats just across the street. Outside the shop, Margaret had set up a booth housing a pair of glass cases under a bright white tent. The two local designers she'd mentioned were there, pointing out their creations to shoppers, while Roger, the store's designer, sat at a small table, consulting with anyone who wanted repairs or custom work.

"That's my son." Harry stopped and glanced at Gabby.

"Really? I had no idea." Just as Gabby said that, Harry's grandson, a tall, lanky boy with long black hair and a perpetual smile, came around the corner, holding a silver tray of tiny slices of cake in one hand. He paused by every attendee, waiting while they took a sample. Like his grandfather, he was affable and friendly.

"And that's my grandson Chad." Harry shot Gabby a suspicious look. "Seems awfully convenient that we're all here at the same time."

"Serendipity, right?" She let out a nervous laugh. This had to work. It just had to. Otherwise, Grandma would slip back into that sad state she'd been in, and Gabby couldn't let that happen. Grandma's happiness was far too important. "Let's go get you that slice of cake."

"I'm not sure this will go well. The last time we were all together…" Harry shook his head. "Gabby, my son and grandson had words. They haven't talked in a long time. My son resents that I took my grandson's side, and my grandson's feelings are hurt."

"They're family. It'll all work out. Trust me." She gave Harry a smile she didn't feel. *I'm not controlling anyone. I'm just trying to keep my family together and happy*, she'd said to Jake, and he'd replied, *Have you ever considered that might not be your job?*

Maybe it wasn't, she thought as they crossed the road toward Margaret's tent. Harry's trepidation was palpable, and she was starting to regret the decision to bring the three of them together in a public setting.

Chad turned into Margaret's tent just as Roger glanced up and noticed both his son and his father drawing near. Roger got to his feet, said something to Chad that Gabby couldn't hear, and then turned and stomped inside the store. Someone took the last treat from the tray, and Chad spun away, his face cracked with hurt. He tucked the empty tray under his arm and charged out of the tent.

Oh no. This wasn't how it was supposed to go.

"Excuse me," Harry said, hurrying toward Chad. He touched his grandson's arm, stopping the young man from leaving. "You okay, Chad? What did your father say?"

Whatever else they talked about was lost as a group of women cut between Gabby and Harry. When the path was clear again, Harry was halfway to the town lawn with Chad, who was shaking his head and talking very fast. Even from here, she could see Harry consoling his grandson and the upset on Chad's face. Roger had yet to come back out to the booth.

Gabby debated running after them but was afraid of making it worse. Nothing she'd done lately had worked out. Not a single thing. She felt a swell of tears in her eyes and pivoted toward Ella Penny.

Across the street, she saw a familiar figure with a familiar khaki backpack slung over one shoulder. Jake had his camera against his face, taking shots of the event, the attendees, and the shopkeepers' wares. She stood there for a second, watching him, realizing how comfortable he seemed with a camera in his hands, far more so than with a briefcase.

She thought of all the trips they'd taken after Jake got the camera, a Nikon he'd saved up for and bought one summer when they were kids. There'd been trips to the park, the zoo, an abandoned building, the waterfront, the cemetery. Half the time, she'd been his unwilling subject when he'd snap a picture of her picking up a shell or wiping the moss off a gravestone. As the years went by, he'd perfected his technique, reading everything he could get his hands on about photography. She watched him now, patient and controlled, waiting for the perfect shot before pressing the button. She had no doubt the photos the *Gazette* ran next week would be brilliant.

Jake started to turn in Gabby's direction, the lens still at his right eye. Before he could see her, she ducked inside her shop. Jake paused when he glimpsed the store. For a second, she thought he'd cross the street and come inside to say hello. Instead, he moved down the sidewalk and disappeared from view.

She wasn't disappointed. Not one bit.

As the day wound down and neither Harry nor Jake came by, Gabby started counting the hours and minutes until she could switch the sign to CLOSED, lock the door of the shop, and go in the back room to cry. She'd barely held it together all day. Heck, she'd barely been holding it together since she stopped talking to Jake. The silence had created a giant black hole in her life, and she was, to put it mildly, devastated and depressed.

It had been the right thing to do, she told herself over and over again. If he couldn't tell her the truth about his job, for Pete's sake, they would never have worked as a couple. She needed to be able to trust the man in her life, and so far, her track record for trustworthy men was...zero.

Might as well go home and enjoy her misery with a glass of wine and a package of Oreos. Tomorrow, she would tally her receipts and thank Lori for her hard work, and try to see the silver lining in all of this. Tonight, she just...couldn't.

Gabby grabbed her phone and was about to head out of the shop when she saw two familiar faces at the door. In a split second, she was a little girl again, in the middle of a storm with chocolate chip cookies and her best friends. "What are you guys doing here?" she asked as she fumbled the lock open and let Margaret and Emma into the store.

"Checking on you," Emma said. "It's not the same as those nights we had at Grandma's, but hopefully this is a good substitute." She held up a bag of chocolate chip cookies, and Margaret hoisted a bottle of white wine.

They'd read her mind. "Aw, thanks, guys, but...I'm fine," she said, the words catching on a lump in her throat.

Margaret scoffed. "You can only get away with saying that when you aren't crying. Trust me, I know."

Gabby laughed and swiped at the tears. "I'm sorry. It's been a hell of a day. Actually, a hell of a week."

Emma's face softened with sympathy. "Do you want to talk about it?"

"No? Yes?" Gabby sighed and dropped onto the love seat at the front of the store. "I think it's over with Jake."

"Did you ever really give it a chance to start?" Margaret asked. She unscrewed the top from the wine, dug a trio of plastic cups out of her bag, and poured each of them a glass. "Because if you ask me, you were betting against him before he even kissed you."

"He's my friend. We would never work." Gabby could see where her sisters got their denial skills from. Clearly it ran in the family. She took a long sip of wine. Then another.

"Yeah, I'm not buying that as a reason, are you, Meg?" Emma said.

"Nope. Not one bit."

"No offense, Gab, but I've seen you two together for more than twenty years, and you have more chemistry than the entire cast of *The Bachelor*." Emma held out the bag of cookies and waited for her sisters to take some. "So it's not that you aren't attracted to him or don't want to jump his bones."

"Emma! I don't." Gabby sighed and thought of his amazing kisses and all the sleepless nights she'd spent anticipating the next kiss. "Well, maybe I do."

Emma turned to Margaret. "You owe me five bucks."

Her jaw dropped. "You guys were betting on my love life?"

"Just the chances of you wanting to be with Jake, like *really* be with him. Course, we all know love is a burn-hot-and-die kind of thing." Margaret gave a sarcastic laugh. "Look at me. Now I'm the jaded older sister."

"Things still rough with Mike?" Gabby asked.

Margaret nodded, and the tough shell she wore began to crack as tears appeared in her eyes. "Not gonna lie, guys, I'm a little worried about us. He told me he wants a separation. He's . . . he's looking at apartments."

"Oh, Meggy." Gabby drew her sister into a hug and held her tight. "Let us help."

Margaret drew back. "You can't. This is on me and Mike. Maybe we'll work it out. Maybe we won't. But you can't fix it, Gabby. You can't fix any of it. Not Grandma, not us."

Gabby didn't hear those words. There was nothing she couldn't fix with her family. Well, losing Momma, but there would be nothing else broken, not on her watch.

"Why don't we have a family night and invite Mike? We'll play Monopoly or something and have a good time like we used to. It'll be no pressure, just the family, and maybe after some laughs—"

"This is about a lot more than a Monopoly game. Emma hung that picture of Momma and Dad on their wedding day in my shop, and they just looked so happy and in love, even with cake all over their faces," Margaret said. "It made me realize that Mike and I have lost that kind of love, if we ever had it to begin with."

"You can get it back," Emma said. "You just have to try, Meggy."

Her oldest sister gave the two of them a watery smile. "I think I'm all out of tries, guys." She sighed. "Sorry. It's just been a bad day. I'll talk to Mike, and maybe we can find some common ground again."

"I know you can." Gabby gave Margaret's hand a squeeze. "You've never failed at anything you've gone after, Meggy."

Margaret scoffed. "Yeah, I'm not sure I agree. Either way, Gabby, it's not your responsibility to take care of me or Em or Grandma or even Jake."

Gabby waved that off. She took another sip of wine. Then she said to heck with it and finished the glass. "Jake can take care of himself."

"Yeah?" Emma said. "Did you just make a relationship decision for him? Because it sure seems to me like you did."

"I did no such thing. I stopped dating him—well, and talking to him—but only because we're not right together. Better to stop this train before it derails."

"I'd say you're more afraid to love someone. Afraid to get hurt." Emma topped off their glasses—well, technically refilled Gabby's—and took another cookie out of the bag. "Because I'm right there with you."

"I'm not afraid of any of that," Gabby said. The wine was going down quite smoothly and taking the edge off her day. Heck, her week. Good thing she lived within walking distance, because she was draining this second glass pretty quickly, too.

Margaret arched her brows in response. "You're not afraid. Really."

"Well, I mean, *maybe* I'm a little afraid of losing someone. But honestly, I'm more afraid that...I'm going to find out that he isn't who I think he is." Like she had with their father. And with Brad. Gabby broke off a piece of cookie. Crumbs littered the floor at their feet.

"Jake? He's the most grounded human I know," Emma said. "He's a what-you-see-is-what-you-get guy."

"Yeah, then why didn't he tell me he's working for his father again?" Gabby hung her head. "I had to find out from *Brad*."

"Whoa, whoa, whoa. Back the truck up." Margaret put up a hand. "When did Jake quit his job, and when did you see Brad?"

So Gabby told her sisters the entire story of running into Brad after Jake told her about his photography business. Of the "extra project" he'd told Leroy and Emma about, and the fact that he wasn't at the paper when she'd dropped off her ad. "So he lied to me."

"Or left something out." Emma shrugged. "Maybe he had a good reason."

Tears burned in the backs of Gabby's eyes. She shook her head. "I can't trust him, or heck, any man. Not even—" She cut off the sentence before she could finish it. That day was between Gabby and Dad. Dragging her sisters into it would only fracture their fragile family more.

"Jake is trustworthy," Margaret said. "Whatever is going on, I'm sure he'll tell you if you just talk to him."

"I don't have time for that. The store, Grandma, this thing with Harry and the column…" Gabby threw her hands up. "Plus, I worry about you guys, and being there for you both. You're going through stuff, Margaret, and someday Emma will. I need to support you."

"In case you haven't noticed, we are adults. We don't need you to worry about us or fix our lives or do anything other than live your own life, Gabby," Emma said. "So go do what makes you happy, like I said the other day. Fall in love, get married, have a bunch of kids that drive you crazy, or run off to Paris and spend a week eating your body weight in croissants."

How tempting that all sounded. Just do whatever she wanted and forget the consequences. She glanced down at the floor. Those damned cookie crumbs sat there, a reminder of the childhood they used to have, the magic that had existed before. Gabby stared at them and felt tears welling in her eyes. "I can't do that," she whispered.

Margaret let out a long sigh. "Why the hell not?"

"Because I promised Momma." She lifted her gaze to her sisters. They were blurry behind her tears, and maybe it was the wine that was rushing to her head making her long for the days of late-night stories in the bedroom she shared with Emma, but Gabby couldn't seem to hold the words back. "I stood over her grave and promised her I would take care of you guys. I swore to her that I would never let her down again."

"Gabby." Emma's voice was sharp. "When have you ever let any of us down?"

"The day she died." The words began tumbling out in a mad, sobbing rush. "Margaret was at Girl Scouts, and I was supposed to remember to bring home Emma's backpack, but we got distracted when we went to the candy store, and I forgot, and Momma had to go back to the schoolyard to get it that night. If I had remembered, she wouldn't have been out there in the rain and the truck wouldn't have hit her and we'd all be all right. It was my fault for forgetting. Don't you guys get that?"

Margaret shook her head. "You were eight, Gabby. It's crazy to blame yourself for that."

"Is it? Because, Meggy, you're like a workaholic's worst nightmare. You work more hours than a human being possibly can and have detached from our family just like Dad did. And Em, you can't stay in one place for more than five minutes. We're not a family anymore. We're fractured and broken, and I'm part of the reason why."

"Don't give yourself that much credit, Gabby." Margaret took the glass out of Gabby's hands and set it on the small glass table. "You're carrying a load that is way too big. We are who we are because that's who we were born to be. Yes, I agree, losing Momma when we were little has had an effect on all of us. But we had Grandma and we had a good childhood, despite all of that. Momma would be proud if she could see how we all turned out."

"You really think so?" Gabby's head was swimming, and she couldn't seem to stop her tears. God, she was a mess.

"Yeah, I really think so. Now pull yourself together or you're going to have a heck of a hangover tomorrow." Margaret swung her bag over her shoulder and plucked another cookie from the bag. "I'm going home."

Practical, structured Margaret saw it all in black and white. Gabby was definitely in the category of shades of gray, but she did as her older sister said and cleaned up the cookies and the wine. "I hate to say that she's right," she said to Emma after Margaret was gone.

"Don't say it to her face. There'll be no living with her after that." Emma grinned. She scooped crumbs off the table and dumped them into the small trash can, then stowed the empty wine bottle in the recycle bin. "Oh, hey, did you ever look at that package of photos I gave you?"

Gabby had to think back. It seemed like a million things had happened since that day in the attic. "No, I totally forgot. Why?"

"Dad said something about wanting a copy of one of them. I think he's going to call you about it."

Just what she needed to top off a difficult week—another conversation with her father. "Great. Can't wait."

Emma opened the shop door and then turned back. "Do you think you did the best job you could after Momma died, trying to keep us together?"

"Well, yes, but I could have done more." Gabby had a hundred things she would have done differently had she known what she knew now.

"Did you ever think that maybe Dad feels the same way?" Emma shrugged. "Give him a chance, Gabs. He's hurting, too."

NINETEEN

The only way to get anywhere was to do something about where he was right now. That had become Jake's new life motto ever since the day he'd kissed Gabby. That moment lingered in his mind just enough to distract him during these impossible twelve-hour days he'd been logging at the law office and the newspaper.

His cousin had left Harbor Cove for yet another business trip, and his father had returned to the office part-time. Jake and Edward barely spoke during the day, with his father holed up in his office and Jake in one down the hall. The digital town-centric version of the *Gazette* was gaining subscribers, which meant more work on Jake's plate every time he walked into the quiet building after hours. At the end of each day when his head hit the pillow, as much as he longed for a deep, restorative few hours of sleep, his mind returned to Gabby.

She'd barely texted and only had two brief phone calls with him over the last few days. Every nerve ending told him this was more than her being busy with the Celebrate

History event. The vibe between them had shifted after breakfast at Earl's, and damned if he knew why.

Hey, he texted Gabby several days after the bicentennial. *I know you've been really busy with the store and the event. I heard it was a huge success, in large part due to your hard work, I'm sure. I think you need a break, so what do you say we meet over at Castle Park and go on a photo hunt? I'd love to get some new pics for the paper.*

There was a long pause. Then, a short, no-emoji response. *Okay. We need to talk anyway.*

Those five words filled him with a deep sense of foreboding. Talk? That didn't sound like a conversation he wanted to have. *See you there in thirty minutes?*

She sent back a thumbs-up, as cryptic as her earlier message. Jake swung by his apartment, picked up his camera gear and an extra sweatshirt, and then climbed back into his Wrangler and headed for the north entrance of the park. Most people went in on the south end, where the ranger station stood and the pretty koi pond gurgled beside it. The first time Jake and Gabby explored this park, they had stumbled upon the northern entrance, really just a dirt road with a metal gate and a grassy path that led into deep, dark woods. A few minutes' walk had brought them to a world of tree houses and forest sprites and adventures as big as their imaginations.

They'd looked for tadpoles, caught crayfish, and held picnics by the creek. In the winter, the park became a wonderland where they had snowball fights or built a family of Frostys. The very first time he'd raised his Nikon to take a picture, it had been in this very park on a languid summer afternoon. He'd saved up for months, keeping the money he earned on his paper route to buy the camera sitting in the window of the pawn shop downtown.

He'd taken a picture of Gabby standing under the shade of an oak tree with sun dappling her hair and the lush greenery bringing out the emerald of her eyes. She'd been laughing and blushing, reluctant to be his subject, and he'd been smitten. It was one of his favorite pictures of her, even though it was a bit out of focus and the exposure was too high, maybe because it had been so natural and easy to make her smile and because that photo was the start of something he loved.

Here he was again, meeting Gabby on a pleasant spring day. They were almost twenty years older, but the anticipation to see her was as strong and bright as long-burning embers. He parked along the dirt shoulder, grabbed his camera from the bag on the passenger seat, and hung the strap around his neck. At the last second, he tucked a water bottle in one pocket and a couple of granola bars in the other, just in case one of them got hungry on the hike.

Gabby pulled up behind him, and Jake's heart leaped. She got out of the car, shrugging into a denim jacket as she did. Her eyes were hidden behind sunglasses, her gorgeous hair in a ponytail and tucked under a Red Sox ball cap. Damn, she was beautiful, in jeans or in a dress, or anything at all.

"I think this is the longest we've gone without seeing each other, or at least running into each other at your grandmother's," he said as he walked toward her. "The store must be..."

His voice trailed off as she leaned against her car and crossed her arms over her chest instead of walking toward him. "You'll never guess who's back in town," she said.

Oh crap. She'd seen Brad. Why was Jake surprised? Someone so ambitious would certainly try one more time to land her heart. "My cousin."

"And apparently your coworker?" She arched a brow, then took a breath, and her eyes welled. "Why didn't you tell me, Jake?"

He sighed. Whatever answer he gave was not going to be enough. He'd kept a secret from Gabby, and the hurt in her face nearly undid him. "Because it was only supposed to be for a couple weeks. My dad had to have a stent put in his heart and take some time off to reduce his stress levels. He asked me to come in and oversee things for a bit. That's all."

"If it was no big deal, why not tell me?"

"Because..." He let out a long breath. It was a question he'd been asking himself all week. He'd told Gabby everything—almost everything—his entire life. Why had he left this one thing secret? "You were the one I called when I agonized over quitting the firm. You told me to stop putting myself in second place. You're the person who gave me the courage to quit. To tell you that I'd gone back there, even for a little while...made me feel like I was letting you down or disappointing you."

"If your dad's sick, why would I be upset or disappointed? I support you, Jake, in whatever you do, whether it's quitting or going back there or going into business for yourself." She toed at the ground, and when she spoke again, her voice sounded choked. "But for me to find out from Brad? I...I thought you and I were friends."

"We are. We were." He threw up his hands. He was beginning to hate the word *friend*. The last thing he wanted to hear was Gabby calling him that. He wanted more, much more. "Honestly, I don't know what we are."

"We're...complicated," she said.

The dark sunglasses hid her eyes and whatever was going on inside her head. It didn't matter because he knew how he felt, and it was way past time that Gabby knew, too. "There's nothing complicated about how I feel, Gabby, and there never has been. For years, I've known I wanted to spend the rest of my life with you because..." He shrugged and gave her a crooked smile. "Because I have been in love with you almost as long as I've known you, Gabby Monroe."

Her mouth opened. Closed. "You...love me?"

"I always have, Bella-Ella. I want to date you and see where this goes."

But she was already shaking her head and breaking his heart. "We'll ruin what we have if we do that."

"Who says we're going to ruin it? What if it becomes something even better?" Birds twittered in the trees, and cars whooshed past on the road, but he didn't notice or care. All he saw was the errant curl that had snuck out from the ball cap and the hurried tick of her pulse in the vein along the slender curve of her neck.

Jake closed the gap between them, cupped both sides of her face in his hands, and traced the outline of her lips with his thumb. She took in a sharp breath. As his finger drifted across her mouth, he felt her tremble. "I have missed this mouth."

"Jake...I..." Her voice trailed off, and all that was between them was the hurried pace of their breath. "I've missed you too, but—"

"I've missed listening to your voice. Hearing your laugh. And most of all, I've missed touching you. And I could be wrong, but it sure felt like you enjoyed kissing me as much as I enjoyed kissing you." He might be an idiot about a lot of things, but he was not an idiot about the way she had responded to his touch.

She shifted closer, as if her body was overriding her

words. A smile played at the edge of her lips. "I didn't enjoy it one bit."

He grinned. "Oh yeah? Prove it."

Amusement flitted across her features. "You want me to prove how much I don't enjoy kissing you by—"

"Kissing me again. Yes, that's exactly what I want."

"That's a crazy idea."

"I think we should settle this once and for all. Don't you?"

"You want me to prove that I can resist your charms? Fine. I will." She rose on her toes and leaned in to him.

Gabby's lips met his, a quick peck, but before she could break away, he wrapped one arm around the small of her back and drew her closer. She let out a little *oomph* of surprise and then stared up at him. "What are you doing?"

"Testing my hypothesis. The right way." He kissed her then, kissed her the way he'd always dreamed of kissing her, long and deep and slow. She tasted of coffee and chocolate and everything he loved. He could take a million photos and not a single one would capture this magical feeling of being with her, like he'd settled on top of a cloud. Yes, he loved her. Always had, and damn it all, always would.

A second later, she put up her hands and pushed him away. A chill filled the space between them, like a winter wind kicking up and scattering the first spring flowers. Everything seemed to slow down and go quiet, from the traffic to the birds. The world that had seemed so green and bright earlier today dimmed into shades of gray.

"No, Jake. We can't do this. We're better off as friends. Then no one gets hurt. I'm sorry."

There was that damnable word again. *Friends.* Hot, searing pain rushed through his veins and into his heart.

His voice left him, stuck behind an enormous lump in his throat. *This is what heartbreak feels like*, he thought. *Like dying, only slower and more painful.* "Are you saying you don't care about me?"

"I do, I really do. And despite what I said, I really love kissing you and every moment of whatever this is. But..." She bit her lower lip and looked away. "No one gets a happy ending. That's just not how it works."

"Of course it does. Look at Margaret. She's been happily married for what...ten years now? And your parents—your grandmother has told me dozens of stories about how happy they were before your mom died, which I believe, just from the little bit of time I knew your mother."

"My sister is talking about getting separated, and my parents.... they weren't the partners everyone thinks they were. Or at least, my dad wasn't." She drew her arms tighter around her body and seemed to shrink against the car. "My parents have always been this perfect image of a tragic true love story, and I'm sure my mother loved Dad like crazy, but I don't think he loved her back."

Impossible. Jake had met Davis dozens of times over the years, and never for a second did he doubt that man had loved his late wife. "I've heard your dad talk about your mom, and I've seen them together. They loved each other. In fact, I've always envied what they had. My parents never once looked at each other the way your parents did."

"Then why did my dad move on to someone else just a week after my mother died?" She swiped at a tear that had escaped from below her sunglasses. "Maybe they did love each other once, but that kind of love doesn't last, Jake. It's like a snowflake. The minute it hits solid ground—or some kind of tough time—it evaporates."

Her voice cracked, and in that sound of vulnerability, he saw the Gabby he knew. The woman who had been so tough and strong for everyone else, even at the expense of her own life. He wished she could see what he did, feel the rightness of them together, know that he would go to his grave before he would break her heart. "You're afraid. I get that. I spent most of my life being afraid of not fitting in, or being rejected, or not being enough. I used all those surgeries and the braces as an excuse, a way to stay in my shy little corner and not get hurt. You know who brought me out of my shell and made me take a risk? You, Gabby. You. And I don't think you did that just because we're friends." He cursed under his breath. She hadn't budged, but he wasn't going to stand here and beg her to love him. Either she was going to take the leap or she wasn't. "Do you really think I would ever hurt you? That I would ever stop loving you? Because I can't. Loving you is all I know how to do. But it's up to you, Gabby, to let go, and trust that I'm going to catch you when you fall."

"I'm not like you, Jake." Another tear slid down her cheek, but she didn't wipe it away. "I can't just believe in the fairy tale."

"I'm not offering you a fairy tale, Gabby. I'm offering you real, honest love, with laughter and tears and all of the messiness in between. Either you're going to take that risk or you're not. I can't decide that for you."

Instead of torturing himself more and hoping for an answer that Gabby wasn't going to give, Jake turned and headed for the path leading into the park, his camera like a lead weight around his neck. It took everything he had not to turn around and see if she was watching him leave. He swore it was a long time before he heard the soft latch of her car door closing.

TWENTY

Gabby knew before she walked in the house. There was a silence over the Bayberry Lane Victorian that seemed heavy and ominous. A million times she had walked into Grandma's house to the scent of baking bread or simmering stew, and a happy, warm vibe. Today, there were no home-baked scents, no seventies music on the radio, and especially telling, no warm greeting.

"Grandma? We came by to say hi." Gabby glanced at Emma. Her little sister shrugged as if to say she had no idea what was up, either.

"I'm in the kitchen," Grandma said.

The girls walked down the hall, their steps echoing against the hardwood floors. Everything was in its place—pillows on the sofa, photo frames marching along the piano, carpets striped with fresh vacuuming lines. Grandma was sitting at the round maple table in her bright yellow kitchen, clutching a mug of hot tea. When the girls entered the room, she merely nodded in greeting.

Emma slid into the opposite chair. "Are you okay, Grandma? What's wrong?"

"I'm perfectly fine." She cupped the mug in her hands and eyed each of her granddaughters in turn. "What I'd like to know is what is going on with the two of you."

Gabby's stomach dropped, and the sense of foreboding multiplied. "We're fine. There's nothing—"

"You're fine? I'm glad to hear that, because you know who's not fine? Harry Erlich." Grandma took a sip of her tea, something she often did while she measured her words. Gabby had learned from experience and dozens of lectures at this very table to wait and let Grandma say her piece. "Harry came to me this morning and said he'd had the oddest encounter at Margaret's booth at the tricentennial event. He said his son and his grandson were there, and that you tried to convince the three of them to talk."

"Oh, well, we just ran into them." Maybe if Gabby kept pretending it was all a happy accident, Grandma would believe it, too. Under the table, Emma gave Gabby's hand a squeeze. "Just a coincidence."

"Do not lie to me, Gabriella." Grandma's features were stern and stony. "How exactly do you know about Harry's grandson?"

"He mentioned him at dinner," Emma said. "Last Wednesday. Remember, Gabs?"

"Yup. I heard that, too."

"But he didn't mention that the relationship with Roger was strained or that his son hadn't talked to Chad in a few years. All of a sudden, a few days after a man who sounds a lot like Harry Erlich sends a letter in to Dear Amelia, you two are moving mountains to bring them all together." Grandma leaned forward, her piercing gaze landing on each of the girls in turn. "What else did you three find in the attic when you were up there looking for your mother's wedding dress?"

Gabby swallowed hard. *Uh-oh.* As she had done dozens of times when the girls were little, Grandma was asking a question she already knew the answer to. There was no sense in lying or pretending. Her face heated, and her stomach twisted. "We...we found the columns, and we put it together that you must be writing them, and you've been really down lately, so we thought maybe if your advice could end well, you'd be happier." The words tumbled out of her in a rush.

Grandma sipped her tea some more. The girls waited while the kitchen clock ticked one slow minute after another. "So you gave Antonia a gift card that you said she won." She looked at Gabby before turning to Emma. "And you babysat Alex so they could go on a date?"

The girls nodded. "We did."

Grandma leveled her gaze on Gabby. "And then you set up Frank with Sandy at the restaurant, making them think it was just a double date with you and Jake?"

"But they worked out great," Gabby said. "They're still dating and seem super happy."

Grandma kept talking, undeterred by the optimistic tone in Gabby's voice. "Then, as if all that wasn't enough, you felt the need to interfere in Harry's life. And in the process, make everything worse."

Gabby had told herself on Saturday that everything would turn out okay. That Harry would talk some sense into his son and somehow mend the rift. She hadn't wanted to accept that Roger storming off meant the plan had gone completely awry or that bringing the three of them together in a surprise meeting had only compounded the friction in the Erlich family. "Worse?"

Grandma's nod was short and serious. "When Roger refused to talk to Chad, Harry was left in the awful position of consoling a grandson who was heartbroken." She unfolded that week's issue of the *Gazette*, already open to the Dear Amelia column. Right there in black and white was the letter from Concerned Grandpa and Dear Amelia's advice. Gabby tried to read her grandmother's response, but the print was too small and the paper too far away. "I admit it took me a minute to figure out how this all happened. When Harry came to me this morning, devastated by what happened on Saturday, I couldn't figure out why you and your sisters would be involved in his family affairs. Sandy has been talking about that double date every time I see her and how Frank had been so desperately lonely that he wrote to a paper for advice. Then as I went to get the mail, I ran into Antonia outside. She mentioned how helpful the two of you were in giving her and Luis a chance to rekindle their love."

"She just seemed so stressed with the baby and—"

"Do not mistake me for a fool, Gabriella." Grandma rarely got angry. In fact, Gabby could count on one hand the number of times her grandmother had even raised her voice. From the quiet, even tone of Grandma's words, Gabby knew she wasn't just angry—she was furious.

"We were just trying to help," Gabby said, rushing to explain, to smooth the waters, while Emma sat beside her, silent and contrite. "You've been so sad lately, and—"

"I do not need your help or your interference." Grandma shook her head. "I can't believe the two of you meddled like that."

"We meant well," Emma said. "We really did."

"And we can fix it," Gabby said. "We'll talk to Roger and Chad—"

"You will do no such thing." Grandma shook the paper in their direction. The black-and-white image of Amelia seemed to shiver with anger. "These are not games to play, Gabriella and Emma. These are people's lives. I take my responsibility to answer their questions seriously. I don't give flippant answers, nor do I force people to do what I think is right."

Forcing people to do what she thought they should do. Grandma's words echoed what Gabby's sisters had said to her the other day about deciding Jake's future for him. She'd had the best of intentions and only wanted to make things better for everyone, to avoid hurting him as much as she wanted to avoid being hurt herself. Why couldn't anyone see that? There had been no malice in anything she did. "I'm sorry, Grandma," Gabby said.

Beside her, Emma nodded. "Me too. We're really sorry. We didn't mean for anyone to get hurt."

But the mood in the room didn't change, and the tension didn't ease. Gabby had never known Grandma to hold a grudge or be angry longer than a few minutes. Judging by the tight lines in Grandma's face right now and the stubborn set to her shoulders, this wasn't something that would simply blow over and everything would be okay again. The thought of her grandmother being angry or disappointed in her caused a lump in Gabby's throat. Tears filled her eyes. "I was trying to do the right thing, Grandma, to take care of everyone and make sure they were happy."

"That's not your job, Gabby. It never was." Grandma got to her feet, turned to the sink, and dumped the rest of her tea down the drain. "Now if you girls will excuse me, I have other things to do today, and I don't need any advice on how to do them."

The bright sunshine outside the *Gazette* office seemed like a wash of white over a world that was still a lot more gray than green. Another week or so and Harbor Cove would be transformed by crocuses and daffodils and the beginnings of hardy tulips. The lawns would begin to come back to life, and trees would thicken with new leaves. Normally, Jake loved this time of year, so full of colors and possibilities, but after the sorta-breakup with Gabby at the park, he'd been far more blue than springlike. He'd finished his time at the law office, now that his father had returned to work full-time and Brad was back in town, and Jake had gone back to spending his days at the *Gazette*. Normally he'd be happy as hell to be sitting at his desk, surrounded by piles of work, but ever since he'd arrived, he'd barely been able to concentrate.

Until the mail arrived at the office this afternoon and a flat envelope with the return address for *Vista* magazine sat on top of the stack. It took a solid five minutes for Jake to open the envelope and another minute for him to believe what he was seeing. Jake stared at the paper in his hands for a long time. *Finalist*. The word stared back at him, shiny and gold against the certificate that had arrived in his mail along with two guest tickets to the awards ceremony.

Finalist.

If there could be a validation that he was making the right decision, this was it. He didn't have to win to know he could make his photography business work. He just needed a thumbs-up from his peers, and this slim piece of paper was it. He felt prouder of this certificate than he ever had of his law degree because this was proof that something he loved was worth the time and energy he'd put into it. That his hobby could be a profession.

Jake took a picture of the certificate and then sent a text to his father. *Awards ceremony is Friday night in Boston at the Park Plaza. I'll leave a ticket for you at the door.*

There was no response. Jake hadn't really expected one. He had, after all, basically told his father that Brad was stealing, and Brad had undoubtedly called Jake a liar. If there was a son to be chosen, whether biological or replacement, Jake had no doubt that his father would side with Brad.

He stared at the second ticket. There was only one other person in the world he wanted to give that to, but he was 99 percent positive she wouldn't accept it or show up. He tucked it in his pocket anyway.

He rapped on the edge of Leroy's office door. "I'm heading out for lunch. You want anything?"

"One of those pastrami sandwiches from Earl's." Leroy fished out some money and handed it to Jake. "My wife is gonna kill me. I'm supposed to be watching my waistline, but damn, Earl's cooking gets me every time."

"Hey, you doing anything Friday night?" Jake asked.

"Is this a date? Because I'm already married." Leroy chuckled. "What's up?"

Jake pulled the certificate out of his inside jacket pocket and dangled it in front of Leroy. "You were right."

"Hot damn! That's awesome, Jake! And I'm not one bit surprised." Leroy rose and clapped Jake on the shoulder. "Congratulations, man."

"Thanks." Jake stood there a second, feeling awkward

and oddly embarrassed. "Anyway, they gave me two guest tickets, and I was wondering if you wanted to come to the awards ceremony. Not that I'm going to win or anything, but you can at least score some free food and drinks."

"I can't, man. I wish I could. It's my anniversary, and the wife and I already booked a B and B in Vermont for the weekend." Leroy cursed. "You know I'd be there otherwise."

"Yeah, yeah, no problem. I'll try to smuggle out a piece of prime rib and bring it back for you. I'll go grab the sandwiches." As he headed out into the sunshine, Jake's phone dinged, and he scrambled to dig it out of his pocket. The insane optimistic side of him was hoping it was a text from Gabby, but it was only a single word from his father. *Okay.*

Not *Congrats* or *I'll be there*, just a vague *okay*. Jake didn't know why he even bothered to hope for change. Edward Maddox was set in his ways and his opinions. Stubborn as a mule in a puddle of glue, Grandma El would say. Every day, Jake told himself that whatever happened at Maddox & Maddox wasn't his fault. That he'd done his best and sounded the alarm bells.

Yet a nagging sense of guilt hung in the background. If the firm his father had worked his whole life to build went under, it would break Edward's heart. He might not have been the best parent, but he was a damned good lawyer who had busted his back to get where he was.

And that meant Jake had to try one more time.

Instead of turning left and going to Earl's, Jake turned right, betting on a hunch that turned out to be spot-on. He found Brad sitting at a corner booth in Bella Vita, enjoying a bottle of wine and a plate of veal parmigiana. When Brad had worked in the Harbor Cove office, he'd come here nearly every day, and Jake figured if his underhanded actions hadn't changed, neither had his eating habits. The restaurant hummed with activity, but Jake's cousin was eating alone, flitting between his MacBook and his phone as he sipped wine and picked at his lunch.

"Let me guess: You're going to claim the wine as a write-off, too?" Jake said as he slipped into the opposite seat.

Brad glanced up, irritation clear in his features. "What are you doing here?"

"You and I need to have a conversation." Jake folded his hands on the table and relaxed the set of his shoulders. Everything inside him wanted to shake some sense into his cousin, but he already knew that wouldn't work.

"If this is about Gabriella, don't bother. She's ancient history." Brad's attention returned to his computer.

The cousin Jake had once idolized had grown up to be a self-centered man who wore custom suits and expensive shoes. A man who cared more about what he drove than what he did to the people around him. For years, Jake had tried to give Brad the benefit of the doubt, but there was no doubt in the numbers Jake had seen. Brad had hurt two people Jake cared deeply about, and that was two too many. "This is about the money you're stealing from my father."

Brad's gaze snapped to Jake's. His brown eyes darkened. "I'm not stealing anything."

"I saw the books, Brad. I know you've been skimming the profits and reinvesting them in a corporation you own. I have to admit, you were pretty clever at first, but lately, you got cocky and careless."

"I have no idea what you're talking about." Brad's voice was a sharp hiss as he lowered it to a whisper.

"And neither do you. You spend, what, a handful of days behind Edward's desk and think you know everything? Hell, you were barely in that office long enough to get a cup of coffee."

Jake was undeterred. It had taken some digging into corporate records to find the links, but once he had, the nefarious path Brad had taken was clear as day. "You made it look like the construction costs ran over. I even saw a few emails to my dad, saying the contractors were charging rush fees. Yet when I went back and looked at the permits and billing, there were no rush charges. Except the ones you paid to a company that turned out to be owned by you."

Brad shrugged. "It was nothing more than my skin in the game. I invested as well. Because I believe in and support your father."

"You got away with that story for a year," Jake said, still calm and collected on the outside, but inside feeling more like a guard dog warning an intruder to stay away from his family. "There were three different office renos and new builds that ran way over the budget. My dad bought your lies every time, even complimenting you for being on top of what was happening and holding the contractors' feet to the fire. Then came the Concord office, which was where you took a lot more than just a few grand here and there. The original bids for the remodel came in at just under a million. Yet Maddox & Maddox paid one point five million. Where'd the extra five hundred thousand go, Brad?"

"You don't know what you're talking about." His cousin's words were all bravado. Genuine fear showed in his eyes and in the way his hand shook against the keyboard of his computer.

Jake leaned forward and fixed Brad with a heavy stare. "I'm here to tell you if you ever steal from my father again, I will personally hunt you down and expose you to the world for the cheating fraud you are."

"Stay out of things that don't have anything to do with you, Jake." Brad's gaze narrowed, and a sneer turned up one side of his mouth. "You couldn't close the deal with Gabriella, and now, because you're jealous that I went out with her, you've got some petty revenge thing you're trying to pull off. You won't win the girl by smearing me with mud. Besides, she doesn't want some weak man who couldn't make it in the law."

The words had no impact on Jake. The days when he looked up to his cousin were far in the past. Jake had carved out his own corner of the world and didn't care if Brad or his father or anyone else approved. He got to his feet and took one step before turning back. "Oh yeah, that reminds me. Only a weak loser breaks up with a woman by text. She deserves better than you."

Brad arched a brow. "And what, you think you're the better choice for her?"

"When it comes to Gabby Monroe, Brad, you don't get to know what I'm thinking. Stay out of her life, stay out of mine, and stay out of my father's wallet."

Brad sputtered a reply, but Jake didn't bother to stay and hear it. He strode through the restaurant and out to the parking lot. His father might not believe Brad was stealing from the company, but Brad knew that Jake was watching him now, and any misstep would be noticed. By exposing Brad's scheme, Jake had hopefully stopped the cash drain.

As he started to cross the street, he heard someone calling his name. Frank came running out of Bella Vita still wearing his apron from the kitchen, his gray hair a wild mess. He was a passionate guy, about everything from his food to his friends, and it showed in his hurried dash to give Jake a quick hug. "Jake! I wanted to talk to you, my friend."

"Afternoon, Frank. Nice to see business is doing well." The last few times Jake had walked past Bella Vita, the parking lot had been full, which was a great change to see after hearing how Frank had been struggling.

"Between Sandy's ideas and your designs, my ads bring in twice the business now. You are amazing, and I am grateful for your patience with this old donkey learning some new tricks." Frank leaned in and elbowed Jake in the side. "And how is that beautiful girl of yours?"

"That's...complicated." She wasn't his, not even close, and didn't want to be, but Jake was in no mood to explain that to Frank or to anyone, much less himself.

"Love, my friend, is not complicated at all. If she doesn't see how smart you are, then use those smarts"— Frank tapped Jake on the temple—"and create an ad campaign she can't resist."

Jake laughed. "I'm pretty sure I can't run something like that in the paper."

Frank rolled his eyes. "You young kids. So literal. I meant in real life. In my day, a man sent a woman flowers, brought her candy, took her out to a nice restaurant."

If flowers and candy were the way to Gabby's heart, Jake would have won her over years ago. He couldn't change the fact that she hadn't fallen in love with him, no matter how many daisies he bought. "Like I said, Frank, it's complicated. Thank you for the advice. I'll give it some thought."

"That girl, I see how she looks at you," Frank said.

"In her eyes is the truth. You look, and you'll see it, too, my friend."

Jake responded with something vague and then headed off to Earl's to pick up Leroy's sandwich. His own appetite had disappeared, and the bright day no longer seemed full of promise. The hardest part of finding out Gabby didn't feel the same way about him, Jake realized, wasn't hearing her say those words.

It was accepting them as truth.

TWENTY-ONE

The next morning, Gabby struggled to get her act together. All she wanted to do was linger in bed and forget everything that had happened over the last month, all the things that had gone wrong or simply broken apart. That day in the attic with her sisters had seemed so promising, like a start to making everything wonderful again. They'd been united in a common goal, just as Gabby had wanted, and then it all...

Went sideways. Their good intentions had worked at first, but the more they meddled, as Grandma called it, the worse things got. Maybe someone who had screwed up her own life and closest bonds shouldn't be trying to give advice to other people, Gabby thought. Because she sure wasn't an expert in anything anymore.

Every day that went by without a text or call from Jake felt emptier than the day before. This silence and distance were what she'd thought she'd wanted when she'd rebuffed him at the park and told him to go back to being just friends, and it was what was right for both of them because they'd never work in a relationship. She kept telling herself that, even as the decision felt more wrong by the hour.

You're afraid, he'd said. Hell yes, she was afraid. Jake had been her best friend for as long as she could remember, and the last thing she'd wanted to do was lose that. Once again, in her effort to do the right thing, she'd screwed it all up. Now Jake wasn't talking to her, Grandma wasn't talking to her, her business was barely hanging on, and both her sisters had gotten distant.

Another bang-up job by Gabby Monroe.

A photo of her mother sat on Gabby's dresser, seeming to accuse her of messing up the very family she'd promised to protect. *I'm sorry, Momma. I'm so sorry.*

There was no answer from the picture. No words of wisdom or hugs of support. All those things she had missed in the decades since her mother had died. What would Momma have done right now?

Gabby honestly had no idea. All she had were snippets of memories: a Christmas morning here, a bedtime story there, a few dresses, and a lot of laughter. Every single day, there had been laughter in the Monroe house, like an endless stream running through all of them.

Momma had been the kind of mother who made animal-shaped pancakes. Who decorated their bedrooms on birthday eves. Who commemorated every event with a picture and a special dessert. She had created moments for each of them, but as the years passed, Gabby's memories began to fade, and all those special times drifted out of her mind because she had yet to find a way to hold tight to those amazing minutes and hours.

She picked up the picture and held it tightly to her

chest while tears streamed down her face, and her heart hurt in a way it hadn't since her mother had died. Regrets and guilt weighed her down, a load that she swore she'd never be able to shed.

Gabby wandered through her little house, passing dozens of mementos from her mother. After the girls grew up, Grandma had given each of them a little something of their mother's. Margaret got the hutch full of the wedding china, Emma got the hope chest, and Gabby got Momma's collection of glass animals and a box of her clothes. She touched each of the little animals in turn, their tiny translucent bodies so delicate that a strong wind could destroy them all.

On the kitchen table, she noticed the envelope Emma had given her after the day in the attic. Gabby had forgotten all about the set of pictures Emma had printed and her sister said Dad wanted to see. She opened the envelope, and a dozen photos spilled out: The girls, hosting the tea parties Margaret had forgotten, with the place mats and napkins that Momma made and Emma had remembered. Her beautiful mother in a red swing dress and heels, with her head thrown back and laughter spilling out of her. Another in a sunshine-yellow sundress with white sandals. A third in a long navy dress, her hair in an elegant bun and sparkly earrings dangling from her ears.

An image of Momma at the dining room table in Grandma's house, a bolt of fabric draped down the long surface and a pile of paper cutouts pinned to each section of the dark green material. A sewing machine sat at the opposite end of the table.

Gabby traced the outline of her mother, the look of concentration on her face. She'd been caught midcut with the scissors in her right hand and the velvety fabric in her left. Momma used to sew every weekend, making all the girls matching outfits every Christmas and Easter and dozens of dresses of her own that she'd created over the years. Every single one of them was as beautiful and unique as Momma herself.

Oh, how she missed her mother, and the sound of her voice as she sang along with the radio while she did the dishes or put the girls to bed. Things had been simpler then, nicer, sweeter. Momma and Dad had been so happy, like the kind of couple you read about in novels, and everyone had believed in forever. Once upon a time, Gabby had thought she could find that same kind of happiness.

Now, not so much.

When her phone rang, Gabby rushed to answer it, which told her pretty much all she needed to know— and was denying—about how much she was still thinking about Jake. That, and the stone of disappointment in her gut when she realized it was her father, not Jake, who was calling.

"Hi, Dad. What's up?" She forced brightness into her voice that she didn't feel.

"Would you like to meet me for a cup of coffee before you open the shop?"

He was asking to see her? Spend time with her? Gabby checked the phone's screen again. Yup, that was her father's name. "Uh, sure. Give me fifteen minutes."

"Thank you, Gabby. See you then."

Gabby threw on some clothes, dragged a brush through her hair, and did minimal makeup. She hurried out the door toward the little coffee shop down the street from the store. Just a few weeks ago, she'd been sitting here with Jake, where he'd ordered her favorite coffee and had it waiting, a thoughtful gesture that she missed in a way she didn't expect.

Loving you is all I know how to do. But it's up to you, Gabby, to let go, and trust that I'm going to catch you when you fall.

But what if she opened her heart to him, and five years down the road they stopped loving each other? Or he found someone else? What if their relationship burned hot and then disintegrated? If anything reminded her that could happen, it was the sight of her father at a table in the coffee shop.

He looked nervous, if that was possible, because Gabby could never remember seeing her father nervous. "Hi, Dad."

His chair screeched as he got to his feet. "Hi, honey. Uh, can I get you a coffee?"

"Janie knows what I like." Gabby nodded toward the barista, who gave her a thumbs-up. "Did you want to talk about Grandma or..." She literally couldn't think of another topic to discuss with her father.

"I just wanted to talk to you." There was a moment of awkward silence with only the hiss of the milk being steamed in the background. Then Dad cleared his throat. "Listen, I know you're mad at me. You have every right to be. I checked out after your mother died and left the burden of raising you girls on Eleanor's shoulders."

She scoffed. "Burden? Is that how you look at us? We're your *daughters*, Dad."

"No, no, I didn't mean it that way." He ran a hand through his hair and let out a long breath. "I'm sorry. It was the wrong word to choose. I'm not good at this kind of thing, Gabby."

She could see the lines in her father's face, the

thinning along his hairline. Dad had aged, and it came almost as a surprise. For some reason, in her head, he was perpetually in his thirties, caught in a time warp from the day Momma died.

"I should get to work," she said, and started to slip off of the stool.

"Gabby, please. I'm trying."

All the resentment that had simmered inside her for two decades came rushing to the surface and hardened her words. "It's a little late, Dad, don't you think? I'm all grown up."

"Are you saying you don't need a father anymore?"

She thought of seeing his arm draped over his young son's shoulders, of the envy she had felt, and the irrational craving for the same kind of easygoing parental love. "You're already someone else's father," she said.

"That doesn't mean I love you less, Gabriella. Or your sisters. Or your mother."

"Really? Because I saw you, Dad. I saw you with Joanna. She was in Momma's kitchen, wearing Momma's apron, and hugging you. Momma had only been gone a *week*, Dad. How could you move on so quickly?"

"That wasn't what you thought. After your mother died, I was..." His gaze shifted to some point far in the distance. "I was so lost, I could barely function. I didn't know how to live without her, Gabby. I didn't want to, either. I got into a pit of alcohol and pills and deep, deep depression. For a while there, I considered... ending the pain. It was so selfish, but I was hurting so much, all I wanted to do was die."

"You..." She gasped. The thought of losing her father, too, nearly broke her heart. "I had no idea. Why didn't you tell us you were thinking about suicide, Dad?"

"You were eight, honey. That's too big a burden to put on a child."

"Still…" She raised her gaze to his. "I'm so glad you didn't."

"Me too." He smiled at her for a moment. "I knew I couldn't do that to you girls, but I also knew I had to find a way to get myself out of bed every morning. To remember to breathe. Then Joanna came by one day with a casserole. I was a mess. I don't think I'd showered all week, and I hadn't been eating or sleeping at all. She took one look at me and told me to sit down, and she'd take care of everything."

Gabby scoffed. "I bet she did," she muttered.

"It was never like that. We were friends for a long time, your mother and I, with Joanna. That day Joanna got me to eat. To shower. To do something other than sit on the couch and cry." Dad reached for Gabby's hand and held it tight. "Your mother was the love of my life, Gabby. She was light and beauty and—"

"Magic."

A soft smile curved across her father's face. "Exactly. I never wanted to replace her, and I know I never can. Joanna was just a friend for a long, long time. Then one day it became something more, and I decided to open my heart again. She's always known that I still love your mother and I always will."

Gabby looked away, just as Janie came by with Gabby's mocha and Dad's plain coffee. It was a welcome break, and as much as Gabby wanted to run out the door and not have this conversation, she thought of the hundreds of regrets she'd woken up with this morning. If she had a chance to make everything right, some way of showing her family how much she loved them, she knew she would take it. Maybe Dad was looking for the same thing. "And you're happy with Joanna?"

"I've learned to be. For a long time, I felt guilty for even caring about another woman. Penny was... irreplaceable." He held on to the mug's handle but didn't drink. "Did I ever tell you the story of how your mother and I met?"

She nodded. "Momma told me."

"Ah, but she told you her version. Mine is different." The clouds in her father's eyes seemed to clear, and his features brightened at the thought of his late wife. "She was the prettiest girl in all of Harbor Cove, I'll tell you that. I was heading into high school, first day in a new school, new town, and I was nervous as hell. Your mother had been assigned to help the new kid find his way around. It was some kind of Key Club thing or something."

"Honor Society," Gabby corrected.

"You're right; I'd forgotten that detail. She was the smart one, wasn't she?" He shook his head, a smile playing on his lips. "Well, she showed me around, but she had a little fun with the new kid, too. She kept telling me that there was an elevator, and it led to the pool on the roof of the school, but freshmen weren't allowed up there."

Gabby sipped at her mocha and gave her father a curious look. "But there's no pool on the roof of Harbor Cove High."

"I didn't know that then because I was new and clueless, but she had me convinced that it existed and that she had been up there many times, even though she was a freshman, too. I wanted to know what it was about this girl that made her so cool that she had been invited up there and could describe this secret place in so much detail." He ran a finger around the rim of the coffee mug, his gaze focused on some faraway moment in the past. "She fascinated me, your mother."

"She was amazing, wasn't she?"

Her father's blue eyes met hers, and he nodded. She could see the shimmer of tears, the bittersweet mix of heartache and love. "Exactly. A true one of a kind, until she had three daughters who turned out a lot like her."

There, in her father's face, was the Dad who had built forts under the dining room table and scooped up his girls every time he got home from work. The Dad who had praised every scribble and read them bedtime stories and told dumb jokes at the dinner table. The Dad she had missed every single day since that stormy night.

"So what happened?" Hearing a new version of a story she'd heard a hundred times was as close to being with Momma as she could get, and today, of all days, Gabby so wished her mother were here to counsel her, hug her, and just love her.

"Well, I didn't want to look like the dumb new kid," Dad said, "so I didn't ask anyone about the pool. I figured if I just stuck with her, she'd eventually get me a pass or the secret code or whatever I needed. I was like a little puppy, following her around every chance I got. We had a couple classes together and a study hall. Within a month, we were pretty much inseparable."

"Like Jake and I," Gabby whispered.

"Yeah, exactly. He's a good kid, that Jake. Reminds me of myself when I was his age."

Would Jake build forts and make dorky jokes with their kids? Would he walk in at the end of the day, a sunburst of joy on his face at being reunited with his favorite girls? "Tell me more about Momma, Dad."

"Well, after a month, I finally got the courage to ask

her out. I took her to the movies. We saw *Big*, you know, the one with Tom Hanks?"

"Yeah. That's a great movie."

"I barely saw it. I spent most of my time watching Penny react. Watching her laugh or smile, or tear up. She was fascinating." His voice caught on the last few syllables, but he cleared his throat. "Anyway, after the movie, we went and got an ice cream. I asked her, so where is this pool and how do I get to see it?"

"She laughed, and said there wasn't one," he went on. "I asked her why she made it up, and she said, and I'll never forget this, 'You were the cutest boy I'd ever seen, and I figured if I made it sound like I was cooler than you, you'd want to hang out with me.' That's the first time I kissed her."

"She never told me about the pool thing. Her version was that she met you and knew right away that you were the one, and that she couldn't wait for you to ask her out, so she dropped a hint one day in Algebra about how much she loved movies."

"Her version was more romantic than mine. You are so much like her, Gabby. So creative and talented."

"Thanks, Dad."

As her father told story after story about those years before the girls came along, she could feel the frayed bonds between them begin to slowly knit back together. It was there all along, that love, buried under decades of grief and misunderstanding. All these years, she had faulted her father for seeking comfort after losing the light in his life. The girls had had Grandma to hug them tight and tell them it would be okay, to remind them that their mother would always be in their hearts. Dad hadn't had a Grandma waiting when he walked in the door at the end of a long, empty, dark day. He hadn't had a person who could hug him and ease a pain that would never completely go away. How could she fault him for one hug? For needing to lean on someone else's shoulders, just as she had with her grandmother and Jake?

Her father took a long sip of coffee. "They have a good brew here."

"Their brownies are even better. Don't tell Grandma, but I think they're better than hers."

"Want to split one with me? Make it a bad breakfast?"

The words echoed off a memory of early-morning laughter and a sunny kitchen. "Didn't we do that when I was a kid? Eat dessert for breakfast?"

"Yup. On Saturdays, your mom liked to sleep in. I admit, I am clueless in the kitchen, so I gave you guys cookies and brownies. She called it bad breakfast, and the name stuck. Of course, I always paid for it later because you three were all buzzing from the sugar, but it was fun." He chuckled.

And then she could see it in her head, her father at the kitchen table, one of the girls on his knee while he doled out cookies or brownies and they dunked them in milk. She could see Margaret laughing, a milk ring around her lips, and Dad tapping her on the nose. "I remember."

"I'm glad, because there are so many good memories from those years." He let out a long breath. "I should have kept doing that after she was gone. But it was just…so hard. Nothing was the same without her. She was magic, like you said, and I couldn't seem to find my way out of the darkness. Eleanor was so good, and helped so much, and I let her. Instead of being the father I should have been. I'm sorry, Gabby."

"You did other things so you didn't have to deal with

your feelings." Like bury himself in work or avoid the people he was close to. Seemed she took after her father in some ways, too. "I get that, Dad. A lot."

"Well, I'm a guy. We make avoiding our feelings into an art form." He cracked a smile. "So tell me about the shop. How's it going?"

They slipped into some small talk, falling into a natural conversational pattern as easily as picking up a loose thread in an old sweater. She promised to drop off a set of the photos at her father's office the next week, and they made plans for another bad breakfast next weekend. After her coffee had gone cold, Gabby glanced at her watch. "Oh, it's late. I have to get to work, Dad."

"Of course. Go ahead and leave. I'll take care of the tab."

She pulled on her coat and got to her feet. Just as she took a step, Gabby turned back to him. In the relaxed features she saw now, she could see the father she remembered on Saturday mornings, the man who had looked at Momma with more love than Gabby thought a person could have for another. "Can I ask you something, Dad?"

Happiness lit his face. "Absolutely. Anything."

"How did you know?" She fiddled with the zipper on her jacket and tried to put words to something she had done her best not to think about. "I feel like I don't have answers to anything. What I want to do with my life, what I should do, or who I should be with."

He paused for a moment, considering his answer. "Nobody has all the answers. Some of us are still trying to figure out how to have relationships with our kids when we're in our fifties. But I will tell you this, something your grandmother said to me when I graduated high school and I was thinking of running off and being a roadie for a band my friends had started."

"You. A roadie?" She laughed at the image of her father with long hair, jeans, and a tie-dye shirt, hefting speakers on his shoulder. "Dad, you're a suit-and-tie guy."

"Hey, I was cool for a minute back in high school." He chuckled. "Eleanor has always been the voice of wisdom, you know? The one everyone should listen to."

"Yeah, definitely." Grandma had been the voice of wisdom for more than just their family. She'd done it for this entire town, for people Gabby loved and cared about. Until Gabby had gotten in the middle of it all and muddied the waters for Harry, Roger, and Chad.

"She said to me, 'Davis, there are things that matter in the moment, and then there are things that matter in our souls.' She told me I was looking at the next five minutes, not the next five years. 'Close your eyes,' she said. 'Imagine yourself five years from now. Do you want to be in some roadside motel cleaning up after some guy who thinks he's the next Mick Jagger, or do you want to be somewhere else?' Well, I thought about it, and I realized I wanted to be with your mother. I couldn't picture my life without her in it."

"Is that when you proposed to her?"

"No, that's when I got a job and went to college. So that I could be the man your mother saw when she looked at me, a man who went after what he wanted instead of taking the easy road. She always saw the best in everybody."

"But how did you know banking was your thing?"

"Because whenever I sat down and got immersed in numbers, the world dropped away. Except for when I was with Penny, nothing else did that for me. It was the right thing for my soul." He leaned in, lowered his voice, and gave her a conspiratorial wink. "And if you tell Eleanor that she was right, I'm never buying you another brownie again."

Gabby laughed. "And it was the same with Momma?"

He nodded. "Whenever I was with her, nothing else in the world mattered. Everything was prettier and brighter and happier. I still love her, Gabby. I will love her until the day I die. Just because I have another life doesn't mean I don't grieve the one I lost every day. Every single damned day."

"Me too, Dad. I miss her so much, and I've missed you, too. I do need my dad."

He scrambled to his feet and gathered her into a tight, warm hug. "Oh, honey, I've missed my little girl, too."

She closed her eyes and held her daddy and forgave everything. They both cried a little, and in the space of that tight hug, she swore she could feel her mother's arms around the both of them. And for just a second, she had everything she'd been missing for so long.

It wasn't until Gabby got home that night, after a long day at work and a lot of thinking, that she saw the envelope tucked under the door, inscribed with handwriting she knew as well as her own.

TWENTY-TWO

This time, the tie didn't feel like it was strangling him. Nevertheless, Jake adjusted it at least a dozen times before walking into the ballroom. Alone. He'd driven to the Park Plaza hotel, splurged on valet parking, and then stopped at the bar to order a beer that he barely touched while he waited for them to open the doors for the awards ceremony. Nope, he wasn't nervous. Not one bit.

The ballroom was decorated with swaths of gold fabric draped from the ceiling and chandeliers, a nice offset to the dark crimson carpet and pale walls. The finalists' pictures had each been enlarged and mounted on easels ringing the room. Jake wandered down the aisle, admiring the artistry and creativity of the other finalists. Some of the photographers had amazing compositions or clever uses of lighting. As he had when he was younger and teaching himself how to take a great photo, he catalogued the information in his head, making mental notes for later.

For next time, he told himself. There was no way he

was going to win tonight, but the simple act of entering had opened a gate inside of Jake. His business cards sat in his wallet, just waiting to be handed out, a business on the cusp of being born.

He made small talk with some of the other photographers and their families, but as he made his way through the room, he noticed more and more that he seemed to be the only one here alone, without a spouse or a family member to cheer him on. Gabby would have come, at least the Gabby who had once been his friend, but—

He'd gone and destroyed that by telling her he was in love with her. His worst fears had come true, and he'd lost her not only as a girlfriend but also as the friend he treasured above all others. A friend who wasn't here, as much as he had hoped and prayed otherwise.

Jake accepted a glass of champagne from a passing waiter and made his way past several other tables before he reached the one he'd been assigned to and tried to pretend he didn't care that there would be two empty seats flanking his own. He sighed.

He was just introducing himself to the woman sitting across from him—who had brought her husband and her teenage daughter—when he heard a voice behind him. "Is this seat taken?"

Jake turned around and stopped cold. "Dad? What are you doing here?"

"I believe I was invited." Edward tick-tocked the ticket Jake had left at the will-call office. "Unless you changed your mind?"

"No, no, not at all. Please, sit down." Jake scrambled to his feet and pulled a chair out for his father. Edward sat, looking a little uncomfortable and stiff, but he was here, and that was enough for Jake.

Edward had worn a dark suit with a white shirt and navy tie, but there were shadows under his eyes and he seemed thinner than the last time Jake had seen him. The heart scare had definitely aged him. Jake wanted to ask about his health but knew his stubborn, proud father would say he was fine no matter what.

"I saw your picture," Dad said. "And, well, I might be biased, but I think it's the best one here. So...haunting."

The praise stunned Jake. He could count on one hand the number of times Edward Maddox had issued a compliment to anyone, never mind his own son. Maybe his health issues had softened him, or maybe he was finally beginning to see his son as something other than a disappointment. "Thank you. I...I didn't know you looked at mine."

His father shrugged, as if it were no big deal. "What made you take that particular photo? Everyone else seems to have bright fields or flowers or, hell, fruit. But yours was completely different, and yet beautiful. I'm impressed."

All his life, he had wished his father would notice him, see Jake for himself, not a mini replica of Edward. To see that Jake's passions and talents had as much value as his father's. To love his son without conditions. Here was that moment, finally. It was, without a doubt, sweet. Jake's throat was thick, and he was grateful when the awards ceremony began and he was saved from some blubbering, emotional answer.

The owner of the magazine, a slight man with a long nose and wide glasses, got up on the stage. "Welcome, everyone, to the fiftieth Vista Magazine Excellence in Photography Awards. This contest has been a wonderful opportunity for us to find and encourage new talent.

Every photographer sees the world a little differently, and what he or she brings us through that lens can change our perspectives on life. There's no greater gift than that. Now let's start awarding these artists for their hard work, because I want to get back to my dinner."

The crowd laughed, and the owner began reading off the winners, working his way from the bottom up, running through honorable mentions, then third place, second place. Each of the award-winning photos was featured on a floor-to-ceiling screen overlooking the ballroom.

Jake watched the others collect their prizes and make a small speech and had to admit he felt a fair amount of envy and disappointment that his name had not been called. But he had his father sitting beside him, and that was better than any prize he could take home.

"I know they say it's an honor to be nominated, but I think that's a load of bull," his father whispered in his ear, as if reading his mind.

Jake chuckled. "True. But for me, it is. I mean, I'm new to all this, and—"

"Don't doubt yourself, Jacob. You are smarter and more capable than you know."

Jake arched a brow. That was two compliments in a row tonight. "Are you feeling all right? Because you're being awfully nice to me."

"Must be the heart meds. Softened me up. Damned doctors." Edward turned his attention to his entrée, but there was a slight smile playing on his lips.

"Maybe you should double your dose," Jake quipped, then gave his father a quick one-armed hug.

"And now, the moment you have all been waiting for," the owner said, "the winner of our fiftieth annual photography contest. The editors at *Vista* are always looking for that one unique voice in the crowd, the photographer who sees the world in a slightly different way from everyone else. And this year, that person, our first-place winner, is Jacob Theodore Maddox. Congratulations, Mr. Maddox."

The room erupted in applause. Jake stared at the stage, sure that he had heard him wrong, but then his photo appeared on the overhead screen, emblazoned with a digital ribbon reading *Winner*. He stared at the image of the empty school, the papers scattered on the floor, and for a moment felt like it couldn't possibly be his photo.

Jake didn't remember getting out of his seat, climbing the stairs, or taking the statuette that was handed to him. Shaking the owner's hand, hearing the words of congratulations and the whoop of the audience were all a blur. When the applause died down, Jake set his award on the small table beside him and gripped the edges of the lectern, suddenly at a loss for words.

The room settled into an uncomfortable quiet. Someone coughed. It made Jake remember all those book reports and presentations in school and the dread he'd felt at having to get up in front of his peers. They would stare at the brace on his leg or snicker about the way he walked. He'd never been more painfully aware of how he didn't fit in than in those moments at the head of the classroom. But here, he was among peers who didn't see him—they saw the art he had created. And they'd chosen it as the best.

"I've, uh, never been the kind of guy who likes being the center of attention," Jake said. He cleared his throat and drew in a deep breath. "So this is kind of my worst nightmare."

The laughter from the audience eased Jake's nerves. He wished he had a paper to read from, because winging it had never been his strong suit.

"I didn't prepare a speech because, frankly, I doubted I was going to win. It really was awesome just to be a finalist. Because..." He glanced to his right and saw his father, beaming and snapping photos with his phone. "Because I was able to realize one of my dreams and enjoy this moment with my father. Thanks, Dad. I love you."

Edward pulled the phone away from his face and gave Jake a nod and a smile. His eyes shimmered with tears, and the hand holding the phone trembled a little. Jake cleared his throat again because otherwise he was going to get all choked up and become a blubbering idiot.

"My father asked me a minute ago why I took this particular photo." He indicated the enlarged version splayed across the screen. "To some people, this image might seem dark or sad. An abandoned building, with its secrets laid bare by the rising sun. But to me, it's much more." He paused. Was he really going to share this story? Expose the past that had once made him feel so ostracized and rejected? He thought about what the magazine's owner had said a moment ago, about the power of a photograph to change people's perspectives. Maybe sharing his history would help someone else— someone who had also felt like a misfit struggling to fit into a world full of other people's expectations—have the courage to be who they were meant to be. "This is where I went to elementary school. They shut it down after Hurricane Sandy destroyed it, but some of my best and worst memories were in this building. It was where I met my best friend"—those two words caught in his throat, but he forced himself to keep going—"and she changed everything about my life, about how I saw myself. She became, in a way, the lens on me.

"I was born different from the other kids. I had to

have a bunch of surgeries when I was little, and I never quite felt like everyone else. I limped, and I had all these scars, and for a long time, I felt like this building, lonely and dark. Then I met Gabby, and suddenly, everything seemed brighter. She saw me as a person, not as the weird kid with the brace. She was like the sun peeking through the fog here, bringing light into everything as her own force of nature." He glanced at the table where his father was sitting and then at the very empty seat where Gabby should have been. His throat clogged, and his eyes burned. "Uh, I'm sorry. I...I told you all I wasn't prepared for this."

A smattering of nervous laughter ran through the room.

He lifted his gaze, and when he did, he caught the outline of a woman, standing by the doors at the back of the ballroom. With the stage lights and the dimmed space, he couldn't be sure it was her. It could be anyone, he told himself, anyone at all. But as he went on, he spoke to that figure at the back, letting his heart show in his words. "That woman," he went on, "has been one of the greatest gifts in my life. She's everything good about me, and she's the reason I'm here today.

"I hope this image reminds you all to look for the sunshine. Sometimes it's hidden behind the fog or just waiting for the night to end, but I promise you, it's there." He hoisted the statuette and tipped it toward the back of the room, toward the woman who could be anyone. In his heart, she was Gabby, watching, supporting, caring. "Thank you. For everything."

Applause carried through the room in waves. Several people stood and kept clapping, blocking Jake's view. As he descended from the dais, the guests began to take their seats, clearing the space. But it was too late. The woman who had been standing by the doors at the back was gone.

"I'll be right back, Dad." Jake set the award on the table by his father, and then dashed out the side door, running down the empty carpeted hall. He made it fifty feet before he accepted that there was no one there.

Jake plodded back to the ballroom just as the waiters were setting out dessert and coffee. He sat down beside his father and picked up the award. His reflection wavered in the shiny brass. "Sorry. I thought I saw someone I knew."

"Congratulations, Jacob. Well deserved. That... that, uh, was a fabulous speech." His father toyed with the teaspoon beside his mug. "I noticed you didn't mention me as being the reason you're here."

"Dad, I..." Jake's voice trailed off. What good would saying the words do? There was no need to add to the scars between them.

"No, you're right. I wasn't there for any of this." Edward waved at the award and the photos lining the room. "I saw only one path for you, from the minute you were born. To get into the law and practice beside me."

"Pretty much forced me into it," Jake muttered.

"Yes, I did. And I'm not making apologies for that."

Jake scoffed. "Why did I think tonight would be any different? Just because I took a different path doesn't mean I hate you or the law or the firm, Dad. I just didn't love that field like you do."

"I was trying to protect you, Jacob, by keeping you close."

"Protect me?" Jake shook his head. "From what?"

"Everything!" The word exploded out of his father.

Then he lowered his voice. "Your mother, those cruel kids in your class, the surgeries, the hospitals—" His father looked away. "Do you know how many times I blamed myself for the pain I saw in your face every time they wheeled you into the recovery room? Every single time you went to physical therapy? And then your mother left, and that pain was my fault, too."

Jake had never thought about how those surgeries must have weighed on his parents, especially his father. How they must have hated seeing their only child scared and helpless. Jake remembered very little of those years, but he did remember the fear he'd felt every time he saw a white coat or a gurney. "I never realized that, Dad."

"I went about it all wrong. I should have just let you do what you loved and had the strength to let you fall or climb on your own." He sprinkled a packet of sugar into his coffee and stirred as he talked, watching the fine crystals dissolve and disappear. "You've been right all along. Right about the kind of job you should be doing, right about me, and right about your cousin."

"You looked into the books?"

Edward sighed as he nodded. "And it's exactly as you said. I confronted him, and he denied the whole thing, saying it was a smear campaign by you. But I knew the truth."

"Because you're good at reading people, Dad."

"At reading everyone but the people close to me." His father gave Jake's hand a squeeze. His hard eyes softened, and a smile wavered on his face. "Thank you for having my back and trying so hard to protect me. Even if I didn't deserve your support."

"Just think of it as me paying in advance for this next chapter of my life." Jake grinned. "Because I'm launching a new business, and I think I'm going to need all the support I can get."

"And maybe a lawyer to draw up your contracts." His father smiled. "I can do that, son. I'll gladly do that."

"I appreciate that, Dad." Neither of them needed flowery words or some big emotional moment. Jake knew that Edward Maddox was a softie at heart, and that he loved his son. He could see the pride and affection in his father's eyes, and right then and there, he shut away all those painful memories from the past. A new perspective, starting right here and now.

Jake turned the award so the lettering faced him. The lights from above glinted off the gold finish, almost as if the award were winking at him. "You know what I love about photography? That you can take a picture right now and take the same picture a split second later, and everything can change. The light can dim or the breeze can blow or the person can move. It's never exactly the same. To me, that says what you see through the lens can change. I think it's time you and I changed the lens we see each other through."

"Very persuasive argument, Jacob." His father gave him a nod. "I don't have a rebuttal."

"Well, I learned from the best lawyer in the state." He gave his father a hug, the two of them a bit clumsy and new to the whole thing. "What do you say we get out of here, Dad, and go get a beer?"

Edward grinned. "I'd say that's something we should have done a long time ago."

TWENTY-THREE

Gabby stayed up long past midnight three days in a row, cutting and pinning and sewing. She ripped out, started again, and then finally struck upon an idea that would work. It took the better part of Saturday for her to finish, but when she got up Sunday morning and saw what she had created sitting on the table, kissed by the sun streaming through her kitchen window, she hoped her mother would have been proud.

She texted her sisters before getting in the car and heading across town to Bayberry Lane. On the way, she said a quick prayer that everything she had done would be enough. For way too many days, her sisters and grandmother had barely replied to her texts or calls. It was as if the world had gone quiet, and if there was one thing Gabby couldn't deal with, it was their silence. She needed her family like she needed her right hand. They were a part of her, and never again, she vowed, would she do something that hurt them.

But before she went to Grandma's, she had one stop

to make. She parked in Harry Erlich's driveway. She got out of the car, walked up the three front steps, took a deep breath, and then rang the bell.

Harry answered the door a few seconds later. "Gabriella, what brings you by today?"

"I...I wanted to apologize. I never should have interfered in your relationship with your son and grandson. My sister and I saw the letter, and we figured out it was you, and we thought..." She sighed. "We got in the middle of it, and we shouldn't have."

"Why don't you sit a spell and we can talk?" he said, gesturing toward a pair of wicker chairs on the porch. "Let me get us some iced tea."

"Sure, that would be great." She sat down in one of the chairs and tried not to fidget while she waited for Harry to return. He had every right to yell at her for sticking her nose where it didn't belong, and as he stepped out onto the porch with a pitcher and two glasses in his hands, she steeled herself for a lecture.

Instead, he poured a glass and handed it to her. "I hope it's to your liking. I make it a little sweet."

"Just like my grandmother does." Gabby took a sip before setting the glass on the end table. "I've learned a lot about family relationships over the last few days. They're complicated and messy, and they can't be repaired with a quick meeting over some restaurant samples. I am so—"

"Stop apologizing." Harry waved off her words. "You may not have gone about it the way I would have, but in the end, it got us three stubborn goats to start talking again."

"Really? But Roger seemed so angry that day."

"He was. And I'm not going to lie—it took some

convincing to get him to calm down. But once I got my son to open up, he said that at the bottom of it all was a pile of hurt feelings because Chad told me before his own father." Harry took a sip of iced tea and sat back in his chair. "The two of them have been at odds most of their lives, even before all this, so it was no wonder Chad felt more comfortable telling me. Roger's got some relationship repairing to do, and he needs to grow a more understanding heart, but the two of them are communicating, and that's a good start."

"I'm so glad." Gabby paused and took another sip of iced tea. "I also need to apologize for sort of forcing you and my grandmother together. Maybe she's not ready to date again."

"Oh, you mean that first dinner invitation?" Harry chuckled. "I knew that wasn't Eleanor's doing. She has told me more than once that she finds me most irritating."

Gabby cringed. "I'm sorry."

"I told you to stop apologizing." He smiled at her. "Your grandmother is a lovely woman, but as stubborn as a fence post. If you hadn't interfered, I don't think she ever would have invited me to dinner. And I wouldn't have the chance to date such a wonderful woman. I have to say, I never thought I'd meet another woman I could care about, until I got to know Eleanor."

"Wait...did you say you guys were dating?"

"Well, I call it dating. She calls it tolerating me." He chuckled again. "Just give her time. She'll come around."

"I sure hope so." Gabby got to her feet, thanked Harry for the tea, and then got back in her car and drove it into Grandma's driveway. The front curtain moved and then closed again. Gabby took her second deep breath of the day, grabbed the bag beside her, and then got out of the car and walked inside the house.

Grandma was sitting in the red velvet armchair that faced the television, her back to Gabby. From the outside, it looked like a repeat of the night Gabby and Jake had been here, trying to matchmake Frank with Grandma. That night seemed a million years in the past, after a million things had happened and changed. Her relationship with her sisters, with Jake, with her father. Some things were better, some things...were works in progress.

Grandma muted the volume on the television when Gabby entered the room. "I'm still mad at you, you know."

Just the tone of her voice told Gabby that Grandma was already softening. Gabby bit back a grin and swung around to face her grandmother. "I don't blame you. I'm still mad at myself."

"You should be." Grandma's face pinched. "That was a terrible thing that you did, no matter how well-intentioned. But I am glad you made it right by apologizing to Harry." She held up her cell phone. "He texted me when you left."

"I'm sorry, Grandma. I just wanted you to be happy." Gabby set the bag on the floor, dropped onto the coffee table, and took her grandmother's hands in hers. "That's all I ever want for any of you guys."

"I know your intentions are good, my dear granddaughter. You were just worried because I've been down a little lately. It's not just about the column or feeling unneeded." Eleanor glanced away. Tears glistened in her eyes, and a breath shuddered out of her. "The anniversary is always so hard. But now, the older you girls get, the more worried I get because you're so close to Penny's age when she died, and I...I can't...I just can't..."

The anniversary. How could she have forgotten? Their mother had died in mid-April, all those years ago. Of course it was a hard day, and with Margaret almost the same age as Momma had been...

Gabby rushed forward, pulling Grandma into her arms. She caught the faint scent of Grandma's perfume and a hundred memories in that tight embrace. "You aren't going to lose us, Grandma. We're going to be right here, eating your cookies and driving you crazy for years and years to come."

"You'd better be." She cupped the back of her granddaughter's head and pressed her cheek to Gabby's. "Or I'll be quite upset with you."

Grandma's tough words were softened by a catch in her throat. Gabby drew back and pressed her forehead against Grandma's until their gazes met, so close, and so similar in color and emotion. "I miss her, too. Every day of my life. I wonder if she saw me graduate from college or Margaret get married or Emma help with all those bridezillas. I wonder if she knows how hard we try to make her proud of us."

"Of course she knows," Grandma said. She ran a hand down Gabby's cheek, and her smile softened. "I tell her about you girls every day."

Gabby drew back and sat on her heels at her grandmother's feet. It was almost like she was a kid again, listening to Grandma's stories about happier days. "You do? How?"

"Did I ever tell you that your mother used to love this chair?" Eleanor ran a hand down the velvety fabric, pushing the pile one way and then the other. "When she was a little girl, she'd sit in it for hours, reading books or playing dolls. She wore the fabric right out, that girl did. And after she died, I spent six months finding the same exact color and then an upholsterer I could trust to make it look exactly as it did when my little girl sat in this seat with me and listened to me read to her." Grandma's voice broke, and her hand gripped the arm of the chair a little tighter, but there was a smile on her lips and a shimmer in her eyes. "Your mother would make up stories while she sat here and tell me the chair was the color of rubies and that it made her think of princesses and queens and magic."

"She was amazing, wasn't she?" No one Gabby had ever met quite lived up to Momma, except for Grandma. Thank God for Grandma, because there would have been no way the girls could have survived without her calm, steady love. And now, the Monroe sisters would hopefully rebuild their relationship with Dad again, and their fractured family would begin to heal.

"Penny left behind three amazing gifts that remind me every single day of her heart and her spirit. I would watch you and your sisters"—Grandma brushed Gabby's bangs off her forehead—"run up and down the halls or play with your dolls, or sit in this very chair and read books, and it was almost as if Penny was right here and I was getting a second chance to be her mother. Only this time, I could tell her three times as often how much I loved her."

Tears streamed down Gabby's face. She couldn't imagine how tough Grandma's loss had been and how bittersweet it must have been to watch three replicas of Penny grow up. Now that the Monroe girls were older, Gabby could see her mother's face in each of them. A reminder that was both bittersweet and precious. "She knows, Grandma. There was so much love in this house, I bet they feel it on Mars."

That made Grandma chuckle a little. "I sure hope so. I sure hope she's proud of how I raised her girls."

"Of course she is. You're the best." How could her grandmother doubt for a second what a wonderful mother she'd been? She'd mothered the three Monroe girls with a firm, loving hand and a lot of wonderful memories. "Heck, even the neighbor kid adopted you as his grandmother."

Jake. A pain fluttered in Gabby's chest. She'd hurt him, badly, and she wasn't sure that she could repair that bond as easily as she had the one with her grandmother. He hadn't replied to her texts or answered her call this morning. Maybe he was too angry to ever forgive her. Either way, she would worry about that later. One broken relationship at a time.

"You know, I sit here in this chair every night before I go to bed, and I talk to her." Grandma swiped at her eyes, but the tears kept on coming, sliding down her cheeks like slow rivers. "I tell her what you three did that day and how you are making her proud and how much we all miss her. I sit in this same spot that she did, and I miss her so much…" A sob caught in her throat. "Oh God, it aches in a deep, deep place inside my soul, so deep I think sometimes I can never fill it again. But then, when I stop talking, I close my eyes, and I listen. I just…*listen*. In that silence I hear her love, as crazy as that sounds. I hear her love and her joy in my heart, and I know my sweet Penny is watching us all, and she's just so darn proud of all of you, she's busting her buttons."

"I hope so, Grandma, I really do." Gabby laid her head on her grandmother's lap, just as she had as a little girl when she'd been sick or sad or just plain tired, and she closed her eyes and listened. There was only the faintest whisper, but maybe, if Gabby listened hard enough, she'd hear her mother, too. Someday. "I'm so grateful I have you, Grandma."

"And I'm so grateful for you, my dear granddaughter. You've made me step outside my comfort zone some in these last few weeks, and I know I should be mad at you, but I'm not."

Gabby lifted her head and studied Eleanor's soft eyes. "You're not?"

"Even Dear Amelia can learn a thing or two from other people." She nudged Gabby up to her feet and drew her into a hug. "Now wipe your face. Your sisters will be here any second."

"How do you...?"

Grandma held up her phone. "The wonders of technology. Less personal, but much faster than letters."

There was a quick succession of knocks and then the door opened, inviting in a brisk wind that ushered Emma and Margaret inside.

"Hey, what'd I miss?" Emma said.

"A bonding moment." Gabby grinned and drew Emma into the hug before yanking Margaret into the same embrace. "I love you guys so much."

Margaret let out an *oomph* but folded herself in with her sisters. "You all are the biggest pains in my butt, but I love you, too. Mike and I are talking, and if it all works out, I'm blaming it on the two of you."

Emma laughed, and Grandma cried a little, and for a minute, there was only love between them. Then the four began chattering and laughing, and Gabby swore her mother could hear them, wherever she was.

"I almost forgot," Gabby said as she reached for the big bag that she'd left on the floor. "This is the whole reason I texted you to come over." From inside the bag, she withdrew three bundles and gave one each to Emma, Margaret, and then Grandma.

Margaret was the first to undo the ribbon and spread out the fabric it had been tied around. At first, she looked confused, but then she recognized what she was holding. "These are...Gabby, they're..."

"Momma's dresses." Gabby smoothed a hand across the shimmery material in Margaret's lap. "I took them all and made them into quilts for each of you guys because I thought you should all have a little part of her to keep close to your heart."

"Oh, Gabs, now I'm mad at you," Margaret said with a frown and a glisten in her eyes. "Because you're making me cry, and you know I hate to cry."

Gabby laughed. "I do, which is exactly why I did it."

"But you've had those dresses for years," Emma said, even as she held hers to her chest. "Aren't you going to miss them?"

Gabby shook her head. She'd thought about this for a long time and knew that her mother would be pleased to see the things that she had made repurposed into a gift from the heart. A gift the three Monroe sisters could share. In the folds of those quilts, they would find memories of their vivacious mother, and the faintest hint of her perfume. All those years of being stored in a cedar box had preserved the material and the scent of history. "I still have a few other dresses, and her wedding dress. Maybe you or I can wear it if we ever get married, Em."

Emma put up her hands. "Oh, hell no. I am never doing that, so you can keep that dress."

Grandma laughed. "I told your grandfather the same thing almost sixty years ago, and it only made him try harder to win my heart."

Good thing, too, Gabby thought, considering how blessed their family had been. Maybe someday Grandma would find love again, but that was a topic for another day. Harry said they were dating, and Gabby wasn't about to press the issue.

"I also decided to take your advice, Em," Gabby said. "I'm going to start sewing my own patterns, based on Momma's insanely good sense of style, and sell them in the store. True one-of-a-kind vintage-inspired designs."

"Now, that's what Ella Penny should have been doing all along," Grandma said. "I think that's a lovely idea."

Margaret nodded her approval, too, and a smile even appeared on her face for a second. "Momma would have liked that," her oldest sister said.

Grandma drew the quilt over her legs and then cocked her head, listening for a little bit. The other two gave Gabby confused looks, but she knew exactly what Grandma was doing. "Your mother says there's no better way to keep her alive in our hearts."

Her sisters and grandmother laid the quilts out on the floor, and as they touched each square, there was a memory to share—some memories that Gabby didn't have, some that she did. As she watched her family laugh and hug and cry, she realized the true warmth in those quilts wasn't in the fabric. It was in the stories they were woven out of.

TWENTY-FOUR

J ake was on the ladder again on a bright, sunny spring day, with a can of paint and a brush, reaching as far as his arm could go to finally finish painting the area under the roof peaks at Grandma El's Bayberry Lane house. He would have skipped doing it altogether, just to avoid running into Gabby, but he'd promised Grandma El, and that trumped everything else.

He'd been miserable in the week since the awards ceremony. Miserable, but busy. Leroy had insisted on doing a full-page spread on Jake's win, along with an interview about the photo and a historical inset about the elementary school. Leroy snuck in an ad for Jake's photography business, and ever since, Jake's phone had been ringing off the hook. Leroy hired an assistant in the graphics department and told Jake to go make something of himself. Then he gave him a wink and a good-natured clap on his shoulder.

Jake had spent more time with his father in the last week than he had in the previous five years. They went to dinner a couple of times, and although the conversations were hesitant and tense at first, they began to ease into talking to each other. It might be many years late, but they were building the foundation of the relationship they should have always had. Brad had quit working at the firm and taken off for Atlantic City, last Jake heard.

But at night, when his phone went quiet and he was alone in his apartment, he found himself scrolling through the dozens of pictures he'd taken over the years, the ones where Gabby was smiling or laughing or simply standing, making the view that much more beautiful. He missed her in a way he'd never missed anything else, and he'd picked up his phone at least a hundred times to call or text her, but in the end put it down again. She'd reached out a few times, but he didn't know what to say back. He wasn't ready to return to being just friends—and might never be able to. Maybe some things weren't meant to be and maybe he needed to hurry up and accept that fact.

He sighed and reached for the far corner of the peak with the brush, hitting it a bit too hard and causing paint to splatter on his wrist. Damn it.

Beside him, he heard the screech of one of the old wooden attic windows being opened. He expected Grandma El, but instead, Gabby poked her head out. "What are you doing?"

"What does it look like I'm doing?" He held up the paintbrush and tried not to look directly at her. Doing that made his heart break a little at a time. Damn it. Why'd she have to be so beautiful, anyway? All crisp and bright in a sunshine-yellow dress with her hair in a clip.

"You weren't supposed to be out here without help." Gabby wagged a finger at him. "You know, to keep you from breaking your neck."

"I'm fine." He dipped the brush and then scraped it along the edge of the can before painting a strip of the siding. Too late, he realized he was repainting what he'd done weeks ago. He kept painting with stubborn strokes rather than stop and admit his mistake. "Really, you can go now."

"Not yet. I wanted to ask your opinion on something." She put up a hand to cut off his protest. "You kind of owe me because you've been part of the whole Dear Amelia thing from the start, and there's one more letter I think we should answer."

Jake kept painting but angled his body just a bit, watching her out of the corner of his eye. "I thought your grandmother got mad at you for doing that."

"Will you just listen to the letter? I swear, you are the most frustrating man I have ever met. And for your information, Grandma and I talked, and we're all good again."

Jake put the brush back in the can before leaning against the outside of the windowsill, now only inches away from her. He kept one hand on the ladder because he truly didn't want to break his neck. Damn, her perfume was so tempting. "Fine, go ahead and read it."

"Good." She dropped her gaze to the paper in her hand, a sheet of notebook paper with handwriting that he swore was familiar. "'Dear Amelia, I have this problem I can't seem to solve. I've been an idiot, and there doesn't seem to be a way to make it right.'"

"Sounds like most people I know."

"Jake Maddox, how are you going to give advice if you don't hear the letter all the way through? Now hush." She shook the paper, cleared her throat, and kept reading. "'I met this guy more than twenty years ago, and at the

time, I had no idea what a great man he would turn out
to be. He asked me out, and we tried dating for a little
bit, but then I got scared and broke it off. I thought I was
doing what was best for both of us, but you see, all I've
done is make myself miserable and maybe hurt him in the
process. I miss him terribly.'" She lifted her gaze, staring
directly at him. Her voice lowered, and her features softened. "'Especially the way he kisses me, and the sound
of his voice in the morning, and the way he looks when
the sun is just behind his head and he's standing on a
ladder and…'"

Her voice trailed off, but her gaze remained locked
on him. Jake grinned, and his heart did a little skip beat.
"You miss me? Terribly?"

"I do." A gust of wind brushed past them, caught
the paper, and carried it out the window. Jake tried to
catch it, but Gabby put a hand on his and stopped him.
"I don't need to read it. I already know the rest of
the letter."

She was holding his hand. He tried not to read anything into that, but damn it, he was reading all kinds of
things in the way she talked about him and touched him
and looked at him.

"'I need your advice, Amelia,'" Gabby went on,
never letting go and never breaking eye contact with him,
sweeping him away with those emerald eyes all over
again. "'I need to find a way to tell this man I broke up
with that I love him. I think I always have. I was just so
afraid of being hurt that I thought it was better to keep
him as a friend. Turns out my life was far better when
he was more than a friend. So how do I tell him how
I feel and make this right? Signed, Silly and Very Sorry
Single Girl.'"

"Well, I think Dear Amelia would say you just did."
He swung his leg over the sill and ducked into the room.
She let out a little squeak of surprise when he hauled her
to his chest. "So you love me, not as a friend, but as
something more?"

She nodded and a smile burst across her face. "I do.
I love you, Jake Maddox."

"And I love you, Bella-Ella." He grinned like a fool
and held her to him, this beautiful woman who had made
his life incredibly sweet. "Hey, I thought you were supposed to bring me iced teas while I was out here putting
in some sweat equity."

She raised her chin and gave him a sassy grin. "And
I thought you were supposed to kiss me right now. Dear
Amelia would say that if a woman tells you she loves
you, you're supposed to kiss—"

He cut her off, bending down and giving her every
one of the kisses he had dreamed about over the years.
He kissed her and loved her and whispered her name, and
she melted into his arms. It was everything he had hoped
for, and a whole lot more.

"You know I'm going to marry you, right?" He
kissed her again, sweeter and shorter this time. "I'm never
letting you go again, Gabby."

"I'm counting on that, Jake. I'm planning on having
you by my side for a very, very long time." She leaned
her head against his chest. He held her tight while dust
motes floated in the attic and the paint dried and the world
moved along. "Congratulations, by the way."

"Aren't you jumping the gun?" He laughed. "We
aren't married yet."

She swatted at his arm. "Not that, silly. Congratulations for winning the photography contest. I thought your

speech was amazing, and your photo was a hundred times better than anyone else's."

His gaze narrowed. "You were there that night, weren't you?"

"I couldn't let the man I love be alone on his special day, now could I?"

He had been so sure that she'd ignored the ticket he'd left under her door, but no, Gabby had been there for him, just as she had for every other moment in his life. "Why didn't you come up and sit with me? Or stay after the awards ceremony?"

"Because I saw your dad there, looking so proud and congratulating you. You two needed that moment, and I wasn't about to step into the middle of it. And...I might have been feeling a little stubborn still."

He arched a brow. "A little?"

She put her fists on her hips and shot him a mock glare. "Jake Maddox, you better be nice to me, or I won't share the cookies I baked for you."

"Wait. You made me cookies? Edible ones?" Of the three Monroe sisters, Gabby was the least handy in the kitchen. The one time she'd baked cupcakes for his birthday, they had been a burned disaster. He'd eaten them anyway, insisting they were delicious because he didn't want to hurt her feelings. Far better an upset stomach than an upset Gabby.

"Of course I didn't make them. I haven't changed *that* much." She laughed. "Grandma mixed the dough, and I dropped it on the cookie sheets and put them in the oven. Hence the baking part."

"Phew, I'd hate to get food poisoning on the day I ask your grandmother if I can become her grandson-in-law."

Gabby rolled her eyes, but he could see happiness

and mirth written all over her face. "You were serious about the marriage thing, huh?"

"I've been serious about that since the first grade, Bella-Ella." Then he kissed her again until she took his hand and tugged him downstairs. Every other step, he kissed her, and she giggled. They were like two teenagers trying not to get caught making out when they stumbled into the kitchen.

Margaret and Grandma were there, holding Grandma's phone up to the window. Emma's face pixelated before reappearing on the phone's screen. "It's Emma," Margaret said. "She's in Nevada at that yoga thing. And you two are...?"

"Crazy in love. I'll tell you more later." Gabby waved at the phone. "Hey, Em! How's the retreat going?"

Emma's face froze; her mouth opened, and then a second later, the video started moving again. "Uh...I think I accidentally got...married."

Everyone in the room froze for a second. Grandma raised her voice and got closer to the phone. "Uh, Emma, what did you just say? I think our connection's poor. Did you say you were in an accident?"

"No time to explain. I'm heading home right now," Emma said. "Gotta go! Love you!"

The screen went black. The Monroe family stared at each other, mouths agape. Gabby leaned against Jake, and he wrapped his arm around her waist. She fit perfectly against him, as if she'd been made for him from the start. Maybe she had—and it had just taken her two decades to realize it.

"Emma's got to be kidding about accidentally getting married," Gabby said. "Right?"

"With this family," Grandma said as she held out

the platter of cookies, "every day is a surprise. And I wouldn't have it any other way."

The Monroe women all started talking at once, their laughter and chatter rising all the way to the rafters of the Bayberry Lane house. It was music to Jake's ears.

Because it was the sound of home.

READING GROUP
GUIDE

Dear Reader,

Some books are closer to my real life than others. This first book in the Monroe Girls series reflects in many ways my relationship with my mother. She passed away when I was in my early thirties, and even though I was an adult at the time, I have missed her every single day since.

I think maybe every one of the matriarchal characters I create is a version of my mother in some way. From the "hundred-dollar lectures" that Grandma gives to the late-night conversations and the busy family dinners, those are my mom and her mother, my nana. Nana was very much like Grandma in *The Marvelous Monroe Girls*: stern but sage, loving, and kind. She was an amazing woman in a million ways—a concert pianist and a dogged survivor. It was no wonder that my mother turned out to be much the same: strong and wise, and beloved by so many people.

I grew up in a small town in Massachusetts, so every time I get to go back there in my fiction, it's like being home again. I love the vibe of a small town and being in the kind of place where you see your neighbors in the grocery store or know the mailman by his first name. The town almost becomes an extension of your family, and that's my favorite kind of community.

Welcome to my fictional family. May it be as warm as my favorite people and places, and may you see a little of yourself in the marvelous, incredible Monroe women.

QUESTIONS FOR
READERS

1. Gabby says that a little white lie never hurt anyone. She and her sisters tell a little white lie to their grandmother to help raise her spirits. Do you think this little white lie was justified? Do you think any lie, no matter how big or small, is ever okay?

2. Jake's mother leaves him and his father when Jake is quite young as she battles her alcoholism. When she returns, their relationship is still rocky for some time. Have you known someone in your own life that was involved in a similar situation? What was your role and how did it affect the other people?

3. How risk-averse is Jake, really? He gives up his law career to pursue a career at the newspaper. Do you think this was brave? Do you think it was the right thing for him to do? What cost did he pay in his relationships for this decision?

4. Grandma Eleanor writes the Dear Amelia column for the local newspaper, but there are now many columnists online, too. Do you read any advice

columns? Would you ever write in to one about a problem?

5. Jake and Gabby are friends for a long time before becoming lovers. Do you think a long friendship is a good basis for a romantic relationship?

6. Jakes thinks a lot about "what-ifs" in the book. What what-ifs do you think about in your life? Do you think these what-ifs have worked out for the best, or are there still some you would like to pursue?

7. Neither Jake nor Gabby wants to ruin a good friendship by trying for a romantic relationship. If a friendship is a solid one, do you think it could be ruined by dating? After kissing, Gabby wants to go back to being just friends, but Jake doesn't. After having a romantic relationship fail, do you think it is possible to go back to being friends and have both parties be happy with friendship?

8. Gabby has been estranged from her father for many years. Who do you think bears the larger amount of blame for this—the father or the daughter?

9. Jake feels a lot of pressure from his father because he did not follow the plan that his father had made for his son's life. Did you follow the path that your parents planned for you? Was this a good thing? Do you think the best parents let their children make their own path? Or do you think

that parents sometimes know their children better than the children know themselves?

10. Emma says, "Life is for living, Grandma. Someone wise told me that once. I believe it was you." Do you think that Emma is living life more because she travels and is not tied down? Or is she fooling herself about how much she is enjoying her life? Do you think that her sisters will live equally full lives by staying in their hometown? What is your definition of living life to the fullest?

11. Grandma tells Gabby, "We can't go back and change the past. But we can't keep living in it, either." In what ways is Eleanor living too much in the past? Why is she doing that? What finally compels Gabby to stop living in the past?

12. When Gabby tries to help Harry, Roger, and Chad, things don't go as planned. Her grandmother thinks that Gabby has meddled too much. Do you think Gabby's actions are wrong? Would you have also jumped in and tried to help?

13. Leroy is a good mentor to Jake at the newspaper. He encourages him to grow in his job and even encourages him to leave when Jake is ready. Have you had good mentors in your life? Who were they and how did they help you? Have you been a good mentor to someone?

14. Davis says that he could not have pictured his life without Penny in it. Who needs to be in the future life that you see for yourself? When Penny died, Davis had to create a new life for himself. In what ways have you had to re-create your life?

15. Eleanor tells Davis that "there are things that matter in the moment, and then there are things that matter in our souls." What are the things in your life that have mattered in the moment? And what things matter in your soul?

ABOUT THE AUTHOR

When she's not writing books, *New York Times* and *USA Today* bestselling author **Shirley Jump** competes in triathlons, mostly because all that training lets her justify midday naps and a second slice of chocolate cake. She's published more than seventy-five books in twenty-four languages, although she's too geographically challenged to find any of those countries on a map.